With This Witch

LEESIDE WITCHES
BOOK 1

ISLA WINTER

To my penguin

And for all of us with a little witch inside questioning whether we are worthy of love. We are.

About This Book

This is a story featuring supernatural creatures. As this is also a story about people who have supernatural abilities, there are real-life experiences built in, and so the following content warnings should be noted:

- Explicit sex scenes
- Swearing
- Death of parents (off-page) and loved ones (on-page)
- Grief (on-page)
- Parental abandonment (briefly discussed on-page)

I appreciate that you have chosen to read this story, but care for yourself first. If any of these elements trigger you, please do not cause yourself any harm by continuing further.

— Isla

CHAPTER ONE

Petra

With each step, the sound of crumbling, crunching leaves soothes her soul. The fallen leaves and crispness in the air are always her favorite part of fall. She's always loved the earthiness of autumn. The smell of decay comforts her as plants and trees ready themselves for the long, cold winter. Her magic thrums under her skin, responding to the nature surrounding, pulling energy from the earth as she crosses the busy street and enters her preferred pub—the Bittersweet Acorn, where her best friend Daisy Hale works.

"Hey Petra, what can I get you?"

Moving her attention from the crowd, Petra looks up at Lachlan Grace, hot man, bar owner, and demon extraordinaire. "How about an amaretto sour?"

"Coming right up," Lachlan responds, turning to grab the amaretto from the shelf. His light brown hair is up in a bun, keeping it off his broad, muscular shoulders and out of his face as he works. His six-foot-six frame gives him a larger-than-life presence behind the bar, and the command of shadows as his demon ability and a mysterious history don't hurt either. Her eyes follow the corded muscles of his arm as he scoops ice for her drink. When he bends over, getting a rag from the bottom shelf, she affords herself a second to glance at his ridiculously formed derriere.

I wonder if that booty is from squats or blessed by the demon lords. She quickly moves her eyes to the shelved bottles before he can catch her staring.

Yelling over the live music, Petra asks, "Have you seen Daisy yet tonight? She said she was working, but"—she glances at her phone—"it's 10:23, and she hasn't manifested yet."

Finishing off the drink with the cherry, Lachlan hands it to Petra, and she catches his knowing smile; yeah, he definitely caught her checking him out. "She's working the private party section tonight, but she should be around shortly."

Petra thanks Lachlan before turning around to join the crowd in front of the band. Daisy had started working at the Bittersweet Acorn two years ago, which was when they both first met Lachlan. Upon hiring Daisy, he immediately became like their older brother, protecting his little sisters when needed.

Petra Rose has lived in Leeside her entire life. Her family was one of the town's founding families, and she often feels the pressure that her name carries. Her mother died when Petra was young, and her father abandoned her many years ago, so it's been up to her to keep the family name worthy under the tutelage of her Gammy, Gladys. It's not an easy task and not always one she wants.

Being a Rose has meant her life has been mapped out since the day she was born. As the oldest of the founding families, and thanks to the tradition of magic being connected to bloodlines, the Roses have the privilege of the

Premier Witch role passing through their family for generations, always going to the oldest child, whether they want it or not. When her father fucked off, abdicating his eventual responsibility as the next Premier Witch and effectively abandoning his family when she was still a child, she became the next in line. As she grew and started to understand what this meant for her future, the expectations started to weigh on her. On more than one occasion, her destiny as Premier Witch caused conflict between her and Gammy, including a multi-night attempted disappearance on Petra's part wherein Gammy had to use a locator spell to find and drag her moody teenage ass home.

Despite the privilege of being a Rose, sometimes she wonders what it would be like not to be one and live more freely; unfortunately, she will never know. At thirty-two, Petra knows her becoming Premier Witch is inevitable one day, though hopefully it won't be for a long time. Gammy took on the role younger than usual at only twenty-eight after her own mother passed unexpectedly when a curse backfired. But Gammy is different. That woman is strong, powerful, and determined. She's been the Premier Witch for nearly fifty years, and Petra hopes Gammy won't be going anywhere soon.

Leeside is where developing witches come to learn more about the history of magic. The local university is a hot spot for magical learning, for humans and supernaturals alike. As Gammy once told her, it is thanks to the council and their governance that supernatural beings are even allowed to attend Leeside University. Apparently, it was one of her first mandates on council that determined a future with humans and supernatural beings co-mingling and living peacefully together. A few years later, the council ruled in favor of inter-species marriage, opening the door for other established communities and their governing bodies to do the same. It's been through these hard-fought battles that the council—well, some of them—have been able to move the community forward.

Petra finally spots Daisy near the private party room door as the band starts a cover of "I Put a Spell on You." She starts singing along as she makes her way over to Daisy.

"Hey!" Daisy exclaims as Petra approaches.

"What's the holdup? You don't usually spend so long in the party room."

"Oh, they were just chatty tonight. Bachelor party and boys trying to prove to each other they still have the moves. Typical." Daisy rolls her eyes.

"So, you had twelve guys hitting on you and being inappropriate? Do you need me to go in and give them a piece of my spark?" Petra asks, holding her hand up and allowing the collected energy to dance across her fingers like a miniature lightning storm.

"I've got it handled. I may have used a spell to make them believe it is last call. At this point, Lach can call them cabs, and they can get out of here." Daisy motions for them to head back toward the bar. "You're still good with your drink?"

"Yep, I think two is my limit tonight. The little tykes wouldn't appreciate a hungover Miss P tomorrow. I'm going to watch the band for a bit. I'll stop by before I head out."

"Make good choices!" Daisy calls as Petra walks back into the crowd around the stage.

Working the closing shift at Bright Mornings Childcare means she can take time to get up and ready in the morning.

It also means there's time to stop by her favorite coffee shop along the way.

She parks on the street a block away from Taster's Delight, a local vampire-run coffee shop and roaster in Leeside. No one is sure how long the establishment has been around; the vampire owners had always altered their appearances every couple of decades and claimed a change in ownership to avoid suspicion from the human residents, back when humans and supernaturals didn't nicely coexist in Leeside. Even now the humans don't seem to like certain aspects, like immortality, to be obvious, which means many of the beings with prolonged lifespans, like vampires and faeries, in Leeside do what they can to minimize its impact or visibility.

Taster's Delight has the perfect espresso, creamy and light but full of flavor, and Petra's mouth starts to water at the smell of the roasted beans as she walks toward it. Placing an order for a macchiato for herself and a latte for her co-educator, she moves to the side, waiting for them to be prepared. As she waits, she looks around the store, noticing the new drinkware available and the mix of patrons, both human and not, sharing tables and laughing together on this crisp, sunny morning. She thanks the barista as she collects her order and winks at Briryn, who is a friend and the gnome council representative, working away on a laptop as she leaves.

The door opens, just as she's about to step through it. Losing her balance, she stumbles out the door. The coffees go flying, and she is caught by a set of strong hands. Very strong hands that have a firm grip on her hips. On a deep inhale in her now-flustered state, she recognizes a familiar bergamot scent even as spilled coffee soaks both of them.

"You alright there?"

She huffs, pulling out of his hold. "Yes, Lachlan. I'm fine. Just covered in coffee now. Don't you look before opening doors?" she snaps, frustrated. She isn't typically one to react so quickly, but she was looking forward to that coffee, and now she won't have time to get another one and head back home to change before being needed at work.

"Good morning to you too, witchling," he says with a grin.

She picks up the cups and shoots a spark at his feet. "Don't *witchling* me." While she's never liked the nickname often given to young witches, and despite her current frustration, the name coming from him isn't completely horrible. It stirs something inside her, but she's not willing to go down that train of thought right now.

He laughs at her. Full-bodied and deep. The sound is like plucking the perfect chord on a bass. As frustrated as she is with him at this moment, she acknowledges that she likes hearing him laugh.

"My apologies. I wasn't aware holding doors open would be so troublesome," he teases. "Would you like me to get that for you?" he asks, pointing to the coffee stain down her front. Before she can answer, shadows creep from beneath her and climb her legs, torso, and chest, leaving goosebumps in their wake as they remove the stain before disappearing again. "Better?"

Looking down, she notes all evidence of the coffee incident is gone. "Yes, thank you."

The gnome with the laptop must have noticed the incident. He strolls through the door, holding out two coffees. "Here, Petra. Looks like you could use some replacements."

Accepting the drinks, her mood shifts from annoyance to

gratitude. "You're the best, Briryn, thanks. I hope you have a wonderful day."

"No problem. And you as well," Briryn replies before returning to his table.

"Sorry about… that, by the way. You caught me off guard," she says to Lachlan.

"No worries. My apologies as well. I'll make sure to be more careful next time," he says, smiling. "Have a great day at work, witchling."

Petra scoffs and is about to retort back, but he's already inside the shop. Lucky demon.

"Hi, friends!" Petra calls out as she enters the classroom, bursting with preschooler energy and excitement for a day of play and learning ahead. Her group of little tykes come rushing over to her as she walks in and puts her bag and the drinks on the counter. The children begin speaking over each other to get her attention.

"Miss P, look! I found a purple rock."

"Look, I have my nails painted! They sparkle!"

"My dad says I have a stinky butt!"

"My mom says Josh is adopted."

"My sister picks her nose and eats it!"

Laughing at all the revelations happening simultaneously, Petra bends down and calls for a group hug before the children rush off again to return to what they were playing with. Working the closing shift means the children have already been awake for hours and have filled that time with more games, stories, and adventures than Petra could do in a month. No two days in childcare are the same, and Petra loves it; it's exhausting but rewarding.

Aside from her friendship with Daisy, this place and these little ones are her primary source of joy and happiness. Their sense of pride as they accomplish new things and their excitement to take on the world is inspiring. She wishes everyone approached the world with the wonder children have, which may be why she laughs to herself while observing Jordan and Tony plotting a dragon attack on Marsha's tower.

"So, how was the show last night?" Shannon, her co-educator, asks as she puts snacks for the children at the table after giving her the necessary updates about absent children and any changes to the daily routine.

"It was good. Their drummer was hot as Hades, so even if they sucked, there was eye candy at least. But the band was good. Very energetic." Petra hands Shannon a drink, and she clasps her hands together and bows before her in praise.

"What does hot as Hades mean, Miss P?" Charlie, ever-observant, asks.

"It means something is very hot to touch, and so we need to be extra careful around it," Petra says smoothly.

"Good one." Shannon chuckles.

"All right, friends! Those of you who are ready to go outside can go to the bathroom quickly, and then we will get our shoes changed and get our coats to head into the world of leaves, trees, and bugs!"

The children collectively yell with excitement and rush to the bathroom.

Petra walks in the front door of her fifth-floor apartment, greeted by the loud meows of Morris, her plump orange tabby. She leans down, scratching him behind his ears exactly how he likes it and coos at him. "Hello, my handsome little dude. I've missed you too." She scoops him up in her arms, nuzzling in his soft fur, and walks into her living room, depositing him in his favorite upholstered chair. As she strolls to her bedroom, she removes the bra under her shirt and steps out of her pants. A late night out on a school night and spending the day with a rambunctious group of fourteen preschoolers means she is Tired with a capital T. She enters the kitchen, grabs a Chinese takeout menu, and texts Daisy.

PETRA

Hey loser!

Ordering Chinese food tonight. Want in?

DAISY

Yes!

Sesame chicken and fried rice, please

Be there in 20!

While Petra waits for Daisy and the food to arrive, she finds a pair of comfy shorts and puts them on, taking a moment to look in the full-length mirror as she passes. She squeezes her belly and turns to look over her shoulder at the cellulite on the back of her thighs. She turns away, sighing, frustrated, and heads to the couch, where Morris jumps and curls up on her legs.

Lounging on the couch, she lets her magic unspool and stretch. Pink-colored tendrils unfurl from her body, reaching for light and shadow. While she understands the power and privilege that comes from being a Rose, she's never fully accepted it or wanted it. Instead, she limits how much she relies on it in her day-to-day life, preferring to feel the satisfaction of doing something through her own strength and ability. Where her power is most often used at work. Being a witch at a childcare that caters to all families, be they human or supernatural, means she's not banned from using her magic at work. So, she prefers saving it for moments when children need a quick hand to stop themselves from getting hurt or to provide additional comfort. Her magic allows her to do cool tricks that make the children giggle, but one of her favorite abilities is to soothe heightened emotions. She spends a lot of her workday outdoors, allowing her ample opportunity to draw energy from the natural world while playing alongside the children.

A knock at the door draws her attention away from her thoughts. She stands and puts down Morris, who gives her a disappointed look. She opens the door and smiles in surprise. Standing before her is her favorite person in the whole world, her Gammy Gladys.

"Hello, my baby girl!" Gammy coos as she walks in the door, past Petra, and into the kitchen.

Petra follows Gammy and then jumps onto the kitchen counter to sit. Her feet dangle and sway below her as Morris saunters in. As Gammy turns to root in the cupboard for some tea bags, Morris reaches up and swats at Petra's foot, making her jump. *Jerk.* Petra hops down from the counter and moves into the living room, sitting at the end of the couch.

"You really should have the tea bags on the counter or at least directly above the kettle for ease of access," Gammy admonishes her, finally locating a box of Earl Grey. She turns and takes the kettle, filling it with water, then turns it on to start boiling before taking a mug from one of the other cupboards.

Petra watches Gammy and knows something is amiss. She's twisting her wedding ring, which she still wears despite being widowed for decades, and tapping her foot lightly. Gammy gazes at Petra and tilts her head ever so slightly to the left, deep in thought.

Petra waits.

"Well, aren't you going to say anything, love?" Gammy finally asks.

Petra smiles and puts her arms out for a hug, which Gammy happily obliges, coming over to where Petra sits. "I am thrilled to see you, of course, but I can see you're worked up about something, and I figured I should give you time to sort out your thoughts before you tell me what's wrong," she says.

"When did you get so smart and so patient? That certainly isn't from me." She laughs as Morris winds himself around her feet, head-butting her shin as he passes. She reaches into the cupboard to find a bag of cat treats and puts a few on the floor for him to eat.

The kettle starts to whistle just as Gammy takes a deep breath and says, "I'm sick."

Petra starts. "What do you mean you're sick?"

Gammy pours the water into a rainbow-printed mug and then places her tea bag in. "I'm dying, love," she says quietly. "I have about a year, maybe less. The illness has progressed beyond the point of a potential cure."

"Dying?" Petra whispers in disbelief. "How could you be dying? Have you gone to the healer? Surely there is something they can do."

"Sometimes these things just happen, darling. Of course I've been to a healer. There's nothing they can do." Petra's eyes well up, and Gammy wraps a comforting arm around her. "Unfortunately, that's why I'm here."

Petra sniffles and wipes away her tears. Her Gammy has always seemed indestructible. Petra catches herself. What is she doing? Gammy is the one dying, likely scared of facing her inevitable and fast-approaching end, yet here she is, comforting Petra.

"What can I do to help?" Petra asks.

"Not much for me at the moment, but I do need to get some things in order and wanted to tell you first."

"Tell me what?"

"The council has requested your presence."

"What! Why?"

"Consideration for the next Premier Witch needs to happen quickly, so they've called an emergency meeting to decide who the potential incumbent is," Gammy says.

"What? I have to go before the council now? Why the rush?" Petra asks.

Gammy rubs soothing circles on Petra's back. "I think they are trying to set up for a certain someone to take the role, but they need to make it appear as though they have followed protocol. But according to tradition, the Premier Witch would pass to you as the next member in the Rose family line. You must be considered and assessed as a candidate."

A knock sounds briefly at the door before Daisy lets herself in. Morris runs to the door and then turns around, charging in ahead of her, meowing loudly as if to announce her presence. Daisy walks into the kitchen and immediately stops, noticing Petra's tear-streaked face and Gammy beside her. "Who died?"

CHAPTER TWO

Lachlan

W alking to his vehicle, Lachlan spots a flash of red ahead. *Petra*, his demon-self breathes. He's felt a pull to her from their very first meeting a few years ago. Over these past few years, they've become good friends, and he's watched her flit from shitty relationship to shitty relationship, her sparkle fading with each new guy. As much as he's wanted to step in and see if he'd have a chance with her, he's been hesitant, afraid to ruin what they have as friends, and wanting to make sure she's ready for him. But thanks to his terrible luck, by the time she seems ready for something new, she finds someone else, and he's missed his chance again.

Instead of being with her, he stands by her. And really, she's never indicated she wants anything more than a friendship with him. As the guy friend, he lends an ear, giving advice or insight into the male view. He might also use his demon abilities as necessary—not that she knows that. When her last dipshit boyfriend bailed on her after six months with nothing more than a text saying, "Peace out,"

Lachlan absolutely did not track the douche down and give him a lesson on how to treat women better while in his demon form.

But damn it all to Hades. When she walked in last night, he would have given anything to put her up against the wall, peel off her clothing, and devour every inch of her gorgeous form. Thinking about her in those jeans and how they perfectly sculpted her curves is sending his dick to attention, causing him to readjust himself. Standing gloriously tall, she still feels small compared to him, but not so small that he thinks he would have chronic neck pain from stooping down to kiss her perfect pink lips. And he knows that her bright red hair would look hot as hell wrapped around his fist while sliding his other hand up her creamy skin.

Stop it. We got shit to do, he thinks, adjusting the growing bulge in his pants again.

Driving down the highway to his younger brother Declan's place, he recalls the first time the fiery redhead came into the bar with Daisy. Daisy was looking for a job, and Petra was quick to tell him why Daisy would benefit his bar. After a trial run, Daisy was officially hired, and Petra continued to regularly visit the bar. Win-win for everyone. Well, except for his dick. He's been with other women these past two years but hasn't been able to shake Petra, despite never having had her.

"Hey, man!" Declan calls out, leaning on his crutches, as Lachlan steps out of his Jeep. "How was the drive?"

"Smooth as ever. There was a little traffic around Highway #9, but otherwise it was good. How have you been?" Lachlan says, walking to meet his brother at the door. The drive to Declan's in Beckton is about an hour, but it can feel much longer depending on the time of day and traffic flow.

"Things have been quiet here since Mom went back to Stanmore. I start work again on Monday, which will help keep me busy and out of trouble."

"That's good. I'm happy Mom could come and stay for a bit to help you after your surgery. You seem to be moving well," Lachlan says.

"I am. It was a bit slow at first because of the swelling, pain, and being drugged to high hell, but mobility is quickly coming back. Doc says I should be good in a couple of weeks." Declan says. "So what's brought you out here? I thought you weren't going to stop by until next week sometime?"

"Can't an older brother come and visit his younger brother for no reason other than to spend time together? Especially after he's had knee surgery after fucking himself up playing a pickup football game and stupidly refusing to see a healer."

"Some brothers could, but not you," Declan jokes, poking Lachlan in the shoulder.

"Ha, ha, jackass," Lachlan responds sarcastically. "Nah, there's nothing wrong. Just wanted out for a bit and decided to stop by."

"Fair enough. Anyways, let's not stand out here like gossiping old ladies. Come in where we can be civilized and gossip in the backyard like normal people." Declan gestures to the open door behind him.

Lachlan nods as he claps his brother on the shoulder. They move back into the house, Declan slowly following behind with his crutches. Lachlan stops in the kitchen to get them drinks while Declan continues through the room and meets up with him again on the patio. They collapse into the chairs beside the pool, crutches leaning against an empty chair, and sip quietly for a moment, enjoying the peace and sounds of nature as birds chirp and insects buzz around them.

Lachlan catches Declan staring at him. "What?"

"You seem… off," Declan says.

"Off? How so?"

"I don't know, but there's just something wrong. How's stuff with the council going?" he asks.

"Meh, usual council bullshit. Though we have an emergency meeting tomorrow," Lachlan replies. As the demon representative on the supernatural council, Lachlan often has to deal with petty and annoying crap from some of the other reps. In particular, the rep for the trolls, Hegnir Grog, has a unique way of getting under Lachlan's skin.

Lachlan was one of the youngest representatives the council had ever had. Despite having left the underworld on a semi-permanent basis, the council voted to keep him as their demon rep because of his bloodline from his father, a former demon lord. So here he is, at thirty-five, now a veteran council member, trying his best to support all community members, even though some other reps do their best to prevent that.

"Any idea why?"

"Nope. They are being pretty tight-lipped about this one. Grog called it, so it's probably safe to assume someone looked at him the wrong way."

Declan laughs fully, the sound bouncing away and into the trees, startling a few birds who launch into the sky. "Yeah, you never know with that troll."

"Anyways, I'll see what happens tomorrow, but hopefully, it's nothing too drastic. I don't feel like bringing out the demon."

Declan laughs, flopping to the side of the chair. "Not the big bad demon-boy!"

Lachlan kicks at him. "Shut up. You're such a dick. Why do I even bother to come see you?"

"Because you loooveee meee…" Declan responds, drawing out the words, teasing Lachlan.

"No, that's definitely not it," Lachlan deadpans, sipping his drink.

Lachlan returns home and changes into his typical bar uniform—jeans and a gray T-shirt—before heading to the Acorn. When Lachlan arrives at the bar, he sees Petra's car, which means that Daisy and Petra are already there. Daisy is stocking the bar with beer, and Petra sits on the bar top, her legs dangling off the edge when he enters.

"Hey, Lach!" Daisy calls as she notices him walk through the door.

"Daisy," he responds with the smallest of head nods. Looking over at Petra, he says, "You alright?"

"Hmm? Oh. Not really."

Daisy turns her head to Lachlan. "She got some other news last night." She shares a silent look.

"Oooh, that sounds juicy."

Petra cuts a harsh look at Lachlan, causing him to flinch. "It's not juicy. Gammy stopped by last night, and apparently, she's dying," she snaps.

Lachlan moves to stand in front of her, feeling like a complete ass. "Shit. I'm sorry. I'm a dick."

Petra looks anywhere but at him, breathing in through her nose and out through her mouth, clearly holding back tears. When she seems collected enough, she continues, "And the council is worried about my ability to be a Premier

Witch, so I've been summoned to an emergency council meeting tomorrow."

"I'm sorry. I didn't know. But damn, now I know why I've been called in," Lachlan responds, keeping his face blank.

"You didn't know?"

He shakes his head. He doesn't like that he's being left out of council plans. He also hopes Grog doesn't have enough gall to try anything super shitty; the troll has never liked the Rose family, especially Gladys.

Petra fidgets with the cuff on her sleeve. "I'm not thrilled about going in front of council, and I'm a little nervous about what will happen."

Lachlan places his hand gently under her chin and slowly raises her head so her eyes meet his. "I know it's scary, and the council can be no joke. But they want something from you, so they will likely behave better. Go in with an open mind and hear them out. Ultimately, they only want what is best for our collective community." He says the words, but he's not sure he fully believes them. He hopes Petra doesn't get caught in the crossfire of whatever political games are going on.

Petra smiles and places her hand on his forearm, giving it a gentle squeeze. She may not say it, but he takes that as a thank-you.

Lachlan turns away, heading back behind the bar to start his opening prep. "Besides, if they want to harm you, they'd have to go through me, and they don't want that." He allows his eyes to quickly flash demon-gold before returning to his usual steel blue.

Petra hops off the bar top and walks over to Lachlan, now at the far end, squeezing his shoulder as she walks behind him. "Thanks, Lach. I appreciate it. But keep the demon in its cage tomorrow. The last thing I need is more council attention than I already have." Petra waves to Daisy, who is out on the floor, and winks at Lachlan before heading out the door, the chimes signaling her departure.

CHAPTER THREE

Petra

Another day with a group of preschoolers proves just as chaotic as usual. While outside this afternoon, in twenty minutes, Charlie fell and got a bloody nose, Max caught a bee and was stung, Seraphina lost her prized stuffy, and Petra herself tripped over a ball that had rolled behind her and fell on her ass.

All day, she tries to convince herself that the meeting tonight will not be an issue. That everything will be okay. And yet, something inside her warns her that something big is coming her way. She pushes these thoughts aside as she returns to her preschool room after her lunch break and plasters on a smile to greet her little ones for the afternoon. She is welcomed back warmly by Max and Seraphina, who rush into her before she has time to close the door.

"Miss Petra!" they exclaim in unison as they bury their faces in the side of her thighs, giving her big hugs.

"I made a castle with the playdough," Max says. "Come look!"

"And I made a dragon that's going to attack his castle," Seraphina tells her.

Petra smiles at them and watches as they run back to the table with the playdough, wondering what the world could be like for them in a few years. Would it be more accepting of their abilities—Max's super speed and Seraphina's fae wings currently hidden under her oversized sweater—or will they still be at risk of hate from the small groups of humans who rally against the magical beings? Could this be something she is able to shape as a future Premier Witch?

Max shouts across the room, "Miss Petra! Come look! Come look!"

Petra joins Max and Seraphina at their table, ready to delve into their world of dragons and castles. Watching these two play together and work so well to create their own world ignites a glowing ember inside Petra. She works hard to guide the next generation and teach them how to care for others and themselves. She knows that the little ones around her are watching everything she does and that she needs to model for them how to approach the world with compassion. Her group of children are a mix of human and supernatural, and every day she teaches them about each other, helping them to understand they are stronger together.

Take, for example, little Seraphina. She's been taught and encouraged to hide her wings, and despite multiple conversations with her family, they continue to send her in restrictive clothing. It dulls her glow and creates shame around her difference. Seraphina once asked, "Miss Petra, why am I the only one with wings?"

"Well, Seraphina, you have wings because you are a fae. Those wings give you special abilities, just like Max's ability to run really fast, or Olive's invisibility. Do you like having wings?"

Seraphina looks down at the table, and Petra can see the hesitation. "I think my wings are pretty."

"They are very pretty. I love how they sparkle in the sunlight."

Seraphina's face breaks into a bright smile. "Me too! But Mommy says I can't show them to everyone."

"I know, love. There may be people who don't like your wings, but your wings are part of what makes you you. Remember how you helped get the baby doll out of the tree when Charlie threw it up there?"

"Yeah! I flew up so fast!"

Petra opens her arms, and Seraphina climbs into her lap. "You were so fast. And if you didn't have wings, that would still be up there. Because of you, we can still play with that doll."

"Yeah. Can I take my sweater off?"

"Absolutely!" Petra says. "Do you want to trace your shadow on paper so we can show everyone your fantastic wings?"

"Yes! Yes! YES!" she replies, bouncing off of Petra's lap and running to the shelf for the big paper.

As Petra watches Seraphina line up the paper under the window and instruct a human friend to trace her, she can't help but feel that ember inside her ignite into a full flame. This. This is what she was meant to do. Help children of all species connect and support each other. If only it were so easy to do this in the larger adult community. Maybe she should talk to her directors about running a community event to bring the families together…

Arriving home from the day, exhaustion spawned by a day of caring for her little friends and having to make a thousand different in-the-moment decisions takes over her body. And she still has to attend tonight's stupid council meeting. She has about an hour at home before leaving, so she decides to make a quick dinner and shower to wash the bad vibes off.

While Petra watched Gammy navigate council politics all her life, the idea of going before them is, well, terrifying. The council is comprised of the most powerful beings from each of the factions within the supernatural community. They are the ones who determine the rules, regulations, and laws the Leeside community would follow, as well as how they could engage with the human world. As much as the human and supernatural communities have been integrated within the last fifty years, there are still policies that dictate what is considered appropriate behavior, which are in place largely to keep humans safe. But it means that the council has the ability to dictate the lives of the community to maintain this order and control.

With a few minutes to spare, she dresses in dark-wash skinny jeans, a lilac blouse, a dark gray leather jacket, and black ankle boots. She tops it off with a long silver chain, small silver hoops in her ears, and her family crest ring on her right hand. She does her best to channel Gammy's strength, hoping she looks presentable but fierce.

She leaves her apartment at seven. Walking down the stairwell, she feels a familiar pull in the pit of her stomach seconds before being whisked away through time and space to the council chambers. She hates traveling through ports. Which means it's probably a good thing that she can't do it herself. Through a collective agreement between the various council factions many years ago, it was determined that porting—the ability to travel magically—was reserved for council members only. The council has always been wary that the other members of the community will misuse the skill.

A wave of nausea washes over her, flipping her stomach as she finds her footing in the chambers, the room still spinning. Someone begins speaking; she's unsure who, but she holds up a finger, silently asking for a moment to steady herself. The speaker stops and waits.

"Are you well, Miss Rose?" the speaker asks.

Shaking her head to try to clear the fuzzy feeling, Petra looks up to find herself in the middle of council chambers, which resembles a courtroom with a bench large enough to seat nine judges rather than only one. There is a small stand, presumably for witnesses, off to the right and two tables behind her. She stands directly between the council members' bench and the tables for arguing parties.

"Miss Rose. Are you well enough to proceed?" the speaker, the vampire council representative, asks again.

Mustering whatever courage she can find, she stands tall. "Yes, Councilor Amare, my apologies." Her magic crawls along her skin, sensing something unusual. *Weird.*

"Good, then let us begin," the Councilor responds. "You have been called here because it has come to the council's attention that the current Premier Witch, Gladys Rose, is fatally ill."

Petra sucks in a quiet breath. Hearing it out loud is a gut punch. She fights the urge to sway, staving off the tilting of her world beneath her feet.

"This means the power attributed to the Premier Witch will be without a host, and as you are next in line, it would appear as though you would be the next vessel. However, the council has concerns about your ability to hold this title and to wield the responsibility associated with this role," Councilor Amare says.

"That's a bit unfair…" Petra attempts to interject but is promptly cut off by one of the other council members.

"You have continued to show your lack of interest in the larger magical community, instead spending time teaching mortal children. You have not spent the required time to train and hone your skills. You are also close friends with a witch who has been shunned from the community," the goblin representative, Councilor Clellugs, states matter-of-factly.

Petra stares, stunned at the bluntness of the delivery and the disdain for others. "Pardon me, council members, but not once have I done anything prohibited. I have always done what is expected of me. I work with children because I find value in helping the next generation develop and grow into accepting and acceptable beings. I am helping to build a world of inclusion that I cannot say has been readily supported among all members of our supernatural community. I also want to clarify for the record that the children I teach are a mix of mortal and supernatural beings. And Daisy has *not* been shunned. Her *family* committed some atrocious acts, of which she had no part, and she has been harshly punished for crimes that are not her own. If anything, I would say you could stand to learn from *me*," she finishes.

She plays back what she just said and pales, realizing how much trouble she's caused herself.

"While that speech was wonderful, if not a sign of your lack of control, you failed to address your willful absence from the community and desire to hone your skills. How do you address these issues, Miss Rose?" Councilor Clellugs retorts.

"I have spent many years practicing magic under the watchful eye of Councilor Rose. She has never expressed concern about my skill level or mentioned that I needed to improve. If her level of expertise as the current Premier

Witch is insufficient for you, then perhaps there is another conversation you need to be having, particularly around the value of the role of a Premier Witch," Petra responds, making sure to look each one of them in the eye, posing a challenge as she does. They know the importance of the Premier Witch and how much the current one has done for the community. She knows they aren't questioning Gammy's expertise; rather, they are trying to make Petra doubt her own abilities.

Gammy and Lachlan sit back and look at her with pride as the remaining seven council members shift uncomfortably in their seats. Petra takes a deep breath and feels she has proven her point. The council and the supernatural community are due for a change. They cannot continue in the current world without learning to live more harmoniously with mortal members of society.

Lachlan leans forward. "I think Miss Rose has proven she is more than capable of fulfilling this position. As the demon representative, we endorse her as the next Premier Witch. She would be an excellent addition to the role and could bring the supernatural community into the current century. Let's settle this quickly. All those in favor of Petra Rose as the next Premier Witch, say 'aye.'"

There is a brief pause as the members consider their votes, followed by a resounding "aye" from the council representatives for the witches, demons, faeries, and gnomes. The vampire, werewolf, shifter, and goblin representatives vote "nay," but the remaining vote, belonging to the trolls, is halted.

"It appears we have a tie," the troll council member, Grog, states. "As the tie-breaking vote, I wish to pose a challenge to you, Miss Rose. A way for you to prove you are worthy of this role and serious about taking on all of the responsibility that goes with it." His sinister tone fills Petra with dread. "You see, we have not had the pleasure of getting to know you on the council since you have spent much of your time avoiding your heritage and responsibility as the next Premier Witch. As such, some of us on the council doubt your commitment to our community and the role you will possess. On the other hand, Miss Sloan Wilks regularly volunteers within the community, helps with council functions, and demonstrates her ambition to possess a leadership role."

Is the mention of Sloan supposed to make me jealous or feel inadequate? What do they want from me? Hesitantly, Petra asks, "What is your request?"

"Ah, you must accept before you find out what it is," he says in typical troll fashion. Petra resists the urge to roll her eyes in exasperation at the poorly veiled manipulation trolls are known for. "Think of it as the first step to show you are serious about becoming Premier Witch. If you accept and meet all conditions by the deadline, all council members will accept your appointment to the position," he says, looking down the bench to see the others who side with him nod in agreement. "However, if you should fail, the title will fall to the next in line after you—Miss Wilks—and you will not only forfeit the title, but also your power. Knowing these conditions, do you accept whatever challenge is set before you?"

Petra looks back and forth between Lachlan and Gammy, hoping to receive a hint as to what she should do. Despite the shocked murmurs from the other council members, Gammy and Lachlan's faces remain stone.

"What happens if I don't accept?" she asks.

"You forfeit the Rose power and Miss Wilks will

immediately become the new Premier Witch," Grog replies with a mischievous gleam in his eye.

He's baiting her and she knows it. He knows she can't and won't forfeit the family power.

What else can she do but agree? Gammy is counting on her to continue the Rose legacy. With a deep breath, she says, "I accept."

"Wonderful," Grog exclaims, clapping his hands together. "Then, the condition is that for you, Miss Rose, to be appointed the next Premier Witch, you must marry within the next thirty days to prove your commitment to this community. After all, it is so very important that the community see you valuing long held traditions. If you are unmarried within the next month, our new Premier Witch upon Gladys Rose's inevitable passing will be Miss Sloan Wilks, and you will be stripped of all power. We expect to receive proof of your marriage within thirty days. Meeting adjourned."

With the call for the end of the meeting, all of the council members except Gammy and Lachlan vanish. Petra stands stunned.

What just happened?

CHAPTER FOUR

Lachlan

Married! She has to get married? Who in their right mind would decide that getting married is a valid test to prove worthiness for Premier Witch? Also, why wasn't this discussed among the other council members? And stripped of all her powers if she fails? Hades help her.

Lachlan fumes. Shadows swirl around him and leak from every corner of the room. The intensity of his rage is evident in the growing blackness and silence of the space. He comes down to the lower floor to go to Petra, but Gammy puts her hand up and erects a barrier to keep him on the far side of the room. Protecting Petra from him. From his anger.

"You need to calm down, Lachlan. I understand you're surprised by tonight's events, and I am too. However, my concern right now is my granddaughter, and you cannot be near her in your current state. Either get out of here and do whatever you need to work out your feelings, or use common sense and control your shadows. I will not allow you to take one step closer until you have a clearer head on your muscled shoulders. Do I make myself clear?" Gladys says.

Lachlan raises a hand to the shield and feels the vibrating power as it hovers around him, closing him in. It would be no easy feat to break through it. A witch with her power is almost limitless in their abilities and strength, and while he is an alpha demon, he knows he would still lose against Gladys's skill and experience. His inner demon growls, rising and pushing Lachlan to shift into his demon form. Lachlan's skin begins to tingle, and the hair on his arms begins to darken and lengthen; his ears start to elongate, dark horns push their way out of his forehead, and black wings poke out from his shoulder blades, tearing holes in his shirt and jacket. The dome Gladys placed around him fills with darkness, hiding him from view.

"NO!" Lachlan growls at the demon as he pushes it back into its inner cage, the internal struggle causing him to dry heave. The pain of stopping the shift is almost unbearable. He dry heaves again. *No, I cannot let it loose right now. Get back down, you bastard, and let us be here to support Petra.* He pushes again and feels his demon relent, just enough to give him room to regain control. A minute later, Lachlan stands back upright, sweaty and spent. The shadows have lessened and continue to retreat tentatively. He looks back to Gladys, hoping she can see he is back in control. For now.

With a nod and the flick of a finger, Gladys releases the shield and allows Lachlan to step forward.

"I'm watching you. One sense of that demon of yours trying to make a break for it again, and I will have you flying so fast out of here you will not know what hit you," she warns.

"I understand." Lachlan cautiously steps toward Petra,

who has stood motionless and silent during this entire interaction with Gladys.

"Now, before discussing what happened, we must leave here. I don't trust Grog as far as I could throw him, and who knows what he has listening. Lachlan, meet us at my home. I will port Petra there." Gladys turns to Petra and takes hold of her hands before they disappear.

He ports himself outside the gates of Gladys's home, the protective charm stopping him from going further. He looks up at the mansion beyond the ornate gates, noting the vines crawling up the front, hiding the dark brick and shutters. Finally, the charm falls away, and he rushes into the house.

"Petra, are you okay?" He manages to stop himself before he does something stupid like wrap her in his arms.

Petra's eyes spark, and she comes back into the conversation. "Okay? Am I *okay*? Of course I'm not okay! What kind of question is that?" she answers, her voice escalating with each question. "I just agreed to get married in the next month to keep the title of the Premier Witch in our family. To keep the Wilkses from getting their filthy hands on the council seat. Of fucking course I'm not okay." She gestures wildly around the room, shooting dark pink sparks with each flick of her wrist. Thankfully, Gladys is quick and puts them out before they land. "And Sloan? Really? They want Sloan? The daughter of the slimiest warlock that is clearly using their family insurance company as a front for something else? Oh, but I guess because they support 'traditional community values' it's ok? Please."

"Of course you aren't. I'm sorry. We can figure out a way out of this." He turns to Gladys. "They can't uphold this, can they? It wasn't even discussed among the council."

"Ah, unfortunately, it was likely discussed among those four naysayers, and we merely 'missed' it," she answers, making air quotes. "They likely got together to discuss it before tonight's meeting with every intent to lock Petra into this scenario, feeling she would never follow through with it and thus allow the title to fall to Miss Wilks as they truly desire. They knew it would never have made it into the meeting if the rest of us knew about it, so we were cut out instead. Unfortunately, with it officially entered in the meeting record, Petra is bound by the terms."

"Which means what exactly?" Petra asks, a thread of hope audible in her tone.

"It means that you, my darling granddaughter, must find a partner and marry within the next month. If you don't, the Rose family line will no longer hold the Premier Witch title. The title will shift to the Wilkses until the council deems them unsuitable to maintain it."

Lachlan catches Petra as she sinks to the floor, defeated. She buries her face in his chest. A sense of longing, of wanting to hold her, but in different circumstances, rises within him.

"I can't get married. I can't get married," she repeats into his shirt between sobs.

"This is asinine. They can't hold her to this. We have to be able to fight it," he says hotly, rubbing his hand along her back.

"They can, and they will. The council is unforgiving, as you know. They are tired of Roses in power. Plus, it *is* tradition for the Premier Witch to be married before receiving the title. While the council at the time made an exception when I took the title because I was newly widowed, it appears that this council will not make any accommodations," Gladys tells them.

"Then we need to help you find a way to prove to them that you are capable. That you can do this without needing a spouse," Lachlan says to Petra, whose tears have slowed.

Lachlan notes a look of realization dawn on Petra's face. "They never said *who* I had to marry. Maybe I can marry Daisy! Wouldn't that be a lovely way to spit in their face? Then, as soon as I have the title, we can divorce. It would help her with being invited back into the community and would solve my problem as well."

Lachlan and Gladys look at each other. "As lovely as that could be—and trust me, I would be first in line to see the look on Grog's face—I think it is important that the marriage appears legitimate," Gladys says.

Petra deflates. "But he didn't say that. All he said was I needed to get married."

"True. But as a future Premier Witch, you are now under great scrutiny and need to ensure you are behaving as such. Which means you can't try and make a farce out of this," Gladys cautions.

Lachlan slowly caresses her back with his hand, drawing circles and figure-eights absentmindedly. *What if…*

"What if I married you?" Lachlan says, posing the question before he can think it through.

Petra bolts upright, pushing away from him. "I can't ask you for that, Lachlan. As Gammy just said, it needs to at least look legitimate. I can't do that to you."

"You aren't asking, I'm offering," he says, confident and sure. He meant it, he realizes. He will happily marry her if it means being able to help her.

Petra takes a handkerchief from Gladys and wipes her face of tears, then takes Lachlan's hand. "I appreciate the offer, but I can't lock you in with me and this trouble. I should tell them I can't do it and solve everyone's problem. Let Sloan have it."

"Petra, you can't let Sloan get this title. This power—" Lachlan holds up a hand to stop Petra from interjecting. "Hear me out. We are, I would argue, good friends and have been for a few years. We already see each other almost daily, thanks to Daisy working for me. We know it would be a fake marriage, but the council won't know the truth." He pauses, thinking it through. "We would have to convince them that this wasn't a rash thing to try and meet their demands, so we would have to be seen in public on dates as if we have a real relationship, but I don't see a problem here. We can always agree to an open marriage later on," he says, winking at her. "It's a win-win for everyone. You get to keep the title in the family, and I get to help a friend in need."

Lachlan lets go of Petra, kneeling on one knee in front of her. He holds out his hands as if opening a box, but of course nothing is in his hands. "What do you say? Petra Rose, will you fake-marry me?"

Lachlan watches the emotions play out across her face. She moves from disbelief to consideration to complete shock. She looks to her Gammy, seeking her approval.

Gladys gives the slightest of nods. "Given your timeline, I think this is your best option, my girl."

Petra looks back at Lachlan. "Why not, Mr. Grace? Let's do this."

"The best answer I could have hoped for." Lachlan laughs.

"Well, with that sorted, we need to start getting you ready to join council!" Gladys exclaims.

It's a bleak-looking day outside the window, and despite the dark clouds and rain streaming down, Lachlan wonders if he will ever see the outside world again. This council meeting refuses to end. Lachlan hadn't paid attention to a word Grog has said in the last few minutes, and certainly hasn't heard what he's just been asked.

"I'm sorry. Could you repeat the question?"

Councilor Clellugs glares at him. "Councilor Grace, I asked about your plan for the werewolves' request to open a new restaurant. Given their nature, how can we be sure that products for consumption would be… edible for the public?"

"Well, I assume they would have to follow the same regulations as any other establishment," he responds, bored and disinterested.

"Councilor Grace, I would be remiss if I did not strongly encourage you to return your attention to the matter at hand. You are not a twelve-year-old boy sitting through a history lesson. It is an honor to be a council member, and you must treat it as such by providing the duties afforded to you with the utmost attention," Councilor Grog admonishes.

"And yet you treat me like a twelve-year-old and continually leave me out of council decisions," he retorts. "If it is such an honor, why then, Grog, do you insist on disparaging it with corruption?"

Grog laughs at Lachlan's insinuation. "Corruption? That is a bold claim, coming from the scourge of the underworld."

Lachlan stands abruptly, leaning over his desk, pointing a finger at Grog as he starts to yell, "Listen here, you good-for-nothing slime bucket, you know nothing of my experience in the underworld." He lowers his voice menacingly, narrowing his eyes as he looks down his nose at him and continues, "And you'd do best to watch how you speak to me. Trolls have a special place in the underworld, and I have many connections who would be more than happy to cash in a favor." Grog's green face pales at this threat.

Lachlan smiles smugly at Grog. He sits down purposefully and leans back in his chair, extending his legs and placing his boots on the desk.

Annoyed that he let Grog get to him and knowing he shouldn't threaten harm on another council member, or anyone for that matter, he can't help feeling that douche canoe deserves it. Grog consistently causes trouble in the council, and with the shit he just pulled on Petra, Lachlan has half a mind to call in some of those favors anyway.

He may not be a permanent underworld resident at this point, but he still has connections. He doesn't talk much about what life was like for him down there because reliving it can be just as hard as experiencing it the first time. Instead, he visits when he needs to. When business or council interactions require it, he goes, staying for as little time as possible. Sometimes, he sends someone in his presence, but he would avoid going altogether if he had a choice.

Grog regains his composure and throws Lachlan a sneer as he sits down again. Councilor Clellugs glances between them. "If you two are done measuring your dicks, I want to close out this meeting." Lachlan snorts, knowing he would win that too. Clellugs turns to Lachlan. "Councilor Grace, if you would look further into the werewolf restaurant plan and report back by the next meeting, we will decide on their request." Lachlan nods his acceptance of the order. "Then, I call this meeting to a close." They bang their gavel, and everyone stands to leave. Grog looks back and sneers again in Lachlan's direction.

"You'd do best to watch your step, demon-boy. It would be a shame if you lost your seat here."

Lachlan's eyes flash gold as he stares Grog down, letting his demon surface. "What are you trying to say, Grog?"

Grog steps closer to Lachlan. "We already know Gladys won't be here to save your ass for much longer. You would do well to choose your allies carefully." Grog smirks before he vanishes into the air.

Fucking douchecanoe.

CHAPTER FIVE

Petra

It's Friday morning, and the sun is streaming through the sheer curtains on the window, leaving a bright patch on the dark hardwood floor. Petra, partially covered in a fluffy purple duvet with her temperature-control foot sticking out at the corner of the bed, rolls over and looks at the clock, thankful that she has the day off. She reaches her arms above her head and stretches out while twisting her torso and reaching out with her toes as she thinks about the day ahead. Morris lets out a soft mew, objecting to being disturbed by her stretching while he sleeps by her feet.

Petra rolls over and sits up, reaching toward her toes and petting Morris as he stands, stretching his little murder mittens out in front of him before moving toward her pillows, where he extends and curls his front paws, making biscuits on the duvet, eventually curling up in a ball and going back to sleep. As she leans to the side to kiss him, she sees a text alert light up her phone.

LACHLAN

There's a present for you in the hallway.

A jolt of excitement courses through her. Her magic belatedly sparks awake, humming with energy as it picks up on the traces of Lachlan's shadows lingering nearby. If it were anyone else, her power would have shocked her awake as it sensed a threat, but being so comfortable with him means he can use his shadows to deposit gifts.

She grabs her housecoat from her bedroom door and slides it on, tying it around her curves, eager to see the gift he left for her. Petra opens the door and spots the elongated box. It's about sixteen inches long, bright purple, with a familiar gold script on top. BellaDonna, a witch-owned florist in Leeside, specializes in arrangements to "let life grow anew" as their slogan says —which means they imbue their bouquets with spells requested by the sender. She smiles, imagining what kind of flowers he chose for her and sends her magic out to sense what kind of spell she may encounter. It never hurts to be prepared.

Sensing a simple "pick-me-up" spell meant to help her have a better day, she picks up the package and brings it inside. She places a hand on each side and lifts the lid, hearing the soft *shhhp* parting sound as the box lid comes off. Inside lays a bouquet of white ranunculus, purple calla lilies, and blush roses with a small white envelope. She opens the note and reads:

Petra,

I can't wait to marry you ;). Let's enjoy a date night to celebrate. I'll pick you up tonight at 7.

- Lachlan

Feeling inspired by the flowers' spell, Petra decides to do something that makes her happy. She spends the morning preparing some activities she wants to do with her preschoolers next week before enjoying some quiet time reading in the mid-fall sun as it beats down on her balcony. As the day shifts into early afternoon, she showers and dresses in dark jeans, a gray T-shirt, and a light jacket before heading to Gammy's.

Gammy's butler greets Petra at the door and takes her to the sunroom where she finds Gammy sitting with a book and a cup of tea at a little bistro table. "Good afternoon, Gammy," Petra says, leaning over and kissing her on the cheek before sitting in the opposite chair.

"Hello, my darling granddaughter. How are you on this wonderful day?"

"I've certainly been better. But the impending marriage thing notwithstanding, I am…fine, for lack of a better term."

Gammy drinks from her cup, letting the silence sit between them long enough for Petra to begin to feel uncomfortable. Finally, Gammy breaks the tension. "It is an unfortunate situation, but I do think it is about time you start showing an interest in the council. Perhaps this challenge, while ridiculous for Grog to suggest, is the exact push you need."

Petra's mouth opens and closes silently as she attempts to find words to counter the verbal slap she just received. "I never asked for this. Or expected it so soon," she finally whispers, eyes on her hands as she fiddles with sugar packets in front of her.

"Neither did I. But I accepted my responsibility to the family and to the community. And you knew it was coming eventually."

"I shouldn't have had to do this for many years yet. It was supposed to be Dad. I'm not ready," Petra all but pleads.

"Yes, but James couldn't handle our world. He chose to abandon his responsibility, misused his power, and ran away. I know I played a role in his actions, and my failure as a mother led to his rebellion. Regardless, now the Premier Witch falls to you. You are the last remaining Rose. It is time you accept who you are as a witch and your legacy as a Rose. I know you love the connections you have made through your work, but you can't avoid this forever," Gammy says. What she says hurts, making her insides burn like a cauldron about to bubble over, but Petra knows there is truth there.

"I understand that this would inevitably fall to me, but what about what I want? I have dreams. I have things I want to do. Doesn't that matter?" Petra asks, tears of frustration building in the corner of her eyes. "Besides, I've seen how the council tears people apart. I don't want to be a part of that."

"Of course you matter, darling. But we have a responsibility to our community. A Rose has been the Premier Witch since the inception of the supernatural council. Through generations, we have helped make decisions that guide our community through times of triumph and challenge. We have facilitated collaboration and healthy relationships with other supernatural factions and helped to develop laws and practices that have made our world, both human and supernatural, safer. You, my lovely granddaughter, are the last in our line. It is your destiny to carry on the work that has been done before you, to continue to carry forth our mission."

It's a nice speech, but Petra doesn't miss the fact that

Gammy ignores her comment about the council tearing people apart. Having spent most of her life under the care of Gammy, Petra has seen firsthand how the council has ruled Gammy's life. Petra, and her father before her, always came second to the responsibility and duty the council demanded of Gammy. And now Petra's own plans for her life feel like they've been hexed.

Petra wants to rise to the challenge, to make Gammy proud, to fulfill her destiny as Premier Witch no matter how early it's arrived, but a part of her is telling her to fight against it. To push back and demand change. Is there any way she can do this on her terms, to make the role more palatable, so it doesn't take over her whole life like it did for Gammy?

Petra lets loose a breath. She's already had to accept the asinine conditions set forth by Grog; what's one more challenge to add to the pile? "Fine. I accept my fate. But I want to be able to find a balance. To still be me, while also finding my way to being the Premier Witch. Is that possible?"

"We shall do our best."

"I guess that's all I can expect. So where do we start?"

"Aside from getting you married, we need to get you using your magic more." Gammy stops Petra before she can protest that she does. "Be honest with yourself, Petra. I know you don't use it as often as you should, and you certainly don't tap into the power that lies within you nearly enough." Petra grumbles to herself. She regularly uses her magic to help the children at work and to do things around the house, but she doesn't do the bigger things – the potions and convoluted spells. She's never been one to showboat and has never shown an interest in the more typical casting that's expected. "The other thing we must focus on is getting you into council circles. Which means attending events and being more visible. Show them that you want this, that you are serious about it."

Petra groans internally. Council events are the worst. She attended a few as a teen when there was no one available to watch her and they were always so boring. She had no patience for the posturing and one-upmanship. Despite how she has felt in the past, she knows Gammy has a point. So Petra nods. "When do we start?"

Gammy grins. "Now. Let's practice your magic first."

"I'm not prepared."

"Then there's no better time. Show me what you can do, unprepared," Gammy says, standing. She waits for Petra to stand as well and then guides them to her conservatory, which contains all her necessary ingredients for potions and herbal mixes. "Let's start simple. Make me a mixture to soothe a harsh cold—coughing, congestion, and headache."

Petra has never made a mixture, let alone one to soothe any kind of illness. "But I've never done this before. Can you show me?"

"No. I want to see you draw on your power. It's there, inside you, the natural tendency. You just need to call for it."

Petra glares at Gammy, wondering if she could fire sparks at her and get away before Gammy could retaliate. Knowing how strong Gammy is, Petra accepts that's not likely. Instead, she closes her eyes, letting her hands fall to her sides. She breathes deep, relaxing her body, and calls to her magic, asking it to show her what to do. She nearly gasps as it responds so readily, telling her everything she needs and how to put together the tea mixture. Within moments, she is combining lavender, chamomile, and rosemary in perfect proportions. She grinds them into a finer mixture and deposits it into a tea bag, then hands it to Gammy for inspection.

Gammy beams at her. "Perfect," she exclaims with pride. "Now, try a sleeping potion."

The afternoon carries on like this, with Gammy giving request after request and Petra calling on her power to fulfill it, surprising herself with each successful attempt. The ability to play with her magic was… fun. And unexpected. It's never been fun for her.

"Gammy, I need to get going. I'm meeting Lachlan in a couple hours, and I need to get ready," Petra says, handing her a potion that causes warts on a foe. "Thank you for the lesson today."

"No, thank you. Seeing you begin to tap into the well of power within brings me such joy, my darling." She opens her arms for a hug, which Petra steps into, wrapping her arms around her slender form. "Now go. You can't keep that demon waiting." She winks.

The second she arrives home, Morris greets her at the door, howling loudly as she hangs her keys on the hook and kicks her shoes off. He scampers ahead, leading her to the cupboard with the treats. He's not a small cat by any means, but with how he screams at her sometimes, you'd think she starved him.

Checking her phone before setting it on the counter to get his treats, she sees she has a few texts from Lachlan. For some unknown reason, her heart does a little skip. Odd. It must be a remnant of her magic use today, causing her body to still feel excited after all of her success.

LACHLAN

I hope you've had a great day.

I can't wait to see you tonight.

. . .

Setting her phone down, she finally gets the treats for Morris, which he happily gobbles up before headbutting her leg in thanks and then sauntering away. Standing there watching Morris leave her, she hears shuffling from her doorway. Rounding the corner, she sees a white envelope slide under her door. *Odd.* She bends down to pick it up, then opens the door and gazes down the hall, but whoever delivered it is already long gone. She turns back, swinging the door shut behind her, and returns to the kitchen, opening the letter along the way.

Miss Rose,

Your presence is requested at the Wilks estate tomorrow at eight o'clock in the evening.

Do not be late.

- The Wilks Family

She reads the letter over a second time. Then a third. The message doesn't change, but with each read her magic sparks inside her more and more, feeling barbed as her frustration grows. "Who the fuck do they think they are?" she seethes to the empty room. "Seriously? The Wilkses are summoning me?" This has to be a setup.

Morris leaps on the counter, sitting in front of her and tilting his head as he examines her. "Sorry, bub," she says, running her hand along his head. He mews at her, accepting her apology, and begins to purr. Taking a breath, she feels her power smooth out and begin to flow softly under her skin.

She'll have to talk to Gammy about this summons tomorrow, but in the meantime she needs to get ready for Lachlan. The thought of a date with him sends butterflies dancing in her stomach and a brief smile to break across her lips. *One thing at a time.*

CHAPTER SIX

Lachlan

Pulling up to Declan's house has Lachlan feeling all sorts of nervous. He knows offering to marry Petra is wild, and he's happy to do it. To help her. To keep her within the community. But he needs someone else to tell him he's not being a complete idiot, and he can only hope his little brother is the one do to that for him.

"Hey, come on in," Declan says standing in the open doorway.

"Thanks. You're looking good."

"Yeah, man. Already feeling so much better. I finally ditched the crutches too!" Declan responds, leading them into the living room. "So what's up?"

Lachlan flops onto the couch, putting his feet on the coffee table. Declan side-eyes him. Lachlan removes his feet and sits up. "I need to tell you something, but I need you to listen first and then give me your objective opinion."

Declan narrows his eyes skeptically. "Okay," Declan responds slowly, drawing out the word into multiple syllables.

"So at the council meeting the other night, Petra Rose

was brought in, and there was a discussion about her candidacy for the next Premier Witch. Gladys is sick, by the way. It's not good," Lachlan says. Declan nods along, taking in the information silently. "Anyway, Grog basically suckered her into a deal to show she was committed to the role."

Remaining stone-faced, Declan says, "Okay. So what was the deal?"

"Petra has to get married within thirty days. Well, now less than thirty days."

"And you're concerned?" Declan asks.

"I am. I think Grog's up to something, but that's not why I am here. Or not completely," Lachlan clarifies.

"So why are you here?"

"I offered to marry her," Lachlan responds.

Declan lurches forward in his chair. "You what?"

"I asked you to listen first, remember," Lachlan says. Declan leans back again, the effort to remain calm visible in his features. "Yes, I offered to marry her. There was no stipulation of who she could marry, and we're friends. I wanted to help. Now I need you to tell me I'm not out of my mind."

Declan takes a deep breath and replies, his voice even and restrained, "Of course, you're out of your mind. You offered to marry her to, what? Help her solve a problem?"

"Kind of, I guess."

"And you've had a thing for her for a while, haven't you?"

"I haven't had a *thing* for her."

"You have. You did this so you could be close to her."

"I did not!" *Liar.* "I wanted to help a friend. Anyway, am I an idiot?"

"Yes, you're an idiot."

"Thanks," Lachlan responds sarcastically.

"But I think your heart is likely in the right place," Declan continues. "It sounds like Grog is trying to trap her. But if you can help her and stick it to him at the same time, it sounds *almost* sensible."

"Thanks," Lachlan smiles. Checking his phone, he notices the time. "Sorry, I have to go. I need to stop into the Acorn for a bit this afternoon. Thanks for the help."

"No worries. I'm always happy to call you an idiot."

"I'm sure you are," Lachlan laughs as he stands. He claps his brother on the shoulder and heads out the door.

As he makes his way to the Acorn, Lachlan can't help but think of Petra, his demon practically dancing inside him. Friday nights at the bar are generally their busiest night. Tourists come in for the weekend and often stumble upon Bittersweet Acorn. The bar also has live music most Friday nights, which is a big draw, and tonight is no exception.

When Lachlan arrives, the bar is already packed, and the first band is just walking onto the stage. He's supposed to be off tonight, but he likes to check in anyway and ensure everything is in working order. Upon entering the building, he walks over to the bar and goes through the side entrance, ending up behind the bar, looking at a not-so-happy Daisy.

"How has it been so far?" he asks her.

"It's been hectic. Being short a staff member hasn't helped," she says. She's never been one to hold back and has absolutely no problem telling him when he's fucked up. Given that he's the boss, it's a risky move, but it makes him laugh. He's not here for long tonight; he's just here to help with the initial dinner time rush, and then Steve is coming in to relieve him, allowing him to port home and quickly shower and change before picking up Petra.

"It seems like you're handling it well," he teases. She

throws a towel at him. "Do you need a moment to decompress? You look like you're about to start shooting sparks," he asks, dancing out of the way of the spark that finds its way to his feet as Daisy walks away.

He turns back to the bar and shelves, taking a quick inventory, noting they'll need more lime wedges, a few more bottles of various liquors, and glasses before the night picks up. He makes his way to the back to collect supplies.

His phone vibrates in his pocket. Pulling it out, he sees a call coming through, the same person who has called him multiple times today. They refuse to leave a message, likely hoping that if they keep calling, he will eventually get frustrated enough to answer. Little do they know, Lachlan is a master at avoiding things. This call will be no different. Daisy returns, catching him putting his phone back in his pocket. "Everything okay?" she asks.

"Hmm?"

"You looked annoyed."

"Oh. Yeah. Just a prank call," he says before picking up an empty glass tray and taking it to back room to fill it up. He hears her grumble behind him, saying something about lying demons, but he chooses not to engage.

A few quick hours later, the bar fills up, and Steve is just on time. Lachlan checks in with Daisy and Martin, one of his other bartenders, to ensure all is good to go before he leaves to pick up Petra.

As Lachlan grabs his coat from the hanger behind the bar, he notices a piece of paper slip from his coat pocket. It's about the size of a business card and has a purple-outlined flower facing up. He bends down, picks up the paper, and flips it over.

COUNCILOR GRACE,

TOMORROW. *8:00 P.M.*

WILKS ESTATE

DO NOT BE LATE.

"What the fuck?" Lachlan states aloud.

Deciding he will look into this later, he returns the paper to his pocket. Right now, his only concern is his date with Petra.

CHAPTER SEVEN

Petra

Nerves settle in her stomach, causing little flutters. Her thoughts fluctuate between excitement and *what am I doing?* as she finishes putting on her makeup. A knock sounds at the door at exactly 6:59 p.m. Leave it to Lachlan to be on time.

She opens the door to find a drool-worthy demon who probably impregnated every woman he passed on his way here, just from them looking at him. Those jeans are hugging his powerful thighs just right, and the blue of his shirt brings out the gold flakes in his eyes perfectly. He looks absolutely edible.

Damn it, Hades! Why does he have to look so good?

"Hi," Lachlan says, a smile spreading across his face as his eyes glow with mischief. "You look fantastic."

"Thank you. You aren't so bad yourself," she responds. "Come in, come in. I need a couple more minutes." She moves back into the apartment as he follows her and closes the door behind him.

"How are you doing?" Lachlan calls out from the living room.

"I'm still rattled. I'm not going to lie. But I think it's because there's been so much over the last few days," she calls from her bedroom while changing out of her jeans into tight leather-looking leggings. *Better.*

"I can understand that. It's been a lot to digest. But I have no doubt that you will be able to handle whatever it is that comes your way."

Petra feels a slight blush creep up her neck. Who knew a demon could say something so simple, and yet it wants her to immediately drop her pants?

"Thanks," she says from behind him as she exits her room.

Lachlan turns, then freezes in front of her. Petra smiles dangerously as she does a spin so he can fully appreciate her outfit. After a moment, Lachlan shakes himself out of his stupor and can only say, "Wow."

"That good, huh?" Petra teases.

"It's so good; I may need a minute before we can go out in public," he responds, his voice huskier.

Satisfied, Petra picks a pair of black heels, a coat, and a purse from the front closet. She turns her back to him and bends over to put her shoes on, maybe intentionally giving him a nice view of her derriere.

"Not fair!" he says, walking up behind her. "Don't get me wrong, it's a gorgeous view, but this is unfair. I didn't know we were playing dirty tonight."

"Well, now you know, pookie."

"Yes, I do."

"If we want people to believe this is real, we need to act like we normally would on a date and as if we are interested in each other. So welcome to a date with Petra Rose." She slides her coat on and places her purse on her shoulder. "You ready, snickerdoodle?"

He takes a deep breath. "As I'll ever be." He opens the door and motions for her to lead the way. "Also, 'pookie'? 'Snickerdoodle'?"

Petra laughs. "Just trying out some new nicknames, pumpkin."

Lachlan's head tips back dramatically. "Ugh… they are only going to get worse, aren't they?"

"I don't know what you mean, turtle dove."

He sighs, shaking his head at her, though she sees the corner of his mouth quirking into a smile as they step into the hall.

A short time later, they arrive at Axe Me a Question, a combined recreation business with axe-throwing, trivia nights, and an arcade.

"Interesting choice," Petra says.

"Well, I know you've had a rough couple of days, and I figured you could use either some old-school fun or the chance to get the bad energy out." He holds the door open for her as they enter the building. "So which would you prefer?"

"Astute observation skills. I approve. They also have a bar, right?"

"Yeah."

"Why don't we grab some drinks first, then maybe we can start with the axe-throwing? I do have some things to work through, and throwing sharp objects sounds like a super fun way to do it. Then, depending on how the night goes," she says, winking at him playfully, "we can go to the arcade and see if you have the skills to win me a prize."

Lachlan sucks in a breath, his eyes flaring with what looks like excitement. "That sounds like a challenge, shmoopie," he says before immediately grimacing. "Nope, nope, nope. That doesn't sound right coming from me."

"Maybe it is." She laughs, feeling lighter already.

"Alright. Well, I'll grab the first round, but the loser gets the next," Lachlan says, stopping mid-turn toward the bar. He turns back toward her and leans in to whisper in her ear. "Oh, and Petra? I absolutely have the skills to win your prize."

As he walks away, Petra sits at one of the high-top tables and fans herself with her hand. *Okay. I see you.*

Returning with two drinks, he sets down an amaretto sour for Petra and a whiskey sour for himself.

"I realized when you walked away that I didn't tell you what I wanted to drink. How did you know this is my fave?" she asks.

"Well, one, I'm a bartender. It's kind of my thing," he says, stirring his drink. "Two, you order this at least once a week when you come into the Acorn."

"How do you remember all this? How many people do you see a night, let alone in a week?" She feels her cheeks warm as her magic sparks under her skin.

"You're kind of hard to forget, Miss Rose."

A spark jumps from her finger in response. Lachlan's eyebrows raise in question, and Petra does her best to brush it off as a misfire. Thankfully, he doesn't question it. Instead, she lets the booze and his compliments continue to take the edge off.

"Well, Mr. Grace," she says with a wink, "why don't we go and try our hands at axe throwing?"

"Sounds like a plan."

The friendly staff member who leads them to their throwing booth keeps glancing at Lachlan. Petra gets it: he's a big man, is objectively attractive, and commands attention wherever he goes. The staff member, Lacey, reviews the safety rules and uses the time giving instructions to touch Lachlan's arm on more than one occasion.

Petra's disapproving magic goes rogue, shooting a spark at Lacey's feet, making her jump. *Oops.*

Lacey, now flustered, looks to Petra, a look of understanding dawning. "I should get back. If you have any questions, please don't hesitate to ask," she says before making a rapid exit, careful not to turn her back to Petra on the way out.

Lachlan gives Petra a knowing smile. "Alright, Miss Rose, you first." He hangs his leather coat on the hook.

Petra smiles and does her best not to visibly pant as she watches him push his long sleeves up, exposing the toned, tanned, muscular forearms. She gives her head a shake to clear her thoughts. Petra will not let sexy-as-fuck forearms distract her. She's in this to win. And to have him buy her more drinks.

She picks up the first axe on the rack, glancing behind her to make sure that Lachlan is a safe distance away. She staggers her legs, placing her left foot forward, and draws her hands up behind her head, both hands firmly holding the axe's handle. She brings her hands down and takes a deep breath. As she prepares to throw, she hears Lachlan behind her say, "Oh, one more thing. No cheating with magic."

She turns and glares at him. She faces the target again, summons her strength, and propels her arms and hands up and forward, releasing the axe. She watches it spin through the air with great speed and precision. Or so she thought. It's like it all happens in slow motion. The axe flips through the air, heading for what looks to be a perfect shot. Only it rotates a witch's breath more than it needs, and instead of landing a perfect bullseye, it makes a loud *thunk* and falls to the floor. When she turns back, she spots Lachlan poorly trying to hide an amused grin behind his hand as he pretends to scratch his upper lip.

"That was just a practice shot," she says.

"Mm-hmm. It looked like a great one." He's barely holding in his laughter as he slides his phone back into his pocket. She swears she catches a flicker of something cross his face as he does. Anger? Sadness? She's not entirely sure, but she doesn't want to ruin the moment and lets it go.

She narrows her eyes at him, moves over to the high-top table, and takes a sip of her drink. "Why don't you show me how it's done then, hot stuff?"

"Hot stuff, huh?"

"Oh, shush! Go take your turn," she says, waving him away.

Smirking like the arrogant demon he is, Lachlan moves to the wall and picks up the next axe in the line. He makes quick work of positioning himself to throw. Releasing the axe with great force, it lands with a solid *thump*, firmly lodged into the center of the target.

"Did you catch that? Or do you need me to show you again?" he teases.

Petra rolls her eyes but smiles. They continue to take turns throwing until they have finished their allotted time. Despite losing, Petra feels calmer and more centered than she has in a long time. This was precisely what she needed. Oddly, the night has been better than she anticipated. It is not that she expected anything horrible, but this is a different side of their friendship. Plus, watching him flex and seeing his muscles ripple with each throw hasn't hurt either.

"So, little lady, what's the verdict? Are you up for some arcade gaming, or is this the end of our short-lived relationship?"

Petra places her hand on his forearm. *So warm.* "I think I could go a bit longer. I am a master at Skee-Ball, and I must redeem myself for that miserable performance with the axes."

They spend the next couple of hours playing various arcade games, including Skee-Ball, which Petra literally single-handedly wins. They cash in their game tokens, and Petra chooses a large plastic ring as her prize, which Lachlan promptly takes the opportunity to place on her left ring finger.

"Sorry, I haven't had a chance to get you an engagement ring yet."

Beaming, she looks at her hand and then up at him. She says, "This is perfect."

As the night winds to a close and the Axe Me a Question staff are pushing them out, Petra can't help but feel that maybe, just maybe, this whole fake marriage thing won't be too bad. She can do this. They can make this work.

Lachlan walks her back up to her apartment, and as they approach her door, Petra begins to wonder how real they'll make this. Will he kiss her goodnight? Does she want him to? Her magic sparks inside her, answering with a resounding *yes!*

"Thanks for a great night, champ," he says, awkwardly moving to stand in front of her as one of his hands lands on the back of his neck, rubbing it.

"No, thank you. I had a wonderful time. It was exactly the night I needed. You were a great fake date," Petra replies.

"Maybe we should do this again sometime?"

"I think if we want to make this believable, we definitely will want to. How does Tuesday sound?"

"Sounds like a date."

She catches him looking at her lips, and he leans in. Time slows. She closes her eyes, leaning toward him to meet him in the middle. As she takes a breath, her nose fills with his bergamot scent. It's comforting and homey. She stops, anticipating his lips on hers. Seconds seem to last minutes. His lips haven't found hers. Oh, Hecate! Did she misread this? When she opens her eyes and pulls herself back, he is looking back at her. His eyes are filled with panic. He thrusts his hand out, clasping onto hers, and shakes it. He immediately turns around and walks back to the elevator.

"Night!" she calls down the hall, both confused and amused.

He raises a hand above his head, waving behind him.

Unlocking her door, she steps inside. Petra scoops up the orange ball of fluff at her feet, burying her face in Morris's soft fur as she says, "What the hell was that?"

CHAPTER EIGHT

Lachlan

I *shook her hand.*
    I SHOOK HER HAND!
    I. Shook. Her. Hand.

Lachlan has been sitting in his Jeep outside of Petra's apartment for the last ten minutes, continually replaying the moment in his mind: the smile, leaning in for the kiss he knew they both wanted, then *thrusting* his hand out to grab hers.

He had no choice. There was no recovering from that humiliation; leaving was his only option.

Looking up, he can see her bedroom light still on. A roiling sensation in his stomach, the manifestation of his embarrassment, keeps him from trying to correct his mistake by going back to her door. Should he send a text? Or is it too soon? Wiping his sweaty palms on his pants, he leans forward, bouncing his head off the steering wheel, accidentally causing the horn to sound. Startled, he looks up again, thankfully not seeing Petra in her window watching his self-destruction.

Why have I suddenly turned into a twelve-year-old boy around a girl for the first time?

This was supposed to be a fake date so they could start to be seen together. Only this date felt anything but fake. He saw a different side of Petra. A side he's been yearning to see for years. And he liked it. He's always found Petra attractive. Since the day he met her, he had wondered what it would be like to date her, but as much as they would flirt back and forth when she came into the bar, he didn't get a sense that she was interested in him in that way. So why did tonight feel so different?

He looks up to her window again, but the light goes out.

Head home, you idiot, his demon taunts.

A buzzing sound pulls Lachlan from his slumber. It takes him a moment to identify the sound of his phone vibrating on the nightstand. With his eyes still closed and his brain foggy, he unplugs his phone and brings it to his face. He opens one eye slowly, bringing the world into focus.

The screen illuminates as he taps it with his thumb, showing a series of messages from Petra.

PETRA

Good morning, sweet cheeks.

I just wanted to say thanks again for last night.

It was fun.

Hope you have a great day.

A smile breaks across his face as he remembers the look on her face when he threw the first axe and then the triumph and joy when she won Skee-Ball. As he is about to begin typing out a response, another message from her comes through.

Oh. Daisy and I are going to the market in a bit. It wouldn't be a bad thing if we also ran into you there.

You know, if you're up for it.

LACHLAN

Sounds exciting.

I need to shower first, but I'll let you know when I get there.

And last night was great.

Awesome!

Hope I didn't wake you.

You did

Oh no! Sorry :(

It's okay.

Also, I'm sorry about the handshake.

No worries.

I like a good handshake now and again ;)

Well, I'm available whenever you feel the need.

Oh god. That did not come out as intended.

> I'm going to drown myself in the shower now.

> Hahahaha

> Please don't!

> I don't want to have to find another husband.

> See you soon!

Lachlan's face hurts from the smile Petra causes. Warmth blooms in his chest as he realizes he didn't ruin things with that stupid handshake. She still wants to marry him. Well, fake marry him.

He rolls out of bed with renewed pep as he goes to shower. When he's done, he puts extra care into choosing his clothes, ensuring he looks good for their "unplanned" meetup. Opting for jeans, a gray T-shirt, and his brown coat, he ties his hair back in a bun, satisfied that he looks casual but decent enough to meet his future wife.

Walking out the door, he spots the little envelope with the summons to the Wilks Estate for this evening. Not knowing why, he puts the envelope in his coat pocket, grabs his keys, and shuts the door behind him as fireflies excitedly dance in his stomach at the thought of spending the morning with his soon-to-be wife.

CHAPTER NINE

Petra

P etra can't help but feel a warm glow from deep inside. Perhaps it's just the magic flowing inside her veins, or maybe it's due to the hot demon she went out with last night. Either way, she'll take it.

It feels like it's been forever since she has felt this light. Given everything going on with her and with Gammy at the moment, a gremlin of guilt hounds her thoughts, taunting her for fleeting moments of happiness. Breathing deep, she pushes the monster down, reminding herself that wallowing in worry and negativity isn't going to help.

Instead, she allows her thoughts to wander back to Lachlan and how good he looked last night. Her magic sparks inside her at the thought of Lachlan, and she reminds herself to keep her feelings in check. *This is fake. He doesn't actually want to marry you.* Even so, she lets the spark sizzle just a little bit longer.

Petra throws her hair into a ponytail and puts on a pair of dark wash jeans with a cream knit sweater and beige wedge boots. With a glance in the mirror, she reaffirms to herself that she looks market-ready and is out the door.

Petra makes it to the market only fifteen minutes late, which has to be a new record. Already apologizing, she strides across the parking lot to where Daisy stands with Lachlan. "I'm so sorry. I got stuck in traffic on the way."

"Yeah. Sure. There's *so* much traffic in the like five blocks from your place," Daisy teases.

Petra holds her hand to her chest, feigning shock. "There was! I saw a herd of elephants blocking the way!"

"Uh-huh," Daisy says, giving Petra the most dramatic eye roll.

"Hey," Lachlan says, giving her a slight nod and a smile.

"Hey to you, too." She hadn't told Daisy about Lachlan meeting them here, as she wanted it to seem more causal and coincidental. "What are you doing out and about so early?"

"I felt like a visit to the market this morning as I haven't been here in a while and happened to run into Daisy," he answers smoothly.

"I figured you wouldn't mind if he hung out with us. And even if you did, well, too bad," she says, playfully sticking her tongue out at Petra as she turns around to enter the market, clearly not over Petra's lateness or the elephants.

In response, Petra sticks her tongue out at Daisy's back, then says, "I *guess* he can stay," as she winks at him.

With Daisy a few paces ahead, Petra turns to Lachlan and whispers, "Thanks for playing along there. I haven't said anything to Daisy yet about our… arrangement. I feel bad for not telling her, but I also worry about too many people finding out and it not working."

Lachlan grasps her hand, and her heart skips. Her magic dances inside her as she holds back its urge to shoot sparks in the air. "It's okay. Just tell her when the time is right. This is an odd arrangement, and if Gladys is right, we have to play it carefully to ensure it comes across as legitimate. So if we need to pretend to have coincidental run-ins, we can do that."

Lachlan releases her hand, dropping it like a hot cauldron when Daisy turns around, checking if they are still behind her. With his hand gone, she feels cold, like an ember extinguishing after a long fire.

She catches what she thinks is the briefest questioning glance in Daisy's eyes. Petra walks into the market side-by-side with Lachlan, Daisy ahead, leading the trio.

The three of them spend the morning looking at the various vendors and their goods, picking up some fresh fruit and vegetables, the odd knickknack, or, in Lachlan's case, a large blanket with David Bowie on it.

"What? He's a legend!" he says, trying to justify the absurdity.

Daisy and Petra shake their heads at him and walk to another vendor with a jewelry display.

After shopping, Petra's stomach growls so loudly that Lachlan, standing three booths over from her, starts acting like a hellhound has escaped. He flails around, looking around corners to find where the sound came from. After a few more obscene rumbles from her insides, they vote to have brunch and make their way to the attached restaurant.

Throughout the morning, Petra did not fail to notice Daisy's periodic looks between Petra and Lachlan. Knowing Daisy and her impatience, it was only a matter of time before the questions would start to fly.

While waiting for their mimosas and food to arrive, Lachlan excuses himself to visit the men's room. Petra waits for it. It doesn't take long.

"What is going on?" Daisy probes, leaning into the middle of the table.

"What do you mean?"

Daisy stares at her. "So we are doing this the hard way, huh?" Daisy can be fierce and direct, and Petra loves that about her. But when she senses something, she's like a vampire following the scent of fresh blood.

"Doing what the hard way?"

"Look, I know something is going on between you and Lachlan. I saw the looks you keep giving each other and the handholding earlier. You two have been attached at the hip all morning."

"That's so not true. And there was no handholding," Petra lies.

"Cool, so now you're lying to me?"

"I'm not lying to you," she lies again.

"Tell me the truth. Are you and Lachlan a thing?"

A blush creeps up Petra's neck, turning her cheeks a heated pink. "Define 'thing.'"

Daisy's eyes widen as her mouth opens in surprise. She enthusiastically points at Petra, shrieking, "I knew it!"

Petra hesitates. She knows Lachlan will be back any moment. Does she tell her the truth, part of it anyway? She doesn't like hiding things from Daisy, so she opts for part of the truth.

"I'm sorry. It's new, and I don't want to jinx anything. Lach and I went out last night and had a great time. I want to see where it goes, but I'm not ready to discuss it. We're just testing the waters a little."

"Look, Lach is coming back and I don't want to make it awkward, but know that I'm excited for you and I will help you bury the body if he fucks up. If you're happy, I'm happy."

"Thanks." Petra laughs.

"No problem. Look, here come our drinks!" Daisy says,

her eyes lighting up at seeing their waitress walking in their direction with a tray of mimosas.

Shortly after their food arrives, the conversation stalls as they dive into their meals. The waitress returns with their bills as their meal wraps up, and they get on their way. Lachlan quickly gathers all three checks before they can protest and walks to the cash register to pay.

He comes back to the table, clearly happy that he managed to pay for their meals without either of them fighting him. As he sits, a small white envelope falls from his hand.

"What's that?" Petra asks.

He releases a resigned sigh and hands the envelope to her. She opens it and takes out the card, seeing the summons to the Wilks estate.

"I wish I could explain. But I can't," he says.

"I had a letter slid under my door with the same invite. What are they playing at?"

"I am curious why you have both been summoned to the Wilks estate," Daisy says, looking back and forth between them. "I don't know what's happening, but you better start explaining."

Petra and Lachlan exchange a look between them. He shrugs and gives her a slight nod of approval. Petra sighs and tells Daisy everything.

"So you need to get married to prove you're capable of being a Premier Witch? That's some archaic bullshit. And you've both been summoned to the Wilks estate, but you don't know why. And you, Lach, think this is a setup and that they have somehow figured out your agreement and plan to sabotage it. Petra, you have been thrust into a role you may not necessarily want, but you also feel a sense of family responsibility *'for the legacy'* to take it on. Do I understand this all well enough?"

"Yeah, that about sums it up," Petra says.

"I have no idea what to say, but how can I help?"

Petra's eyes immediately well up with tears, and she dabs a napkin under her eyes. Daisy scoots out of the booth and sits beside Petra, wrapping her arms around her in a soothing embrace.

"You know I'm your ride-or-die. Just tell me what to do, and I will do it. This deal they made is beyond ridiculous and does nothing to show them how dedicated you are, nor does it speak to your capability to be a Premier Witch in general. So whatever you need from me, whether it's to help tear them down or to show them up, I'm your witch."

Petra sniffles and wipes her eyes again, lifting her head from Daisy's shoulder. "Thanks, lady. I'm sorry I didn't say anything sooner. It's been a rough week, and I wanted to keep this close."

Something flashes across Daisy's face, but Petra doesn't quite know what it means before it's gone. "It's all good," Daisy responds as Petra sits up and regains her composure.

"So, with that said, what's our plan for tonight at the Wilkses'?" Lachlan asks.

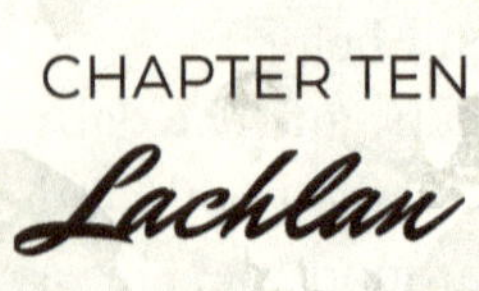

CHAPTER TEN
Lachlan

Lachlan bids Daisy and Petra a quick goodbye at the restaurant and kisses Petra on the cheek, much to everyone's surprise, even his.

"Oh, Hades. I'm sorry."

Daisy and Petra giggle. Petra places her hand on his arm and says, "It's okay. An honest mistake, I'm sure."

"Yes. A mistake," he says, placing his hand on the back of his neck. "I'm going to go before I do something else to embarrass myself." He walks away, trying to determine when he became such a bumbling fool around Petra.

By the time he's made it across the parking lot and into his Jeep, he has a couple of texts from Petra.

PETRA

Lach, it's okay.

Please don't worry about it.

I'll see you tonight.

A feeling builds in his chest as he starts the engine. Could this be anticipation? He's just left her after spending a few wonderful hours together, yet he's already looking forward to seeing her again.

While this is a fake arrangement between them, Lachlan knows deep down that he offered her this deal because he didn't want it to be fake. Is it deceitful? Maybe. Does he hope it works out in his favor and she magically chooses to be with him? Maybe a little. Maybe a lot.

He drives away, feeling an overbearing sense of loss, like he left behind a piece of his heart in the parking lot.

Lachlan arrives at the Wilks estate at exactly 7:59 p.m. As he walks up to the house, he sees Petra standing at the door, looking down at her phone. She raises her head and smiles at him as he approaches. As the clock on her phone flips to eight p.m., the door to the estate swings open, Sloan Wilks greets them formally. "Welcome, Councilor Grace and Miss Rose, to the Wilks estate. We are happy you could join us tonight." She ushers them inside and takes their coats, handing them off to the butler, who has just appeared as if from thin air.

Sloan gestures for them to follow her as she moves into the house's interior. Lachlan looks around in awe of the grandiose nature of this home: the large open-floor plan with cream and gray marble surfaces, the grand staircase, the ornate chandelier hanging in the main entry, and the oversized family portraits. Sloan notices his impressed gaze. "It's a bit much, isn't it? But my family, like the Roses, has been around for a long time, and this house has been here just as long. Each generation has done updates and renovations, which I think helps it be a nice blend of history and modern times."

"It's a lovely home," Lachlan responds politely.

Lachlan and Petra walk side by side, and he reaches out to squeeze her hand in what he hopes is reassurance. Petra turns her head to him and smiles before facing forward again. He places his hand on the small of her back, letting his thumb caress her bare skin exposed by her backless dress. He can feel her shiver at his touch.

They follow Sloan through the house and spy even larger, ornate rooms along the way. Lachlan is pretty sure he even saw a door to a movie theater along the way. As they continue to meander through the home, it seems she's taking the scenic route to either show off the estate or to confuse them so they won't be able to escape. Either option seems possible.

"Welcome to the grand library," she finally says, extending her right arm forward and stepping to the side for them to go in ahead of her.

It's as if a fairytale has come to life. The space itself extends three floors with staircases on either side leading up to the floors above. The back wall alone features built-in cherry wood bookshelves that must be at least twenty feet tall, bursting with books. Lachlan notes the various ladders leaning against the shelves. He half expects woodland creatures or animated furniture to emerge, offering assistance. The room is full of people, ranging from council members to community influencers and bigwigs; he spots Councilor Clellugs and Councilor Amare huddled in a corner in what appears to be a heated discussion, as well as various business owners floating around the room as they mingle.

Sloan quickly excuses herself, leaving them alone. Petra, needing some liquid courage, moves toward the bar, and Lachlan, curious about their collection, begins perusing the shelves. He removes a leatherbound book from the shelf, and as he opens it, a finger trails up his arm.

"Hello, Councilor Grace," the owner of the finger says.

Francesca Wardwell. Like the Wilkses and Roses, she's part of an old Leeside witch family.

Lachlan clasps the book in both hands, turning his body away from the offending touch. "Good evening, Miss Wardwell. To what do I owe this pleasure?"

Francesca smiles in a way he assumes is meant to be seductive, though it comes off as constipated. "I was hoping to have a few minutes with the most handsome demon in the room. And please, call me Franny. All my friends do," she says, batting her eyelashes.

"Are you well, Miss Wardwell? It looks like you might have something in your eye."

"Pardon?" she sputters, running her finger under her eye. "Oh. Yes, I'm fine. There must have been some dust in my eye. Thank you for your concern. I am happy to see you here tonight."

"Were the Wilkses not expecting me to come? This room is full of council members and community leaders. It seems natural that I would attend, especially as I was personally invited."

"Were you not wondering why they have asked for your presence?"

"I have no reason to think there are any hard feelings between us. While a council member, I have not had the pleasure of crossing paths with the Wilkses in my regular council duties," Lachlan responds, trying to determine where this conversation is headed.

"Well, I welcome you to the house on behalf of the Wilkses and hope they do not disappoint. Can I get you a drink from the bar?" Franny asks.

"I would love a scotch neat, please."

"Any preference for distillery?"

"Whatever you think is the best."

"I know just the one. I will return shortly."

Lachlan nods as Francesca turns on her heel and leaves. What a strange encounter.

He wonders if this is nothing more than a song and dance to try and impress him and the rest of the council. To highlight that Petra doesn't have what it takes. The Wilks family has money and influence, it's clear by the gamut of attendees, yet they don't seem to realize that Petra doesn't need an ostentatious house.

Francesca returns with Lachlan's drink, handing it to him and snapping her fingers to produce a folded piece of paper.

"Here is your drink, Mr. Grace, and I also have this for you," she says, slipping the folded paper into Lachlan's open hand.

Lachlan looks at Francesca and tilts his head, narrowing his eyes as he scrutinizes the witch before him.

"Thank you for the drink," he says warily, taking a sip. A part of him wonders if he's about to be poisoned but also feels it would look bad for the Wilkses if he suddenly dropped dead. "Should I be concerned about what is on this paper?"

Francesca lets loose a shrill laugh, the sound piercing his ear drums. She reaches over, placing her hand on Lachlan's bicep. "Wow. You must be so strong," she says stepping close enough that he can see her mascara goop at the corner of her eyes. "It's merely a letter of character."

"A letter of character?"

"Yes, for Sloan. I was asked to pass it on to you, with you being a council member and all. We know the Premier

Witch space is in consideration, and we hope we can count on your support."

Lachlan stands silent for a moment. He stares at Francesca's hand, which still rests on his bicep. She laughs sheepishly and removes her hand, but not before giving his arm a playful squeeze. The audacity of this witch to touch him so openly and to try to bribe him on behalf of the Wilkses. He looks across the room and spots Petra in conversation with the owners of Taster's Delight. Francesca is not the witch he wants touching him. Bringing his attention back to her, he looks down at the paper in his hand and moves to hand it back to her, but Francesca raises her hands. "No, no. Please, keep it."

Placing the book back on the shelf, Lachlan pulls himself up to his full height, allowing his eyes to flare gold and his shadows to circle their feet as his demon rises. "I want to be very clear here, Miss Wardwell. I appreciate the Wilkses' hospitality, but I will not be bribed and will not base my decision on character references from a candidate's friend. I thank you for the drink, but I think it's time I speak to some of the others here tonight."

Francesca squeaks and jumps away from him, noticing the shadows beginning to wrap around her legs. His eyes follow her as she finds Sloan.

Drink in hand, he mingles around the room, chatting to various business owners he has helped get started and whom he has personally advocated for at council. As he chats with the owners of Taster's Delight, his eyes find Petra again. Sloan and Francesca are with her and the look on her face nearly breaks him apart. He excuses himself from the conversation and goes to her.

CHAPTER ELEVEN

Petra

etra winds her way through the various community members present tonight, shaking hands with some and awkwardly waving at others as she moves to the bar. She's never been one for the schmoozing. It seems so fake to be friendly with people she wouldn't talk to on a regular day. After years of seeing Gammy having to place that Premier Witch smile on her face at these events as she promised one thing or the other while Petra sat by hoping for a shred of that attention, doing this herself now feels dirty. Like she's compromising a part of herself.

She makes another quick lap of the room, saying hello to the other council members – narrowly avoiding Grog – and conversing with some of the business owners she knows. She's only been here a short while, and already, her chest feels tight. Beads of sweat begin to form on her brow as she realizes the number of eyes that have found and tracked her movements through the room. Of course, two sets of those eyes belong to Sloan and her minion Francesca. Petra notes Francesca chatting with Lachlan and the way she touches him. Francesca looks completely enamored, using every opportunity to caress him in the same way Petra has imagined doing.

She orders a glass of champagne and a whiskey neat, intending to bring the latter to Lachlan. Despite whatever is happening with Francesca, Petra is glad she is here with him tonight. Before she can step away from the bar with their drinks, she is greeted by Francesca's high-pitched, nails-on-chalkboard voice. "Well, look what the broomstick dragged in."

"Good evening, Francesca. Hello again, Sloan," Petra says, attempting pleasantry. "This looks like a lovely gathering you and your family have put on. I am honored to be included."

Sloan smirks, picking up a glass of champagne from the bartender. "The pleasure is all ours."

"It's also an easy way to scope out the competition," Francesca says, gazing at her manicure, already bored with the conversation.

"Now, Franny. Play nice," Sloan admonishes.

"What? It's true. Little Miss Thing here might as well know what she's in for."

Petra, choosing to channel poise, ignores the bait from *Franny*. "The invite is still appreciated. It is so nice to see a part of Leeside history." As the second-oldest family in Leeside, next only to the Roses, the Wilkses are well-known throughout the community, and their estate has been a major landmark in Leeside for well over a century.

Francesca, choosing to ignore Petra now, turns to Sloan, loudly sharing for everyone around them to hear, "It's not like she really has a chance anyway. Everyone knows they just included her in the running so that they didn't piss off her grandmother."

The jab is like a spark to her insides, twisting and

burning her stomach, hitting at her insecurities. Francesca turns back to Petra, popping a candy in her mouth nonchalantly. "Oh, sorry! Was that out loud?"

Petra's eyes start to well. *No! Not here.* Forcing the tears back causes her fingertips to spark, the hurt manifesting as anger instead. As much as setting Francesca's dress on fire sounds like a good idea, she fights the urge to let a spark slip from her fingers. She looks across the room, spotting Lachlan talking to some man who looks like the stereotype of a university professor.

"I've heard about the, uh"—Sloan pauses, searching for the right word—"*challenge* the council put upon you. Do you think you will satisfy the requirements?"

"I will do my level best to prove my worth," Petra responds, her voice tight.

Sloan snorts, slowly rotating the champagne flute in her hand. "But that doesn't mean you *can*. I mean, you haven't had a serious partner for how long? According to the coven gossip channels, your last relationship—I mean, if you want to call three dates a relationship—was months ago and ended when Caleb ghosted you. Finding someone who likes you enough to get married in the next few weeks seems insurmountable. I'd bow out now if I were you." Behind her, Francesca bounces almost giddily as she puts her hand out and mimics dropping a microphone.

"And I would find some better company to keep if I were you," Petra snaps back. The response takes them both by surprise. *Damn it.* Sloan's knowing smile shows that she knows she got under Petra's skin.

Hearing heavy footsteps approaching, Sloan turns, noticing someone coming up behind them. "Looks like someone else wants to speak with you," she says, grabbing Francesca's hand and steering her away.

"Good evening, Councilor Grog. What a pleasure to see you," Petra says, failing to hide the hint of annoyance in her tone. She feels Lachlan's hand settle on her back reassuringly as he slides in beside her.

"It is so very nice to see you too, Miss Rose. And you, Councilor Grace," he says in a saccharine tone. "Checking out the competition, are we? How is that search for a marriage prospect coming anyway?"

Petra does her best to maintain her composure and plasters on the fakest of fake smiles. She straightens her posture, summoning confidence and power, before saying, "I thank you for your concern, Councilor. I assure you I am taking this whole archaic agreement seriously and will do what I can to ensure that the honor of Premier Witch is passed on to the most deserving candidate." She feels a flare of anger again as her magic responds to her emotions. She pushes it down, keeping the spark at bay for now.

Councilor Grog narrows his eyes at Petra. "Archaic? Is that really what you think about our time-honored traditions?"

Against her better judgment, she snaps back, "Is it really a time-honored tradition if no one has ever been asked to do it before? And yes, I think it is archaic. Would you have asked a warlock to get married if he were under consideration for this position?" Grog begins to sputter, trying to find a response. Before he has a chance to get his thoughts together, Petra continues, "I doubt it. But because I am a woman, you think you can force me into a marriage, which is also a time-honored tradition," she finishes, taking a satisfying sip from her straw as she looks up at Grog, feigning innocence.

His disgusting hand lands on her arm, squeezing it tightly. It hurts, and she winces but doesn't pull away. She's not going to show him a single weakness tonight. "Now listen here, you useless witchling," he begins in a low tone. "I am a revered council member who could make your life a living hell. You would do your best to show me the respect I am due." Grog huffs angrily at her, spit flying and landing on her exposed shoulder as he releases her.

Lachlan smoothly hands her a handkerchief to clean the spittle off and takes a threatening step toward Grog, using his considerable height to intimidate Grog to remove his hold on her. "As a fellow council member, I want to remind you, Grog, that you are to remain impartial for these proceedings as we decide on a new Premier Witch. I also want to remind you that should you continue to degrade an upstanding member of our society, which Miss Rose is, I will be forced to bring you in front of our fellow council members to review you and your position. I advise you to think carefully before your next words, and," Lachlan continues, his voice lowered menacingly, "if you touch Miss Rose again without her permission, I will *end* you." Lachlan steps back and casually sips his whiskey.

Grog's eyes flash with surprise, then calculation. He looks pointedly between Lachlan and Petra. "I should watch what I say, hmm? Well, it seems as though someone else is having difficulty being impartial." Tilting his head condescendingly, he leans toward Lachlan. "Maybe it is you who will need to come before the council and be sanctioned, Mr. Grace. I am sure it is unethical for you to be in a relationship with one of the candidates. What would the other members think, hmm? I wonder." He leans back to an upright position with a sinister look. "It was truly a pleasure to see you both this evening. It has been…enlightening." He turns on his heel and walks away.

Petra can feel the magic rumbling under her skin in fury,

ready to explode. Lachlan places a hand on her arm and strokes her lightly. Soothingly. His hand is warm, the skin soft on her arm.

She feels her magic respond to his, instantly relaxing and flowing more smoothly inside her. Typically, it feels sharp and ready to stick to whatever she needs. But around him, it is smooth and almost fuzzy, like a velvet cloak, as if it was welcoming him into her warm embrace.

Lachlan softens his gaze, looking into her soul. "Are you okay?"

She nods gently, looking up through her lashes at him. "I am. Thank you. I'm not sure how I would have handled him without you here. I am sure that whatever I would have done or said would not have helped land me Premier Witch."

He softly cups her chin, ensuring that he has her full attention and that she has his, "I would jump into a fire for you, Petra Rose. We are a team, and he was seriously out of line. He needed to be reminded of his place." He brushes his hand across her cheek and down her arm.

Her cheeks warm as a blush rushes up her body. She holds his gaze for a moment longer than she should before saying, "Speaking of which, was what he said true? Is it unethical for us to be doing this? Will it hurt your position as a council member? I won't do this if it does. I can find someone else." She shivers, more as a stress response than being cold, but Lachlan catches the movement. Without asking, he removes his suit jacket and swings it behind her, placing it on her shoulders. The warmth from his body still captured within it, wrapping her up like a fresh cinnamon roll. Taking a breath, she breathes in his scent: bergamot with a hint of honeysuckle. It's heavenly.

"Don't you dare," he growls. "He's just trying to scare

you. I will deal with him and the council. You focus on making sure you get the title, which is rightfully yours, despite anything he may say."

Petra stands back and takes a long look at Lachlan. "How did I get so lucky to land you as a friend, Mr. Grace?"

"Clearly, the Fates had a hand in it." He looks around the room. "I'm not sure about you, but I have had enough of these people for one night. What do you say we get out of here and get a burger?" Lachlan asks, putting his elbow out for her to loop her arm into.

"That sounds magnificent," she responds, accepting the invitation by guiding her arm into his and allowing him to lead her out. As she walks out, she knows she will need to tell him about her conversation with Sloan and Francesca, but for now, she wants to soak in this moment with him. She smiles, trying her best not to focus on how her power swirls and dances where Lachlan's body is making contact with hers and failing miserably.

CHAPTER TWELVE
Petra

Petra, kneeling on the floor, marvels at the now empty and spotless fridge. Cleaning is much easier and quicker when magic is involved, but there is something to be said about the satisfaction of doing a deep clean with your hands. The monotony of the task lets her get lost in her thoughts, giving her time to process and find solutions to any problems she faces. Admittedly, an unhealthy portion of the day has been spent ruminating on the previous night's conversations with Sloan and Francesca. These two witches made it abundantly clear that Petra had no place in their world. After spending so much time since leaving their presence, playing the conversation repeatedly in her mind, she begins to question whether they are right.

Questioning her ability comes easy. She's never really wanted this. Yes, she loves being a witch and the relationships gained because of it. But she's never wanted the spotlight, and it seems like everyone knows this. The glory that comes with the title, nor the responsibility, has never been appealing. For the last twenty years, she's watched Gammy managing all of the politics and frustration that comes with being Premier Witch, and it's just never been something that made her think *I want that*. Petra knows it is not hard to believe that Sloan and Francesca are right, and she wonders if the community would be better served by someone who wants it. Someone with the drive and desire necessary to handle the role. Someone who isn't her.

But then the Rose family legacy would end with her. The expectation that she would take on the Premier Witch role and create a little witch of her own one day adds to the pressure she already feels. While she's never thought of taking over as Premier Witch from Gammy, she's also never considered having children. She likes working with them but also enjoys being able to go home and not have her own to care for. Would she be mandated to procreate, much like she's being ordered to marry? Is that something she wants?

All of these thoughts swirl in her brain as she moves to clean the bathroom. Then, there's the added complexity of Lachlan and whatever is happening between them. The thread between them seems to be strengthening, and she feels it tugging her toward him more and more. He's offered to help her, but at what cost to him? What dreams does he have? How will their…*arrangement* change his life and change their relationship? She doesn't want to lose his friendship. She scrubs the shower roughly, working out her frustration and confusion. Can they keep their friendship intact after this fake marriage? Can she keep these feelings growing for him locked away?

Her phone rings in the kitchen, pulling her out of her reverie. She looks at the number and sees it's the lobby of her building; someone wants in. She answers.

"Hello?"

"Hi, sweetie," replies the visitor.

"Come on up," she responds, surprised, as she pushes

the button to open the door before hanging up. She unlocks her front door, knowing Gammy will walk right in, and returns to the kitchen to start the kettle.

She hears the door open and Gammy call out, "Where is my darling granddaughter?"

"I'm in the kitchen. Pardon the…mess," Petra says, forgetting about the chaos she caused in her cleaning frenzy.

"Hello, love," Gammy says as she enters the kitchen.

Petra hugs Gammy, holding on a little longer than usual, trying to soak up her presence. It was only two weeks ago that Gammy broke the news of her impending demise, altering the course of Petra's life completely. Not that Gammy is at fault.

Gammy gives her a big squeeze and rubs her back in soothing circles. "It's been a rough week, hasn't it?"

"More than you know. But let's not talk about me. What brings you here?" Petra asks.

Gammy gasps, placing her hand on her chest in fake alarm, "You wound me! Can't a grandmother visit her only granddaughter whenever she feels like it?"

Petra can't help but let a little smile through. Many people don't get to see this silly side of Gammy, and Petra will forever be grateful that she is one of them.

"Was that a crack in the armor I saw? Please share why you are so guarded that I could feel your shield across town."

"You could *not* sense my shield across town," Petra shoots back, side-eyeing Gammy before pouring their tea.

"No, I could not. But you admit you are shielding right now. Let us go have a seat and discuss what has my granddaughter so worked up," she says as she turns around and sees there is no place to sit, as every surface has been buried under…something. "Or we can stand here instead?"

Petra shakes her head and flicks her wrist, sending everything in the living room back into its rightful place. Books fly off the table and back on her bookshelves, dinnerware soars back into the cupboards, and blankets fold themselves as they return to the linen closet. With another flick of her wrist, steaming cups of tea, perfectly prepared for each of them, appear on the counter, and Petra hands Gammy hers.

Petra gestures toward the sofa and chair set in the living room. She sits on the soft pink and puffy, oversized chair, and folds herself into it, making herself as small as possible. Gammy sits on the couch, bringing her feet up beside her, then turns to look at Petra and tilts her head as she takes in her granddaughter's protective posture.

"What's all this about?"

Petra sighs, deciding where to start and what details to share—wondering how she protects herself, her Gammy, and their legacy. As a member of the council, Gammy is privy to more information than Petra is, but she wonders how much she truly knows about the other council members. She appreciates that Gammy sits patiently, giving her space and time to form what she wants to say.

"I'm just having a hard time with processing everything and what it means for any plans I had," Petra finally says.

"Yes, I know a lot has been thrown at you this week, and I can understand your need to shield, to feel like you need to protect yourself. But you must remember that when you build a shield as thick as I'm sensing, you protect yourself not only from harm but from others getting close to you."

Petra looks down at her hands in her lap and watches her fingers as she repeatedly weaves them together and apart. She tries her best not to sound broken. "I know. The shield was not intentional. It developed after I left the Wilks estate last night and appears to have continued to grow in intensity since. My magic feels…off." Petra looks up as she finishes her statement and sees the tiniest flare of surprise in Gammy. *Interesting. She didn't know I was there last night. Did she even know about the party?*

"When did your magic start to feel different?" Gammy asks, ignoring the mention of the Wilks family.

"It was fine last night, but it hasn't been quite right since I got up this morning. I figured it was due to stress. Why? Do you think something is wrong?"

"Perhaps. We must wait for your shield to dissipate before we truly know."

"Okay…" She tries not to be concerned or let the thoughts from earlier infiltrate her visit with Gammy. "Can I ask you something?"

"You can ask me anything, my girl."

"You looked surprised just now when I mentioned being at the Wilkses'. Why?"

Petra can see the gears turning in Gammy's head. There's something there, something deeper than just the long-standing competition with the Wilkses. "I was both surprised to hear there was a gathering, as I imagine it was a last-minute venture, and that I was so conveniently left out. Which makes me wonder what their angle was. Who all was there?"

"Everyone. The other council members, community members, business owners…"

"Interesting. I assume Grog was in attendance?"

Petra swallows. She doesn't want to repeat the swill that Grog said to her last night, but she nods her head in answer.

"Curious. I wonder…" Gammy says, her words trailing off as a look of deep thought emerges on her face.

"What is it?" Petra asks.

"I wonder if Grog is behind this. Trying to put Miss Wilks front and center," Gammy responds, reaching forward and picking up her drink again.

Petra shifts, unfolding herself and sitting upright with her legs crisscrossed on the oversized seat. "Why do you think he's orchestrating it?"

"Grog and I have…a bit of history," Gammy begins. Petra senses this will be a lengthy story, so she picks up her teacup and leans back, settling in. "Hegnir was already on the council when I joined as the newly appointed Premier Witch. Your grandfather had recently passed, and your father was only a few months old. I had a lot to manage at the time since my own mother had passed during this time as well. She was a formidable witch who had an unfortunate run-in with a group of angry shifters, and it didn't end well for her. Anyway, I digress. One of my first votes as Premier Witch was on an issue close to my heart. The council had been working toward a more integrated society with the human world. They wanted us to co-exist with the humans and actually be able to support each other. Well, some of them did. When I joined the council, Hegnir took it as an opportunity to sway the vote to his side—the anti-integration side. He always felt that humans didn't deserve to benefit from our abilities and believed that we needed to stay separate. The council, of course, voted in favor of the integrated community, and he believed that it was my fault. That my vote was the deciding one, and had I have voted with him and his cronies, then our world would be the better for it."

"Wow. So he's always been a hateful prick?"

Gammy snorts. "That's one way to put it. But yes, he's always been… challenging, and traditional in his beliefs. He was so upset that he cornered me on a walk with your father in a pram one evening. He threatened me and said I would live to regret what I've done. Hegnir has been a thorn in my side for nearly fifty years now, always pushing against what is best for our community, both human and supernatural. He fails to see the progress we have made and instead continues to try and send us back to a time of witch hunts and troll dungeons."

"That's a lot of resentment to carry for so long. So what does this have to do with the Wilkses and their party?"

"I don't know. But I sense that he has gained followers with the Wilkses and is going to try and use their influence in the community to push against you as the new Premier Witch so he can have a guaranteed vote on the issues he wants put through council. How he will accomplish this, I am not sure, but unfortunately, I think he's going to do his best to remove the Roses from power," Gammy replies, years of battle suddenly visible in every wrinkle of her expression.

At least now Petra understands why Grog has been so insufferable and why it feels like he has been personally attacking her. "So what do you think I should do?" Petra asks. She feels the heavy weight of all of these years of resentment settling on her shoulders.

"To start, make sure you meet his conditions for becoming the next Premier Witch."

"And then?"

"And then? Then you show him who he messed with, my dear," Gammy says, fire lighting her eyes. "Now. About why I came today. This marriage to Lachlan, are you certain?"

Gammy looks at Petra, concern written all over her face. She leans over and grasps Petra's hands. "My darling girl. We can find another way if you don't want to do this. We can look again for a loophole in the agreement. We can create a clone. Goddess, we could blow up the council if that is what it takes." Petra smiles at that. She certainly would have liked to do that to Grog last night. "Tell me what you want, and I will use all my power to help you make it happen."

Petra can feel tears welling up. "Oh, Gammy. I love you. I know you would move heaven and the underworld to help me. The problem is that I don't know what I want."

"I know. But maybe this is what you are meant to do. Maybe this is all for some greater reason that only the Goddess knows."

"Maybe," Petra responds. She pauses and gathers the courage to admit the next part. Barely above a whisper, Petra voices her greatest fear. "Maybe… maybe… I'm not good enough."

"Hades and Hecate!" Gammy exclaims. "What gives you that idea?"

Petra doesn't answer.

"You are a *Rose*. You have more power in your pinky nail than any other witch your age. While yes, you haven't traveled the depth of that well of power yet, that does not mean you are not capable and worthy of the title," Gammy insists.

Petra remains silent, feeling tightness in her chest as the negative thoughts from earlier reemerge. Gammy was made for Premier Witch. How could she understand how inadequate Petra felt?

Gammy stands up and moves over to sit at the end of the coffee table directly in front of Petra. She grasps Petra's chin firmly and makes her look her in the eye. "You, Petra, are no mere garden gnome. You are a powerful witch who can do whatever she wishes. You come from a legacy and a

Leeside founding family. You are my granddaughter, and my granddaughter is worthy."

Petra's lips quaver. "What if I don't want to be worthy?"

"Well, it's a little late for that. You have always been worthy, even if you choose not to accept the Premier Witch title. But there is power in your blood. You will need to reckon with that someday." Gammy lets go of Petra's chin and stands up. She collects her purse and coat from the kitchen counter and walks to the door. She places her hand on the doorknob and turns back to Petra, still curled up on the chair. "While I will support any decision you make, I will not sit here and watch as you wallow in self-pity because you can't process your privilege. It is an honor to be a Rose and an honor to be even considered for the Premier Witch. Let me know your decision and if you wish to move forward with the wedding by the end of the week." She shuts the door firmly behind her.

Petra buries her face in her hands and weeps. As she does so, she feels her shield add another layer. Another brick in place to keep herself safe. Another wall to shelter her from the world trying to decide her life for her.

She flicks her wrist again, and everything that flew back into place returns to the heaps and piles they were when Gammy first arrived. This suits her. The chaos, the destruction, the lack of order. She's always felt out of place in this supernatural world, so it only makes sense that she feels comfortable when things around her match that.

She doesn't belong here, and the community will never accept her as the Premier Witch. Maybe Sloan and Francesca were right after all.

CHAPTER THIRTEEN

Lachlan

I t's been a few days since the night at the Wilks Estate and just as long since he's seen or talked to Petra. He's thought about texting or stopping to check on her, but he keeps convincing himself not to. The other day, he received a call from Gladys, which he has yet to return. It's never a good thing when she calls, and he'd rather someone else deal with whatever problem she's got right now. At that thought, he hears a loud clang behind him and whips around.

What the hell?

Standing there as if he summoned her, is the Premier Witch herself.

"Good afternoon, Lachlan," she says, smiling in a way that hints at trouble.

Lachlan reaches up, runs a hand through his hair, and rests it on the back of his neck, trying to pass off the fact that she actually startled him. "Nice of you to… pop in. To what do I owe this pleasure, Gladys?"

"My granddaughter."

"Petra sent you? I didn't realize we were using messengers these days."

"No, she didn't send me. I am concerned about her and our quickly depleting timeline," Gladys informs him, picking up a dusty trinket on the desk beside her.

Lachlan's eyes flared wide, giving away his surprise.

"Ah, so she hasn't talked to you. Interesting. Very interesting."

"Why is it interesting?"

"Because I thought she would talk to you about what's bothering her. But it appears she is keeping that shield up, perhaps reinforcing it," she answers, replacing the trinket and then wiping the dust on her fingers onto a handkerchief she pulls from her coat pocket.

Lachlan leans against the door frame behind him and crosses his arms across his chest. Something is wrong with Petra? Guilt creeps in. Something is wrong with her, and he couldn't get over himself enough to go check on her.

Gladys takes his continued silence as an invitation to push forward. "Seems maybe you two aren't quite in sync yet. You need to talk to her about your arrangement. You are already close to two weeks into this conditional agreement, and you need to move forward with the marriage if we want her to secure the Premier Witch title."

Lachlan's phone vibrates on the counter. He silences the call coming through.

"Do you not want to take that?" Gladys asks.

"No. It can wait." She quirks an eyebrow at him and then nods.

Lachlan lifts one of his hands and runs it down his face. "Anyway, about Petra. I can talk to her, but I won't push her into something she doesn't want to do. We can find another solution if we need to," he says firmly. *As much as I would prefer she chooses me.*

"She needs to make that decision sooner rather than later."

"I'll go talk to her."

"Good. Help her break the shield down. Keep me informed on the progress of the rest of it."

"Yes, madam witch."

With that, Gladys turns. A quick *pop* sounds, and she's gone, leaving no trace that she was ever here in the first place. Lachlan lets loose a sigh. "Alright, shower first, save Petra second," he says to no one, turning down the hall toward the bathroom.

When he arrives at Petra's apartment, the hairs on his neck stand on end. He can feel the shield she has erected around herself from the hallway and see a faint hint of the dark pink shimmer. He's never seen such a protective force before, and he's unsure he can break through it if she turns him away. Seeing the shimmer from the shield, he knows this can't be good. He's only ever seen her physical magic turn from its usual light and airy pink to dark and dense when she's deeply upset or stressed.

He raises his fist, knocking three times on the door and calls out, "Petra, it's me."

Silence answers him.

He raises his fist again and knocks harder this time. "Petra, it's Lach. Can you let me in?"

He receives no response again.

After a prolonged moment, he hears shuffling from the other side. The handle turns, opening to reveal Petra in tight shorts and an oversized sweater. Her eyes are puffy and red. Yet, despite this raw appearance, he feels she could not look more beautiful.

Mine! his demon commands. "Calm down," he tells it.

"What was that?" Petra calls, already heading back into the apartment.

"Nothing," he responds quickly.

Pulling out his phone, he opens a new conversation with Gladys as he follows Petra.

LACHLAN

I am at Petra's.

That shield is strong.

She's a mess.

GLADYS

Good boy.

Stay as long as is needed to help her work it out. Keep me updated.

Will do, boss.

Petra picks up the used tissues that litter the living room floor as he sits at the far end of the couch, not wanting to infringe more on her space than he already has by his mere presence.

"Do you want to watch something?" Petra asks, finally sitting at the other end.

Lachlan stretches his arm along the back of the couch, crossing one ankle over his knee, hoping he looks more relaxed than he feels. Despite being relatively comfortable around each other for some time, this is new territory for him, being the concerned partner. His last and only serious partner, Desi, was also a demon and more forthcoming than

Petra. Desi never hesitated to tell him when he fucked up or if something was on her mind. So, having to figure out how to navigate a relationship with a partner or soon-to-be partner who was more introspective was different.

"Sure. What do you have in mind?"

"Something scary?"

"Sounds good."

"Cool. You scroll through the various streaming platforms and see if you find any contenders. I'll make some popcorn," she replies, going to the kitchen.

As he sifts through the different options, he keeps an eye on her, noting how she keeps wiping at her eyes and nose, trying to hide evidence of tears. She doesn't need to keep a strong facade around him; she should know this. The question is, does he call her out on it or see if she will broach it herself? When she returns with snacks and a glass of soda for each of them, she settles on the seat next to him, curling her legs underneath her, the bowl of popcorn nestled between them.

"So, we have a few options," he begins. "In the classics category, we have *Nightmare on Elm Street* or *Halloween*. In the gory category, we have *Saw* or *House of 1000 Corpses*. And finally, for the more psychological horrors, we have *Get Out* and *Misery*."

She sniffles and puts on a smile. "Let's go classic, and…" She pauses as she decides. "*Nightmare on Elm Street*."

"Good choice," Lachlan says, setting it to play. "Do you need anything?"

"Maybe for you to hold my hand at the scary parts, but that's it."

He laughs. "I think I can manage that."

They make it halfway into the film before Petra has to pause for a bathroom break and snack refill. She's jumped a few times, and he has taken advantage of it to be able to touch her, even briefly, as she squeezes his hand and hides her eyes. Given she's looked away so many times, he's a bit surprised she wanted to watch something that scares her, but at the same time, he's content to share the moment with her. Hell, they could be dangling off a cliff, and he'd feel the same way.

Her sniffles have become less frequent as they get further into the movie, so maybe she's just trying to distract herself from crying or whatever it is that has her upset.

When she returns, he decides to see if she will open up to him.

"Can I ask you something?"

"I guess," she responds hesitantly.

Looking up at her, he places his arm on the back of the couch again, allowing him to touch her. Touching her cheek softly, he says, "When I arrived, it looked like you had been crying for a while. Do you want to talk about whatever it is that's upset you?"

CHAPTER FOURTEEN

Petra

She huffs out a breath, leaning into his touch as he brushes his thumb along her cheek. "I was hoping you wouldn't notice. Guess I wasn't as good at hiding it as I thought."

All the emotion— the pain, the frustration, and the pity — she has been shoving down over the past few weeks bubbles over inside her. She can't hold it back any longer. A loud sob escapes her lips as her chest heaves, trying to gather air. Lachlan flinches in what she can only assume is surprise at her drastic escalation, but then he has one arm around her back and another under her knees and lifts her onto his lap. He doesn't ask what she needs or what's wrong. He wraps his muscular arms around her as she continues to sob, quietly giving her space and time to feel.

She doesn't know how long it takes her to calm herself or how long he holds her. All she knows is that he's still there when she finally stops crying, waiting for her without a complaint or demand.

"I'm not going to pressure you into talking about what set all this off," he says, motioning to the space around them, "but I am here for you. I'll stay as long as you need and listen as long as you are willing to talk. If you need to just sit in silence, I can also do that."

Petra smiles at him, at the truth she knows deep in her bones. This man would go through fire for her.

"I appreciate that. I think I can talk about it. Looking back at it, it doesn't seem like such a big deal—"

"No, don't do that. Don't minimize your feelings. What you are feeling and experiencing is valid and important. Sorry, I don't mean to interrupt, but I don't like seeing you make yourself smaller. You deserve to take up space."

Petra blinks at him in surprise. No one has ever said anything like that to her before. She hadn't ever thought of it that way, of taking up space, of allowing herself to exist in all of the ways she wanted to and should. She feels something within her start to shift.

"Thank you for that." She smiles and then suggests, "Why don't we make some tea? This may take a while to work through."

"Sounds like a plan," he replies, getting up to turn on the kettle.

"Make it a big pot. We might need it."

After the water is boiled and the teapot filled, Lachlan brings it along with mugs on a tray and rejoins Petra on the couch, sitting just far enough that she can rest her feet on his lap. One of his hands finds its way to her calves, and he absentmindedly strokes his thumb along her skin as she starts to talk. Her skin warms to his touch as her magic flows underneath his hand, begging for connection. Morris contentedly snores by her head as if he can feel Lachlan's soothing caress.

"Obviously, you know this started after the visit to the estate. I know that you were talking with Francesca a bit while we were there, and then we had the interaction, let's call it, with Councilor Grog. You don't know that I spent part of that horrible evening having a conversation with Sloan and Francesca that was about as fun as a puking spell," she says.

Lachlan tenses and puffs up his chest as if ready to battle for her. He opens his mouth, but she stops him.

"Please, just let me talk it through. No interruptions." He takes a deep breath and nods in agreement. His hand is like an ember on her skin, slowly heating her from the outside. Her magic floats inside her, pooling where his skin meets hers.

She takes a sip of tea and then takes a deep breath. "As I was saying, Sloan and Francesca had me cornered at the bar. They did the typical mean girl act and made it appear as though we were having a polite conversation, but it was anything but. Francesca immediately picked up on my fears about my ability to be the Premier Witch. She said I was only considered basically as a favor to Gammy, and to be honest, that thought has certainly crossed my mind on more than one occasion over the past few weeks. They latched onto my ideas of inadequacy, all but confirming that I am incapable of being Premier Witch." She sighed and took another sip of her tea. "Look, I know it's stupid and so high school, and I shouldn't let them get to me. But these past couple of weeks have been rough. I know I am meant to be the next Premier Witch, but there's that seed of doubt in my brain that seems like a fully grown stalk some days. It's hard to ignore, and then the added pressure of having to get married to someone I don't necessarily love to prove a point is... well, it's gross. On top of all of that, my magic is misfiring because of all this stress, and I don't know how I can be Premier Witch when I can't even control my power."

"What do you mean your magic is misfiring? How?" he asks.

"I swear to Hecate that I went to simply make some tea yesterday and my power decided that turning my entire living room into a field of tea plants was a better idea. Do you know how long it takes to clean that up when you can't just reliably magic it away? I had to call Daisy for help."

Lachlan gazes at her, his eyes filled with empathy as he waits to see if she's done.

"You can speak now," she says, an amused laugh escaping her lips.

"Thanks." He gives her a wink. "As I said, your feelings are valid. You've had a lot to try and process and make sense of in a short period, and that interaction with them didn't help in any way. I won't diminish your feelings by saying just ignore them because that doesn't help."

Warmth pools in her chest as she listens to him. Demons are often perceived as brutal and vengeful, and while that is certainly possible with Captain Shadow here when he is crossed, he's just such a softy inside. His ability to respect and value the feelings of others is inspiring. How did he get this way? She knew his father, Damian, by reputation was not nice and spent so much energy instilling fear to maintain control. It's truly a wonder how Lachlan came out the way he did.

"Instead, you need to recognize where you see your strength and power. What impact do you want to have on the community? On the world at large? Yes, your family has a legacy, but what do you want *your* legacy to be? And, of course, the big question is, do you even want to be Premier Witch?"

"The *want* is the hard part. I don't know."

"Then you need to figure that out."

"But how?" Petra asks, frustrated and exhausted.

"Only you can determine that. But you're running out of time. The deadline for the thirty days is a little over two weeks away."

"I know. There's this ticking clock above my head, constantly reminding me of this life-altering decision," she says, flopping her head back dramatically and staring at the ceiling.

"I understand. But what do you want to do about it?" he asks.

"I don't know. I still have a hard time not believing everything the girls said to me. I keep thinking that I'm not good enough, that I shouldn't be the Premier Witch, that I should just let Sloan have it because she wants it more than I do right now."

"I promise you that you are more than worthy. I have watched you over the past few years—not in a creepy way," he clarifies quickly when she raises her head to look at him. "Your compassion and love for the supernatural community speaks volumes. It's louder than you probably realize. Working with human and supernatural children allows you to build inclusive communities from the ground up, and you're making an impact already. We could certainly use someone like you as a leader in our world. I believe in you, but you need to believe in yourself."

Lachlan reaches beside him to the box of tissue on the table and hands it to Petra so she can wipe the tears that have escaped. This man is something else. She uses the tissue to dab away a final tear. "I'm working on it. What do you think we should do?"

"Well, *we* have a couple of issues. One is Sloan as a competitor, waiting for you to fail, and two is the conditions set forth by the council to prove your readiness."

"You mean getting married?" she asks, a heat working its way up her neck.

"Yeah. I'm not trying to pressure you or tell you what to do. But… I think we can potentially solve both problems by addressing the second. If you—*we*—get married, the council will have no reason not to follow through and deem you the new Premier Witch. Upon doing so, you will gain the Premier Witch power and can use that to help deal with the Wilkses. If you choose not to get married, then, well, that provides an answer to what I asked earlier: what do you want? And Sloan then takes the title, and she'll join the council and push her own agenda through," he says. "So it's really up to you and what route you want to take."

"If, *if*, we get married, we need to set some ground rules first," she ventures. "We need to make sure that we can come out of this unscathed."

"Ok. What are you thinking?"

"We need to keep our friendship at the forefront. Regardless of what happens, we are friends first, and it is important that we stay friends after."

"Ok. Stay friends. Easy. What else?" he replies, the corner of his mouth quirking up ever-so-slightly. Is he amused by this?

"Gammy said this needs to appear legitimate or at least that I am taking this seriously. So I suggest that *if* we get married, we remain married for a period of two years to make it appear real and not just something that was done for the sole purpose of getting a title. After two years, we can get divorced and go back to our pre-marriage lives. Oh, and with that, because this needs to look real, we can't date anyone else while we are married."

"Got it. Stay friends, stay married for two years, no affairs. Anything else?"

"That's all I have. But you need to get some benefit out of this as well. So what are your demands?" she asks.

"Aside from getting to marry into the most powerful witch line? Nothing."

Petra scoffs. "Don't try and flatter me. No, you are sacrificing yourself for me, and I need to know that you are getting something out of our arrangement, too."

He smirks at her, clearly enjoying this. "Being married to you also helps me appear more devoted to the council. It shows that I'm willing to attach myself to someone, and as an added plus, it gives me a reason not to return to the underworld. And it shows that I could potentially be a part of creating a new demon-witch power spawn." Petra opens her mouth to add a comment, but he cuts her off. "I don't want children, and I'm not suggesting we have any. But the outer world doesn't need to know that." He pauses. "Anything else?" he asks.

"No. I think that's it."

"Okay, then, Petra Edaline Rose, will you marry me?"

Petra sits in silence, running through the options in her head. Her head tells her to do the logical thing and just give Premier Witch to Sloan, recognizing that this decision shouldn't be something she wavers over. She should want it completely, without a doubt. But then she thinks of her Gammy, newly widowed with a young infant, taking on the role. As great as she's been as the Premier Witch, she likely had her own self-doubts at that time.

On the other hand, her heart is pulling her toward Lachlan, the Premier Witch title, the family legacy. It tells her to take this challenge and to follow the line that leads to power, but also leads to pride in herself and love of others. It tells her that her path to Premier Witch is unconventional but the right direction for her to take.

After a painstakingly long time, she opts to go with her heart, trusting that it won't lead her astray. "Yes. Let's do it."

"Do what?" he asks, clearly fighting an excited smile that wants to break across his perfectly shaped lips.

"Make me Premier Witch. Let's get married."

CHAPTER FIFTEEN

Lachlan

Lachlan beams from ear to ear. It's been nearly two days since she agreed to marry him, and he hasn't stopped smiling. When Petra decided to follow through with the wedding, he swears his heart did a jig in delight.

After their conversation and Petra's decision that night, she asked him to stay the night "as friends," stating she didn't want to be alone. He was happy to see she appeared to be in better spirits the following day. He's not ashamed to admit that waking up next to Petra was perfect. He woke with her curled into his chest with his arm wrapped around her middle.

At that thought, he feels his phone vibrate in the back pocket of his jeans. He takes it out and looks down to see Petra's name. They've been messaging pretty much constantly since they parted ways yesterday morning. He opens up the message from Petra, already smiling, and reads:

PETRA

Good morning, fluffy.

So, I know Gammy wants a big wedding to show everyone publicly, but I've been thinking…

LACHLAN

Good morning, witchling.

What schemes have you been cooking up?

Well…

What if we got married today?

…

Is that a no?

Not at all. It's a surprise, that's all.

When and where?

There is an opening at city hall at 4:30. Does that work?

Sounds like the perfect time to get married :)

Great. I'll book it.

See you soon, future husband.

See you soon, future wife.

Lachlan sets his phone down on the counter and pumps his fist. "Fuck, yes!" he shouts before realizing he is not at home but at Taster's Delight, which is currently filled with people getting their morning brew. Quickly apologizing to the people in the dining area, he picks up his coffee and heads out the door with an extra pep in his step, the bell above the door chiming happily behind him as he steps into the brisk fall wind.

CHAPTER SIXTEEN

Petra

Goddesses' gonads, I'm getting married.

Surprised that Lachlan agreed to such a quick wedding, Petra starts scrambling to get everything in order, which is made more complicated by the fact she has to work today. But she feels goddess-blessed that she had the early shift. Before she leaves her apartment, Petra makes sure to pack her makeup and mother's veil in her car.

Thankfully, Daisy is off today. When she called to tell Daisy the plan for the day, she immediately went into witch-of-honor mode, asking for a list of things she needed to do before meeting Petra at City Hall.

On her lunch break that afternoon, she heads out to the play yard for some quiet so she can call Gammy.

"Hello, my darling granddaughter," Gammy says after answering the call on the first ring like a monster.

"Hi, Gammy."

"How are you doing, love? Are you eating and sleeping well?"

"Yes, yes, I'm okay. Thank you. And thank you for trying

to help me sort through everything—and for sending Lachlan."

"Hmm. I'm glad it all worked out."

"Anyway, I don't have much time since I'm on my lunch break, but I wanted to let you know that Lachlan and I decided to get married."

"Yes, I know, darling. Remember, I was there when we devised the whole marriage plan."

"No, no, I meant we are getting married *today*."

"Oh. Wait, today?"

"Yes, I booked us at city hall at four thirty. Will you please join us?"

Gammy is silent on the other end. It takes her a moment before she finally answers. "Yes, of course, my darling. I wouldn't miss it. Is there anything you need me to do or bring?"

Petra almost sighs audibly in relief. While she was ninety-nine percent sure Gammy would agree, Petra certainly thought there would be more of a fight or at least some questions. "Do you have a dress I can borrow? I want something more vintage in style."

"I have the *perfect* dress," Gammy says excitedly.

"Thank you. Love you."

"Love you too, darling," Gammy replies before Petra ends the call.

Petra stands, brushing off dirt from her butt, and heads back to care for her little gremlins. *Holy shit, I'm getting married today.*

When three thirty hits, Petra is out the door like her broomstick is on fire—not that she actually rides one.

Thankfully, a few of the kiddos were picked up early, so she didn't have to worry about staying late due to ratios. Working in childcare is no joke, and with them constantly being short-staffed, it's not unusual for the early shift to have to stay late as they wait for little ones to be picked up and for the mandated staff-to-child ratios to be acceptable to be able to leave.

Parking her car in the first spot she can find, a block away from City Hall, a magic rush flows through her. Every inch of her tingles as power pulses in response to her nerves. She pushes down the apprehension and worry that builds alongside it as she collects her purse, makeup, and her mother's veil from the back seat.

With her arms laden with necessities, she locks her car and walks the block to City Hall. She notices the colorful fall leaves on the trees planted along the street, the oranges, reds, and yellows making it look like a path of fire as she makes her way to Lachlan. She stands outside of City Hall for a moment, gazing at the gothic architecture of the building where her life is about to change. Another power rush and a pink magic tendril urge her on. Gathering her courage, she climbs the few steps to the front door, where Daisy and Gammy greet her. They lead her to a family bathroom where she can change.

She does her makeup quickly, opting for a natural look with a soft pink lip. After setting her makeup, she changes into her dress and swaps out her regular gold studs for the drop-pearl earrings Gammy has lent her. She takes a final look in the bathroom mirror, appreciating the simplicity of the look, before opening the door to the glowing faces of Daisy and Gammy.

Their eyes are alight as they take in Gammy's simple, ivory satin halter dress that hits just below her knees. The ruched bodice flows down from the strap of fabric that loops around her neck to a cinched waistband, opening up to a softer, flowing skirt. It clings to her in all the right places as she moves and twirls in front of them to reveal the open back, showcasing the sapphire pink swirl and rose tattoo that climbs her spine.

"You are gorgeous," Gammy says softly, holding her clasped hands up to her chest, tilting her head to the right as she takes Petra in.

A tear starts to well in the corner of her left eye, and she dabs at it with her finger before lightly admonishing Gammy. "If you keep looking at me like that, I will break down completely, and I can't do that right now."

"You know, I heard once that if you clench your butt cheeks together, it will stop you from crying," Daisy shares, earning an amused snort from Gammy. "What, it's true. I've been doing it this entire time, and not a drop. Your brain can't focus on the two things at the same time. Try it!"

Petra laughs at her friend. "You… you are…" she says between giggles. "Thank you for being… well, you," she finishes.

"Anytime, babe," Daisy responds with a wink and a finger gun.

Gammy looks down at her watch and then back to Petra, "It's almost time, love."

Petra takes a steadying breath. Like many women, she has looked forward to getting married for much of her life. As a young girl, she dreamt of what her wedding would be like. It didn't exactly involve getting married to someone as a fake arrangement to meet some arbitrary, archaic patriarchal ruling by a supernatural government. But this is clearly what the Fates had in store for her. They must have a bigger plan for her, and who is she to argue with the Fates?

She looks between them, staring at the door before her. Turning to Gammy, she asks quickly, "I'm not making a mistake, am I?"

"Absolutely not. I think this is the smartest decision based on the circumstances."

"But will there be issues with me marrying another council member?"

Gammy pauses, thinking. "I don't think it has ever been done before. But I can't think of any regulations that prohibit it. You two will be trailblazers, that's for sure. There's certainly no laws prohibiting inter-being marriage, so you are allowed to marry a demon."

"You can take a moment to think this through, you know. It's a big decision, and you are being forced into it. If you don't feel ready yet, we can come back tomorrow or every day after for as long as we can," Daisy says.

Waiting only a brief second, Petra gives them a quick nod. "No, I'm ready. Let's do this."

Then Lachlan walks around the corner, and suddenly she forgets how to breathe.

He strides forward confidently in a navy suit, ivory shirt, brown shoes, and a pink pocket square combo, gazing at her with a huge smile on his face. He has no right to look as good as he does, but damn if he doesn't cause things to stir inside her.

Reaching her, he gallantly puts out an arm for her to hold. "Well, witchling, shall we get married today?"

Her core warms, turning her insides to liquid. She smiles back and gives him a quick nod, words escaping her.

"Let's go and get you Premier Witch," he says, taking a step forward and bringing them into the ceremony room.

CHAPTER SEVENTEEN

Lachlan

The officiant looks between them before turning to Lachlan and asking, "Do you, Lachlan Grace, take Petra Rose to be your lawfully wedded wife, in sickness and health, in both good and challenging times, from now until you both should expire?"

"I do," Lachlan responds without hesitation.

The officiant now turns and looks at Petra, repeating the vows for her. He knows she repeats them, but he is too focused on Petra and how perfect she looks in her dress. Her fire-red hair cascades down her shoulders, and it takes great restraint for Lachlan not to reach out and wrap it in his hands. To pull her closer to him. Her soft pink lips are plump and enticing as he eagerly counts down to the moment where the officiant says they can kiss. She looks up at him, and her eyes sparkle with what he thinks—he hopes—is affection. As he continues to gaze at her, his heart nearly beating out of his chest, he can only think it should be illegal to be so beautiful. He can't help but thank the Fates for allowing her to be his, no matter how brief or unusual the circumstances.

"I do," he hears Petra respond. A genuine smile breaks across her lips, and he catches her licking them ever so briefly.

"It is my pleasure to announce, for the first time, the new Mr. and Mrs. Grace-Rose," the officiant says before finally saying what Lachlan has been waiting for. "You may now seal your union with a kiss."

Lachlan releases Petra's hands and steps toward her, placing his hands on either side of her face and guiding her to look up at him. He leans down, placing his mouth on hers. He feels her relax into him, and he moves his left hand down to her back, tipping her back so she raises a foot from the floor as she wraps her arms around his neck. Beneath him, she parts her lips slightly, bringing her tongue forward to meet his. Literal sparks fly in his peripheral vision as their tongues connect. The kiss is brief, lasting only seconds, but it feels like a lifetime to him. He already knows he never wants to stop kissing this magnificent woman.

Near them, Gammy, his mom Fenella, and Declan clap loudly while Daisy has her fist pumping in the air as she whoops, celebrating their official seal as a married couple.

He tips Petra back to a standing position, bringing his hands to the side of her face. "Hello, wife," he whispers, resting his forehead against hers before giving her another small peck and then turning to face his friends and family, both old and new.

He raises their clasped hands and notices her blush. *My wife,* his demon roars. He smiles at her, bringing her hand to his mouth and kissing it softly. *She's my wife.*

Hands clasped and fingers entwined, they proceed down the aisle together. They did the right thing. He knows it down to his soul, which he would happily offer up to see her continue to glow the way she does now.

In the hall, they are quickly surrounded by their small crew in a group hug as they share their excitement and congratulations. With how they respond, he can almost believe this isn't a marriage under false pretenses. They celebrate as if they are here for marriage between two people in love. Lachlan may have feelings for Petra, but as he watches her receive a hug from Daisy, he can't say if they're reciprocated or not. For now, Lachlan will revel in the excitement and celebrate Petra being his for the next two years.

Daisy claps her hands and looks around the group. "Alright, we need to celebrate the newlyweds." She holds a hand up to stop Petra's protests. "No, you don't get to be all coy here. You just got married. To a demon with a magnificent ass, if I do say so myself." Daisy winks at Lachlan. "We are celebrating. I was thinking of dinner and drinks at Skylight?"

"Sounds wonderful!" Gammy and Fenella agree.

"I'm in!" Declan declares.

The five of them turn and look at Petra, who is chewing her lip. Her glow has softened, but Lachlan can still see it there. She needs this. She needs them.

"What do you say, wife? Let's go celebrate with our little miscreant family."

She raises her beautiful green eyes, and he sees a softness there that could maybe, one day, be love.

"Dinner sounds lovely," she agrees. She squeezes his hand quickly and rests her head on his shoulder before Daisy calls for everyone to follow her.

"Are you okay?" he asks gently.

"Yeah. Yes. I'm good. And thank you, Lach. For everything."

"Anytime, love." He squeezes her hand. "Shall we go

before she notices we aren't behind her?" he says, motioning toward Daisy halfway down the stairs out front.

"Yes. Definitely. Rule number one with Daisy, never get in the way of her and food," she jokes.

Hades, her smile could heal the world, he's sure of it. It's already healed him. Putting his arm out for her, they walk out, arms linked, a united force against the world.

CHAPTER EIGHTEEN

Petra

Dinner with their small, tight-knit group was exactly what she needed. As much as she could do without being the center of attention, it was nice to share this moment with everyone. Plus, the longer she gets to look at Lachlan in that gorgeous suit, the better. That man is beyond beautiful. His blue eyes could melt the most frozen of hearts, and the navy in the suit makes them pop perfectly. Seeing him in this suit has done something special to her nether regions. Looking at him now, you'd never know he was a golden-eyed demon with giant black horns who could decimate this entire block with the snap of his fingers when in his true form.

Oh, and that kiss at the altar? Her stomach flips just thinking about it. The way his lips possessed hers, hinting at the beast under the surface. It looked innocent, but there was such heat between them that nearly had her knees buckling underneath her.

She attempts to protest again when Daisy and Gammy settle the bill. They couldn't agree who between them would pay for the celebrations tonight. However, with some coaxing from Declan, they decided to split it. As she watches the scene before her, her chest warms with love for everyone here. She's genuinely grateful to have all of these wonderful people in her life. While she may not know Declan and Fenella well yet, she's happy to gain them as a fake family-in-law.

Petra rounds the table and hugs Gammy, Daisy, and Declan, thanking them for coming today and for this celebratory dinner. She turns to Fenella to thank her for welcoming her into the family. "I am so happy for you two," Fenella says. "Lachlan has filled me in, and while your union may be unconventional, I think this will be good for him. I think *you* will be good for him."

"Thank you," Petra replies, taken by surprise.

"I know you and I don't know each other well, but I know of your family. If you are anything like your grandmother, then you will do great things."

Petra smiles, appreciating the vote of confidence. Fenella pulls her into a hug. It's warm and comforting. The way a mother's hug should feel.

"I can't tell you how much I appreciate all of… this," she says, motioning to the space around them. "I am so lucky to have you all in my life, and Declan, I am happy to finally have a brother."

"Anytime, sis," Declan responds, putting his arm around her shoulder. "Don't be afraid to put him in his place. He needs it." He laughs as Lachlan lightly punches his shoulder.

Petra grins at Lachlan. "Oh, no worries there."

Gammy and Daisy wrap Petra in a final group hug, and then Gammy holds Petra's face in her hands, looking deep into her eyes.

"You are chosen, my love. Don't ever forget it," Gammy says, before releasing her and walking toward the door.

Chosen for what? Gammy is just being overly sentimental today.

Daisy, Fenella, and Declan follow closely behind Gammy while Lachlan and Petra take a moment to themselves before following the others out.

"Holy Goddess, we got married today," Petra says.

Lachlan beams. "We did."

"Now what?"

"Now we go home."

Standing outside Lachlan's large century home, Petra side-eyes him. "You know when you said 'go home,' I didn't think you would take me to *your* home."

He leans back against the black railing on the front porch as he crosses his arms across his broad chest. Though he smiles softly, his eyes say something mischievous is happening inside his head.

She narrows her eyes at him, trying to decipher his plan and what's happening inside his head. "I guess we should have talked about this and how our 'married life,'" she says, making air quotes with her fingers, "was going to work. I wasn't expecting us to live together."

"I know we haven't talked about how we want this to work, but I think it makes sense for you to move in here. One, it's bigger, so you'll have lots of space, should you need to get away from me. Two, if we are posing as a married couple to the council, then it makes sense that we would be living together since that is generally what married couples do," he explains.

Petra moves to stand next to him, leaning over to rest her forearms on the railing. She gazes down at the garden on the other side. "I mean, I guess that makes sense. I hadn't thought about it. I just figured we would return to our regular lives."

"We could, but if we want the council to buy this relationship, we need to make it look real. We both know if they get even a whiff of this being for convenience, they will find whatever loophole they can to pass on the title to Sloan."

"True. I just don't get what they have against me and why they are trying so hard to ensure I don't become the next Premier Witch."

"I'm not sure what Grog's motive is, but I think there's some lingering animosity between him and Gladys. Only time will tell Grog's true agenda, but until then, we can do everything possible to ensure that you are the chosen candidate."

"Gammy's told me a little, but it seems like such a long time for Grog to hold a grudge. Maybe I should brush up on my Gammy history and find out what's really going on underneath it all," Petra responds, spinning her new wedding band on her finger.

Lachlan turns and reaches for her hands, gently clasping them in his own, stopping her nervous fidgeting.

"Spending time with Gladys and learning more about her sounds wonderful. Not that I want to ruin what has been a fantastic day with a discussion of her passing, but we know she's on borrowed time, and I think it would be beneficial for both of you to spend as much time together as you can," he says carefully.

"I know." She tries to hold back the deluge of tears waiting at the thought of her Gammy no longer being with them, but a couple slip out.

Petra feels him release her hands before he pulls her into

his chest, wrapping his strong arms around her. She rests her cheek on his chest, and he sets his chin on her head.

"I will be here for you every step of the way," he promises. "By the way, you'll want to send a copy of the marriage license to the other council members before the deadline next week."

"Thank… thank you," she sniffles.

"Why don't we go inside, change into something more comfortable, and watch a movie?" he prompts.

"With popcorn and M&Ms?"

"Absolutely."

"That sounds great," she responds as they approach the door. "But I don't have any clothes here, and I need to feed Morris."

He smiles warmly at her, placing his hand on the small of her back. "I had Daisy drop off clothes for you earlier today, and I personally went and collected Morris and all of his things while she was there."

She pushes away from him just enough to gaze up into his beautiful face while her magic sizzles under his touch.

"Despite the break and entering, you are something else, Mr. Grace."

"That's Mr. Grace-Rose to you now," he says as he leans down and kisses her forehead before sliding an arm under her legs and carrying her over the threshold.

"Welcome home, witchling."

CHAPTER NINETEEN

Petra

Over the next few days, Petra makes sure to notify the council of her marriage and verifies that she met their stupid condition. When she doesn't get any response back, be it congratulations or complete outrage, she figures she has sufficiently met their condition which signals her acceptance of her destiny as the next Premier Witch. If only things were that simple.

On the fifth day of being married to Lachlan, a letter arrives.

Dear Mrs. Grace-Rose,

We, the council, thank you for notifying us of your successful marriage. While this means you have met the condition set before you, some concerns have been brought forth by some of the members regarding your chosen partner and what that means for the council and community at large. As such, your presence is requested at a council meeting in two days' time.

Councilor Amare

"Well, shit," Petra says.

Lachlan appears from around the corner and stands beside her at the kitchen counter. "What? What's wrong?"

She hands him the notice and watches his face as he reads. She expects some kind of reaction from him—frustration at being left out of council proceedings, anger that she is being called in, anything really. But his features remain infuriatingly neutral. It's as if he read something that holds little meaning for him. Maybe it does? Maybe it means more to her than it does to him?

"Interesting," he eventually says.

Petra stomps down the building spark inside her. "That's it? Just 'interesting'?"

Noticing the sparks at her fingers, Lachlan takes a few steps back from her and leans against the opposite counter, crossing his arms over his broad chest. "Have I done something wrong?"

"This clearly can't be good. Why am I the only one here who seems to see that?"

"I didn't say anything about it. I don't understand why you are so worked up over this."

"Please explain then what you find so interesting," she replies sarcastically. To be honest, she's not entirely sure why she's so worked up either. It's not like it's the first time she's been called before the council. Though that generally doesn't end up going well for her.

Lachlan takes a breath and then begins speaking slowly,

choosing his words carefully. "I find this interesting because you notified them a few days ago. I have been in the chambers since then, and nothing was said. As far as I'm aware, no one even looked at me differently. So to me, that means they met without me there, and I would assume without Gladys as well. Again, that's interesting. As it means there is something else going on that we're being left out of."

"Oh," she says.

"Yeah, oh. I wouldn't be surprised if they try to argue against our union."

"But I don't have time to find anyone else." And she didn't want to marry anyone else. Being married to Lachlan—at least the first five days—had been great so far.

"And you won't have to. Remember, they didn't have any stipulations about who you could marry. So this marriage is valid." He begins to raise his arms up to open them for a hug, but he stops himself and instead stands awkwardly in the space. "Feel a little better now?" he asks.

"Yes. Sorry. I was expecting more of a response and the flat 'interesting' seemed like you didn't care."

"Petra, when it comes to you, I *always* care. I just can't go flying off the handle at everything."

Feeling her cheeks warm, Petra turns to face the counter. "I guess that makes sense." She looks around for something to do, trying to make it look less awkward, but all of the dishes are clean and put away and the damn kitchen is spotless.

While she can't see him, she knows he's closer than he was. His breath brushes past her neck. "Would you like some pancakes for breakfast?"

"Sounds good," she squeaks. She steps away, rounding the counter, and sits on a stool on the other side, putting a safe distance between them.

Gammy's house is bustling with activity when Petra arrives. The house, normally quiet, is bursting with all sorts of mystical and magical beings. As she works her way through the large home trying to locate Gammy, Petra passes faeries, gnomes, shifters, and she's pretty sure someone who is part giant. As far as Petra knows, there was no event planned for today, so seeing so many beings here is surprising.

Finally locating Gammy out in the garden, surrounded by gnomes and fae, Petra stops, standing back as she takes in the scene and the story Gammy is in the midst of sharing.

"See, my friends, there was a time when we were not allowed to gather in celebrations such as this. Many rules existed that prevented large gatherings of magical creatures, let alone smaller mixed groups. There was great fear about what would happen should our powers combine. I believe there was also fear that we may actually like each other and decide to work together against the controlling council at the time—but you didn't hear that from me," she stage-whispers, earning a ripple of laughter from her audience. "What the council didn't know was that our community was already meeting and mingling in secret. This led to many of the great and lasting bonds that we see today. For example, the witches and fae have long relied on connections with each other, the fae sharing their abilities in nature and growing plants, and the witches providing their experience with potions and salves for healing. A wonderful partnership that would not exist today if not for those rebels. It is with this and many other rebel partnerships in mind that we gather here today to celebrate who we are and the bonds we hold so dear." A resounding applause erupts as Gammy finishes, which Petra happily joins.

Gammy looks up and finally notices Petra standing in the distance, a broad, warm smile breaking across her loving face. As the group separates, moving on to other areas in the garden and home, Petra steps toward Gammy, observing her slightly tired expression, an added slump in her posture, and the cane resting on the stones beside her. Gammy conjures a chair and slowly sits.

"Hi, Gammy. That was a wonderful tale," Petra says, leaning down and kissing her grandmother on the cheek before sitting on the low stone wall beside her.

"Thank you, darling."

"I didn't know all this was going on today. Why didn't you tell me?"

"I knew you were working today, and I didn't want you to feel obligated to take time off. Plus, I knew you were stopping by so you would see it anyway. It is such a wonderful way to mingle with community members and let your presence as the next Premier Witch be known," Gammy explains.

"You still could have told me. I was a little surprised when I pulled up and there was a flood of people here."

"Sorry, darling. Next time I will be sure to let you know in advance." Petra goes to nod in acceptance, but then realizes she doesn't know if there will actually be a next time. It's only been a little over a month since Gammy shared she was sick, and from the looks of it, she is already deteriorating. The thought of not having Gammy here creates a tightening sensation in Petra's chest, like a hand has found its way past her ribs and is gripping any organ it can find.

"Love, are you alright?" Gammy asks, placing a comforting hand on Petra's leg.

"Yes," Petra replies, clearing her throat. "Yes. Sorry. Anyway, how are you doing?"

"Better now that my granddaughter is here."

"You look tired after all this excitement. Do you want some help going somewhere to lie down?"

Gammy waves her off. "No, no, I'm fine. Tell me, how have your first few days as a married witch been?"

A strange blush rises, causing Petra's cheeks to warm. She and Lachlan haven't done anything so she really has no need to blush, but the idea of being married, and then thinking of who she's married to, seems to be enough to set her off. It's as if she's a teenager again, trying to hide the naughty things she did from her Gammy. "It's been… an adjustment."

Gammy tilts her head, examining Petra. "Is that good or bad?"

Petra hesitates. It's not horrible, but it's also different. She's never lived with someone other than family. "It's a bit strange," Petra says. "This is a new thing for me, and we are still figuring out how it's going to work between us with us living together."

"How would you like it to work?"

"I don't know. I've never lived with someone before, so I'm not really sure of how this is supposed to work," Petra says, looking down at her feet as she swings them. "And I don't want to risk our friendship, and I think we need to make sure to keep that intact. But…" Petra trails off.

"But what?" Gammy asks, the corner of her mouth quirking up.

"But I feel there's a thread between us. A connection that binds us together."

"Maybe there is?"

Petra looks at Gammy, taking in this woman who has guided her throughout her life. "What would that mean, though?"

"It means the Fates have something bigger in mind for you two, my dear. It is best not to question these things and just follow the road before you."

Maybe all of this, this challenge to prove herself, to show commitment to her world and the Premier Witch role is for something bigger. If only she knew what that something was.

"You ready?" Lachlan calls from the hallway.

"Just gotta put shoes on," Petra calls back, running past the sexy demon in a suit. She feels her nerves slip into place and the tension held in her body as she slides her boots on. The last time she was at a council meeting, she ended up married to Lachlan, which, while so far not at all bad, wasn't exactly what she had in mind for her life at the time. "Good to go," she says, standing up and fixing her shirt and coat.

Lachlan steps around the corner, and now that she can get a better look at him, she doesn't understand how looking so good in a black suit and black shirt isn't illegal. She wipes her hand across her lips, checking for drool, and thankfully it comes away dry.

"Alright, let's get this over with," he says, extending his arm for her to grasp so he can port them to the council chambers. She prepares herself for the pulling sensation by taking a deep breath and closing her eyes, hoping that she won't get as dizzy as last time.

It doesn't help at all. It takes a moment for her mind to stop spinning once they arrive in council chambers. Lachlan holds onto her shoulders, and when she opens her eyes, his steely blue eyes stare back into hers. His eyes are soft and caring, and seeing herself reflected back in them is perhaps the best thing she has ever seen.

"Welcome, Councilor and Mrs. Grace-Rose. Thank you for joining us this evening," Councilor Clellugs says. "Please, if you could have a seat," they say, motioning to the center of the room where two chairs and a small table have appeared.

"Thank you and good evening, everyone," Petra responds as they sit. After settling herself, Petra looks up at the council members and finds Gammy's eyes shining back at her. She knows there is so much love there, but even sitting here now, after having married Lachlan to meet the demand set before her, she questions whether she wants a life like Gammy's. Petra's done what she needs to do out of obligation and a sense of family loyalty, but is it worth it?

"We have called you here this evening as we have some concerns about your marriage," Councilor Clellugs explains. Petra leans forward to begin protesting, but is stopped by the councilor's hand rising in the air, cutting off her ability to speak. "You will have your moment to address any concerns after. We appreciate that you have been forthright and informed us of your marriage as soon as possible, and we are all in agreement that you have met that condition as set forth by Councilor Grog." At the mention of his name, Grog's chest puffs up in pride. Petra fights the urge to roll her eyes and instead shifts her attention back to Clellugs. "However, we do have concerns about your chosen partner."

Councilor Amare leans forward, laying her hands down

on the table in front of her. "It is unheard of to have two council members married to each other. As this is unprecedented and could lead to potential challenges in important votes and rulings within the community, we have decided to put your marriage under review."

Clellugs puts her hand down, allowing Petra to finally speak. "Honored council members, I can appreciate your concern. However, the stipulation in my agreement was that I needed to marry, to show my commitment to tradition and to the council. I have done so. Who I married was not a concern. Since I have met the requirement, and done so within the allotted time frame, I see no reason for my union with Councilor Grace to be called into question." She looks to Lachlan as she finishes her speech, and he takes her hand under the table, squeezing it gently. The touch warms her skin, sending sparks up her arm and into her stomach, setting fireflies fluttering inside.

"No need to be so sensitive, Mrs. Grace-Rose," Councilor Grog chimes in, his voice sliding over her like worms slithering through wet soil. *Sensitive?* Does no one else hear the condescension? "After being notified of your marriage, the council discussed what this union could mean, and upon identifying some potential dangers to the community, and considering how it will be perceived by our esteemed peoples, it was decided that we need a deeper review to determine if this can continue."

"And what happens should you, objectively, decide that our marriage is unacceptable?" Petra asks, attempting to keep her tone even. She must have failed, as Lachlan squeezes her hand again, a signal to pull it back.

"We will address that should it come to that. Which I doubt it will," Gammy firmly responds, the threat evident in her tone.

"Is there anything else we need to be aware of? How long do you anticipate this review to take?" Lachlan asks.

"A few weeks to a month at most. We will reach out to the community and collect feedback, as well as determine potential parameters to keep in place should your union remain," Councilor Amare replies.

"That is all for tonight. Thank you again for coming in," Councilor Clellugs states.

"Oh, and before you go, Mrs. Grace-Rose…" Grog slides in as Petra and Lachlan stand.

"Yes, Councilor Grog?" Petra responds, her body tensing as she waits for a final blow.

"Miss Wilks has been doing wonders creating a knowing presence in the council circles through her volunteer work in the community and support with council functions. Being married to a council member is not the only thing that makes a strong Premier Witch candidate. You would do well to show your community that you actually care about them."

She cares for the children in the community. Petra can't think of any better way to show she cares than to support the next generation.

She turns and glares at him, willing her magic to strike him where he stands. Only she is ported out of the chambers and back to Lachlan's home before she has a chance.

Dick weasel!

CHAPTER TWENTY

Lachlan

His phone has been ringing all morning, and every time he sees the name on the screen, he silences it, refusing to deal with whatever is wrong. Is it healthy? Probably not. But he has distanced himself from that world for a reason. The underworld that his father left him is not a pleasant place. His memories of being there are painful and fill him with shame. So he avoids visiting as much as possible, leaving much of the work to Selene and Viktor, two of his father's former staff.

When Petra enters the kitchen, coming to check if he needs any help, his phone vibrates across the counter again, the face lighting up with Selene's name. Petra doesn't know about Selene, or about his past. He reaches for his phone, trying to silence and pocket it before she can see, but he's not quick enough.

"Who's Selene?" she asks, handing him his phone just as it stops vibrating.

"No one," he replies curtly.

She raises an eyebrow at him but doesn't push it. He feels his chest tighten at the lie, but it's just not time yet.

When would be a good time to tell your wife *about your past, hmm?* his demon mocks him. He tightly closes his eyes, fighting the urge to spill everything.

"How has Gladys been doing?" he asks. "She looked a little off the other night."

Petra takes a deep breath as if she is preparing herself. "She says she's fine, but I don't believe her. I noticed it too, but she brushed me off. When I was at her place for more magic and council lessons yesterday, though, I could see she was tired and in pain. I'm worried it's progressing faster than she originally thought, but she won't talk to me about it."

He sees her soul practically deflate as she talks. It's hard, he knows. And he imagines it is even harder when it's her last connection to her family as she knows it. The desire to go and hold her as he sees her shoulders slump is almost too much. But he needs to keep his distance or risk scaring her away. Little touches here and there have been okay. They've been friendly. He's not sure how she will react if he attempts something more intimate than a consoling hug. "She is a tough witch, and I can understand not wanting to show weakness, especially with Grog already looming over you. She likely doesn't want to give him any more power."

"Yeah," she agrees weakly.

Shit. Why did he even bring this up? Now he's ruined this night by trying to talk about something upsetting. He's such a fuckhead. "I'm sorry for bringing it up."

She sniffles softly. "No, no, it's okay. Maybe if I mention to her that others are noticing she will actually open up."

"Worth a shot," he replies.

"Anyway! Let's go watch some pirates!" she says, trying to sound excited. He'll go along with whatever makes her happy.

He follows Petra into the living room. She's chosen *Captain LongBeard,* as their movie for tonight, which, in his opinion, is one of the best films ever made. With the arrival of winter and snow, they have spent many nights doing exactly this. They take turns choosing which film to watch, and Lachlan makes sure to have popcorn and M&Ms on hand for Petra's perfect sweet-and-salty treat.

Even though Petra finds a way to snuggle into him during their movie nights, she has maintained the friendship boundary line, never venturing further than a friendly cuddle.

He's caught her on more than one occasion, conveniently walking by the home gym and watching him as he works out, and he maybe makes sure to grunt louder and flex harder when she does. He sees the heat in her eyes when she looks at him and notes how her gaze lingers. She keeps saying they're just friends, but he can only hope that she might want something else one day. Every time her voice turns breathy, or her eyes flare with desire, his dick twitches, wanting to make his and her thoughts a reality.

As they reach one of the best points in the movie, a part that terrified Lachlan as a child, where Captain Longbeard punishes one of his crew by placing them in a scorpion-filled box, he notices Petra has run out of her popcorn and candy mix. Pausing the movie so he doesn't miss it, he jogs to the kitchen, refilling her bowl and his drink. When he sits back down, Petra lays her feet on his lap and spreads a blanket over the top, assuming her standard position. He hands the bowl back to Petra, and she immediately digs in her hand to gather another clump of salty-chocolatey goodness. Lachlan catches the adorable, happy humming noises as she eats, and his face heats, wondering what else would make her hum.

"Did you know that's Svetlana Severn as the pirate who gets put in the box?" she tells him.

He banishes those thoughts aside so he can banter with her. "What? No! There's no way that's Svetlana."

"It is," she reiterates, rewinding and pausing on the close-up of the pirate's face. "Look! If you remove the beard, you can see that's her!"

Lachlan leans forward to get a closer look, and sure enough, he sees it. "Damn. I've never noticed. Now I have to wonder who else is hidden throughout."

"You really shouldn't question my movie knowledge," she says as she stuffs another handful of popcorn into her mouth, dropping an M&M. Lachlan's eyes follow it as it rolls down her chin and under her shirt. "Witches' tits!" she exclaims, pushing herself upright, bringing her body closer to him as she tries to fish out the rogue candy.

Spotting the candy as it rolls out from the bottom of her shirt, landing beside her hip and in perilous danger of falling between the back of the cushion and the couch, he leans toward her, reaching for it. She turns, trying to locate the wayward treat, putting her face and her perfect, plump lips inches from his. She spots the M&M and picks it up, turning her head to face him, and her eyes widen briefly in surprise to find him so close before softening at his heated gaze. He catches her eyes drop to his mouth. Unconsciously, he licks his lips. She bites the corner of hers.

"Sorry, I was trying to get the runaway chocolate," he says, moving to lean back.

"Don't."

"Don't what?"

"Don't move," she says, her voice low and breathy.

Lachlan freezes. A curious smile breaks across his lips as she continues to take him in. Her hand reaches out and brushes his loose, shoulder-length hair out of his face, tucking it behind his ear. He leans toward her touch, and she rubs a thumb against his cheek. Her eyes dip down to his lips again as she licks her own. She leans forward, bringing her face close to his. Too close.

He feels her breath on his skin as she hesitates. The warmth from her breath and the anticipation of what he hopes is to come sends goosebumps racing over his body. Alarm bells start to sound in his head, warning him of a line about to be crossed. Fuck it, she's worth breaking the rules.

"Lach…"

"Hmmm?"

"Kiss me."

That is all the direction he needs. His eyes flare with desire as he scoops her into his lap to straddle him. She gives out a surprised squeak as she lands. One hand stays on her hip as the other roams her body, finally landing to cup the back of her neck and pull her down to him so he can place his lips on hers. As their lips meet, his world tips on its axis. Everything he has wanted slides into place.

Is he just some way for her to distract herself? Likely. But he'll take anything from her.

Cautiously at first, not wanting to scare her away, his lips find hers. He forces himself to take it slow. His hands slide down her back and settle on her luscious ass. He has longed to sink his fingers into it, and maybe his teeth too. Resisting the urge to latch on, he gently squeezes her tender flesh.

She leans into him and places her hands on either side of his head. Her lips part, opening her up as her tongue comes forward to tangle with his. She tastes sweet, like the lingering chocolate, and it spins his head with depraved thoughts.

He takes the invitation as she parts her lips further. The

kiss turns hungry, a mix of tongues and lips. Nibbles at her bottom lip elicited a small whimper from Petra. What he wouldn't give to hear that sound and any others she makes as he brings her to the brink.

Petra runs her hands through his hair. Grasping it, she pulls his head back, using the movement to deepen the kiss. She runs her tongue along his lips, and he captures it between them and sucks. She moans, grinding into him. His hands grip her ass firmly, fingers digging in hard enough that she may have bruises tomorrow, and he pushes his hard bulge against her.

"You are incredible," he rasps, kissing down her neck to her chest. One of his hands slides under her shirt to her stomach, and rests on the side of her ribs with his thumb under her breast. She's soft and warm against his rough hands. He's dreamt of this moment for months. No, years. Since the day she walked into his bar. He's imagined this so many times, and already it's better than anything his brain could create.

Crossing her arms in front of her, she grasps the hem of her shirt and pulls it off. Lachlan groans again at the sight of her. A dark purple lace bra barely hides her pink nipples. He places both hands on her back, pulling Petra into him. Lachlan's mouth finds one of her perfect peaks and sucks it through the fabric, running his tongue over the sensitive flesh, earning another whimper. She grinds into his hardness again.

His hands splay on her back while he continues to suck, and he thrusts his hips up to match her. He's surely going to come in his pants if she continues this for much longer. Only Petra could get him this close to the edge with most of their clothes still on.

She writhes faster on top of him. He picks up the pace

to increase the friction and buries his face in her breasts, nipping and sucking whatever flesh he can find. She tangles her hands in his hair, pulling him, claiming him. His hands find her ass again, giving her more power and leverage as she rides him.

He feels her tense as sapphire tendrils swirl around them. She whispers his name against his ear, riding out her release and sending chills down his spine. Hearing her say his name as she comes on top of him is mind-blowing. It sends shockwaves down his spine, making his cock grow impossibly harder. She grinds into him a final time, burying her face into his neck. Her breathing is heavy. His cock pulses, mere thrusts away from his own release. She lets out a short, embarrassed giggle, the wind from her breath tickling his dewy skin while she pushes into an upright position.

"Where do you think you're going?" he asks, digging his fingers into her plump ass cheeks and pulling her against him.

She looks away in embarrassment, reaching for her shirt. "Sorry, I'm sorry. I didn't mean for it to go that way."

"Petra, I want to be clear: you never have to apologize. I will happily let you ride me all day, every day," he answers, placing his finger under her chin to make her look at him. "Besides, watching you come undone is by far the best sight I have ever seen."

He sees her eyes spark with an idea, and she begins shifting off of him.

"Well then, I think it's only fair I get to see what you look like as you come," she says, kneeling before him. She rubs her palms up his leg and hooks her fingers into the top of his sweatpants and boxers, pulling them down as he raises his hips. His dick springs free at last. Her eyes widen.

"Oh, fluffy, you've been holding out on me."

Snorting at her, he palms his thick dick, stroking it slowly, watching her eyes darken with hunger.

"That thing is huge, sir."

He laughs again. Seeing her kneel before him is hotter than he thought it could be. He longs to feel her around him if she wants to do it, but he won't force it. He won't do anything she doesn't want to do. "I appreciate the confidence boost, witchling."

She stops his hand and pulls it away, replacing it with her own. She has barely touched him, and his breath is already hitching. "Will it fit?" she asks worriedly.

"You don't need to do this. We can stop here. It's not tit-for-tat," he says, barely containing himself with her touching him.

"Oh, I know. But I want to see this tat and have it all over my tits," she responds, licking her lips as her hands firmly grasp his hard, throbbing cock.

He lays his head back on the back of the couch and groans. Fucking Hades, his wife is incredible. She leans forward and wraps her lips around the head of his cock, the heat instantly enveloping him as she slides him down to the back of her throat. "Perfect. Fit," he grunts, resisting the urge to thrust into her.

He can't help but look back down at her. Her mouth stretches around him, sliding back and forth with her hand, creating the best friction. He was already close, and he knows he won't last long. She's too good.

"Witches' tits, you're so fucking hot," he growls, wrapping a hand around her ponytail. He pushes down the urge to use the new grip to guide and dominate her. Instead, he lets her continue to lead and holds on for dear life.

Her tongue slides up and down the underside of his

dick, flicking the end of his head each time. Tension builds at the base of his spine, and his left leg twitches slightly. Petra laughs around his cock, and the added vibration brings him to the edge.

"I'm gonna come," he rasps.

She pulls away quickly with a *pop* sound as if she is releasing the most delicious lollipop. She moves her hand down, grasping his balls, and pulls on them gently as he wraps his left hand around his shaft and pumps. One, two, three. Three pumps are all it takes before he shudders and spreads his hot come all over her chest as requested. She holds her gorgeous tits in both hands, still in her bra, squeezing them together, scooping up his deposit.

He gazes down at her as they both admire his artwork. She runs a finger through his come and licks it off her finger. If he hadn't just come all over her, that would make him instantly hard again.

He leans forward, capturing her lips with his, and groans into her mouth, tasting the sweetness of her mixed with his saltiness. "You, my wife, are perfect," he says, conjuring a warm cloth to wipe his deposit from her glorious chest. Her breath hitches as his shadows move over her, cleaning up his mess. *More* his demon demands. *Later* he responds internally.

He can feel her magic thrumming beneath her skin while he traces his fingers up and down her arm. It's like a little network of bees, humming and buzzing underneath.

As the movie finishes, she looks up at him, smiling sleepily while her hand draws circles on his chest.

"So, what now, witchling?"

"What do you mean?"

"Well, it seems as though you are ready to fall asleep," he says, getting a sleepy "hmm" back in response. "While I have enjoyed every minute of tonight with you, I don't want you to feel pressured to share a bed with me."

Petra takes long enough to respond that he is sure she has fallen asleep. He closed his eyes while he waited and absolutely did not start to doze off.

"I enjoyed tonight as well. I don't want you to think otherwise," she replies, picking at the fluff on her shirt.

"I wouldn't dare," he says, winking at her even though she can't see it.

"But I think I will sleep in my room," she says hesitantly, as though trying not to disappoint him.

They will need to talk about what tonight meant for them. If it meant anything at all. He sees her nervous picking and fidgeting, and it lets him know she's not near ready for that, but the time will come. Kissing the top of her head, he reassures her, saying, "That's okay. I didn't expect any of this"—motioning around them with his free hand—"to happen tonight. I only want you to be comfortable."

"Thanks," she says, pushing herself off him. He instantly misses her warmth and weight on him. How long will it be before he can feel it again? He can only hope it's not long, as he isn't sure how to survive without her in his arms now that he has had her.

"Truly, Lachlan, thank you. For everything."

"Anytime."

She walks away from him, moving down the hall toward the guest room, and he feels his heart leave with her.

CHAPTER TWENTY-ONE

Petra

Entering her room, Petra leans back, resting her head against the closed door, sighing, both thankful for how well things between her and Lachlan have been going and scared of how good everything felt with him tonight. How *right* everything felt.

This wasn't meant to be a serious arrangement. It's a fake marriage, and only until she gets her Premier Witch title. But tonight… no, tonight definitely did not feel fake. It felt more real than any other relationship she had ever been in, including the two-year relationship with Liam. Liam was good at the start, and even though she thought he was the love of her life at twenty-two, he made sure to let her know she would never be good enough for him before he left her. Their sex was decent, but the heat and passion were nowhere near as hot as it was with Lachlan. Which, of course, means she needs to shut it down and keep to the friend zone so neither one of them gets hurt.

She pushes herself away from the door before she does something stupid like going back out there to find him. Pulling back the covers, she crawls in, sinking into the soft, pillowy mattress and pulls the light gray fluffy duvet back over her.

Holy goddess, this is the most comfortable bed ever.

She lays on her back and raises her arm above her head, tucking it under the pillow. A pleasant, satiated feeling starts to overcome her, but thoughts of Lachlan keep running through her mind. How his rough hands roved over her skin, his mouth on her nipple, the feel of his kisses on her lips and body, the feel of his perfectly thick dick in her mouth. This leads to imagining what it would feel like in other, more sensitive places. Magic tingles under her skin, flowing toward her core as it responds to her lurid thoughts, setting her back on edge.

While she may be lying on a cloud, she tosses and turns for what feels like hours, unable to find sleep. Giving up, she pulls herself out of bed again, deciding that maybe a glass of water will help settle her mind and nerves. Opening her door, she finds Lachlan standing there, fist raised, about to knock.

She jolts in surprise as they both begin to laugh. "Hi."

"Sorry, I didn't mean to scare you. I was coming to check and see if you were alright before I headed to bed," he says, raising an arm and leaning against the doorframe.

"What time is it anyway?"

"One thirty."

"Wow. Why are you up so late?"

"Bar life. I'm used to being late, so it's just a habit now."

"Ah," she says. "Well, I'm just going to get some water. Unless you'd like to join?"

"Oh. Yeah. Sorry," he responds, moving out of her way so she can pass. "And water sounds… nice."

She giggles softly to herself as she walks down the hall. He's so confident and commanding as a demon leader, yet he fumbles his words here. It's endearing. They've been friends for years, and yet she's never really seen this side of him. It's nice to see beyond that tough demon persona that he usually employs.

She gets them both a glass from the cupboard and goes to the water dispenser in the fridge to fill them up. Handing him his drink, she takes a sip from hers, catching his eyes flick away from her quickly.

Working with young children means she is often up early, and while they have lived together for a couple of weeks now, she's usually fast asleep at this hour and when he would normally be coming home from the Acorn.

"So what do you typically get up to when you are up this late but aren't working?" she asks, filling the silence as he leans down, resting his forearms on the counter.

"Mostly watching movies. Though sometimes I'll play a video game."

"What did you get up to tonight? You know, after I left." Maybe he couldn't stop thinking about her too?

"Nothing," he laughs. "I was replaying the day in my head and lost track of time." He looked up at her with a gaze so heated her panties, if she were wearing any, would be scorched.

A knowing silence settles between them. Rather than risk that heated gaze becoming an inferno, Petra excuses herself and returns to her room. Lachlan follows closely behind her after putting the glasses in the dishwasher.

Lachlan's room is just down the hall from hers, and he stops outside, looking at her as if he wants to ask her to come in. She doesn't give him a chance. Instead, she quickly wishes him a good night and closes her door firmly behind her. She lets out a deep breath and then gets back into bed.

Sleep finds her quickly this time, but she is left dreaming of Lachlan and all the ways he could make her come.

Petra wakes late the next morning and momentarily forgets where she is and all that transpired the day before. As she stretches and notices her surroundings, excitement and hesitation flood her system. Sapphire tendrils flow through the room, lifting random items from shelves and opening closet doors.

"Put that back," she tells her magic as it takes a turtle figurine from one of the corner shelves and places it on the bed. She watches as the responsible tendril sags reluctantly and perhaps with a bit of attitude as it wraps around the figurine and puts it back on the shelf.

While she gets dressed, she can hear Lachlan moving around in the kitchen. She hoped to slip out unnoticed, but the fates have decided against it and would rather humiliate her. After a final look at herself in the mirror and double-checking that there are no loose tendrils of magic floating around, she takes a deep breath and opens the door, greeted by the tempting smells of waffles, bacon, and coffee.

Lachlan clears his throat as she walks into the kitchen. "Good"—he checks the clock on the stove—"morning. How'd you sleep?"

"Good. I immediately passed out when I went back to bed. Apparently, all I needed was some water."

"Good. Good. I wasn't sure what time you'd be up, but clearly"—he gestures to the plates of waffles and bacon—"I made brunch. If you can grab the berries and whipped cream from the fridge, I'll get some syrup, and we can dig in."

Petra opens the fridge, spotting the fruit containers and whipped cream, and carries them over to the table, which has already been set for two.

"This looks lovely, Lach. You didn't have to do all this," she says.

"I know. But we both need to eat, and I need to show that I can provide for my wife. Even if it's just waffles and bacon," he responds, winking at her as he rounds the table to sit.

Petra laughs lightly, sitting down opposite him. "Well, you're off to a great start."

They each load their plates with the delicious meal Lachlan has put together and eat, enjoying companionable conversation, during which Petra learns that Lachlan had to train to hide his demon form and that it's not something that every demon is capable of.

"So, I've always been curious about why you own Bittersweet Acorn. I mean, as a high-powered demon, son of a demon lord, a council member, and from seeing this place, you clearly don't need the money. So why a bar?" she asks, cutting a slice of waffle and bacon and swirling them in the maple syrup on her plate.

"Honestly, I like that it makes me feel useful."

"But aren't you useful in your everyday life?"

"I am. But this is different. My usefulness at the bar doesn't depend on my ability to persuade, dominate, or instill fear. It's not about me as a demon and how much power I have or the power I can lord over others. It's simply about providing a service and being a listening ear."

"I guess that makes sense," she responds, tilting her head as she processes his answer.

"It also helps that when people and creatures drink, they tend to talk, so I learn all sorts of different tidbits about humans and the supernatural. And information is always useful as a council member. So, it helps me to stay connected to the goings-on in the community, which was a perk I didn't think of at first. I just applied for the business license because I wanted something just for me."

"I can understand that. It's hard being from our world and living in the human world. Finding that balance of purpose and responsibility while also trying not to terrorize the humans."

"Absolutely."

"Can I ask something else?"

"You can ask me anything," Lachlan responds, leaning forward so she knows she has his full attention.

"Why did you really offer to help me? Why do you care so much that I take the Premier Witch role?"

"Aside from the fact that I wouldn't want any of the Wilks family in the role—can you imagine what harm they would do to the community?" He shudders, "I care about you. I know you would be great in this role and would help facilitate some of the change we need within the council. Believe it or not, there are downsides to some council members living century-long lives. Your compassion, patience, and empathy are desperately needed, as much as your youth is."

Petra blushes, unsure of when she last had something so positive said about her. She's always seen herself as someone willing to help others and would do whatever she can. But she's never seen herself as anyone extraordinary.

"Okay, but why help me? Why not let me find some other sucker or leave me to my own devices to find a loophole in Grog's plan? You offered yourself so quickly and without hesitation."

Lachlan laughs, leaning back into his chair and crossing his arms across his chest. *Goddess, save me from those forearms.*

"First, no one who marries you would be a sucker. You are the smartest, most beautiful woman I know. You got sucked into a shitty position by a council member with ulterior motives, and I can't stand by and let that happen. You being linked to me will say a lot in our community. Second, you're my friend, and I am nothing if not loyal. Third, I would steal the moon for you, Petra."

Petra's eyes go wide. She's pretty sure he just confessed to something more profound than friendship. She pushes her plate away, giving herself a moment to gather her thoughts and to control the hum of her magic flowing through her as it responds to Lachlan's words. She feels him grasp her hand in his, running his thumb against hers, scorching her skin with his touch.

"Lastly, Petra, you are worth it. Whatever comes of this, of us, of the council decision, you are worth every second of it," he says softly, looking deep into her soul as he does.

Witches' tits.

After brunch, Lachlan has to go to the Acorn, so Petra spends most of the afternoon reading in Lachlan's home library, which is something else she learned about him since moving in—that he's a big enough reader to have a home library. Seriously, who is this man?

The circular room was likely once a conservatory, boasting lots of natural light through the large windows that look out onto the pool deck and lawn. It's a space filled with built-in dark wood shelves and flooring, soft contrasting couches, and oversized chairs to lounge in. Books of every genre, new and old, line the shelves. Upon finding an intriguing-looking thriller featuring a serial killer making their way through a busy city, she plops into one of the oversized chaises. She remains there for the next few hours, losing herself in the tale and mystery. She is so engrossed that she doesn't even notice when Daisy arrives. She also doesn't see Daisy choose a book and stretch out on the couch nearby. It isn't until Petra puts her book down to get a drink that she sees Daisy out of the corner of her eye and screams.

"Goddesses' gonads!" Petra exclaims, slapping her hand against her chest. "When did you get here?"

Daisy falls into a fit of laughter. In between wheezes, Daisy says, "Did you… just say…'goddesses' gonads'?"

"Yes. Because you scared the crap out of me," Petra responds, now laughing at Daisy and herself.

"Oh, my goddess. You are the best," Daisy says, wiping away tears. She picks up her phone, wakes it up, and continues, "Anyway, I got here about an hour ago. You were in such a trance you didn't even respond when I called your name and waved my hand in front of your face. So I grabbed a book and joined you."

Shaking her head, Petra chuckles at herself.

"How are things going between you and the Lach-ness-monster?" Daisy asks, wiggling her eyebrows suggestively.

Petra sits back in her chair, running her hands over her face, deciding how much to divulge.

"Good. It's taken a while, but I've settled in and feel more at home. We had a movie night last night and watched *Hook*…"

"A classic, of course," Daisy cuts in.

"Of course," Petra agrees, smiling at her friend. "And we may have made out a little during the movie."

"I knew it!" Daisy shouts, waving her arms in front of her and pointing her fingers excitedly at Petra. "Goddess save me, but I knew there was something between you two. I mean, Lach wouldn't agree to marry you if he didn't have feelings for you."

"There's nothing between us," Petra insists.

"Uh-huh. Keep telling yourself that."

Petra continues to deny that there are real feelings between them, but Daisy refuses to believe her. While Petra and Lachlan shared a nice moment this morning, she can't let herself get her hopes up and can't allow herself to explore what could be there. She knows a tough road lies ahead of her with losing Gammy, claiming Premier Witch, and whatever comes with that. Gammy has led a very solitary life, with council being her priority, and Petra expects she will need to do the same. So, no, nothing is going on between them. It was a one-time thing, and it won't happen again. They just had to get it out of their systems.

"What time is it, anyway?" Petra asks, pulling herself out of her thoughts.

Daisy looks at her phone again. "Just after four, why?"

"Wanna go for some afternoon cocktails?"

"Ab-so-fucking-lutely."

"Great. Let me go and change quickly, and then we can head out."

"Sounds good. I'll meet you out front. Oh, and Petra?"

"Yes?"

"Don't think I didn't notice the convenient change of subject."

Petra smiles at her friend before heading to her room. Daisy is like a scrying witch; she isn't going to let this go. However, if Petra can keep her distracted with other things, maybe, just maybe, she can get through this without having to acknowledge the buzz in the air and her magic when she's around Lachlan.

CHAPTER TWENTY-TWO

Lachlan

As much as Lachlan wants to spend every waking moment with Petra, he knows she needs time to process. Their arrangement and her staying with him is a big adjustment, and given everything she is dealing with right now, he assumes she will be better off if he isn't hanging around all the time. Thus, in an effort to give her space, he pulls up to Declan's home, planning to spend the afternoon here.

Declan always got the shorter end of the stick when they were younger. With Lachlan being the eldest, more attention was paid to him as the heir, and more pressure was on him to succeed. Unfortunately, this meant that Declan was often left alone and not trained to the same extent as Lachlan. As Lachlan got older and started noticing the disparities between them, he did his best to fill those gaps, especially after their mom took off with a random shapeshifter and their dad passed. They both have a great relationship with their mother now, but it was challenging for a while as they figured out their roles in the family post-Damian.

It is only with the guidance from Lachlan that Declan

has been able to become the demon he is today. It's also because of Lachlan and his position on council that Declan has his auto shop. Sometimes there are perks to having a family member in politics. Despite being more of a father figure than a brother to Declan at times, spending time with his little brother is one of his favorite things to do. And he's thrilled to be able to do it today, even if it's just a means of distracting himself from his new wife and what happened between them last night.

"So, how is it being a married man?" Declan asks, handing Lachlan a cold beer as they sit on opposite patio couches under the open umbrella with the heat lamps nearby. The shift to cooler weather, while not unexpected, is never one of Lachlan's favorites. Being of the underworld, he is more accustomed to the heat and steady warmth. Declan refuses to acknowledge winter is a thing and thus insists on the patio being an all-year space. Thankfully, he finally invested in the heat lamps this year, meaning that with a warm coat and layered clothes, it's almost tolerable to be sitting out in the cold and snow.

"It has been interesting."

"Just interesting, huh?"

"Yep." Lachlan takes a sip and hopes Declan won't push further.

"Why don't I believe that?"

Declan lifts his leg and rests his ankle on his other knee, creating a figure-four shape, as he leans back and rests his opposite arm on the back of the seat. Cocking his head, he smirks at Lachlan, waiting for Lachlan to break. When Lachlan doesn't, Declan finally says, "I think there's more to it than 'interesting,' but you're afraid to say anything. You're just trying to play coy so you don't freak out over it."

Lachlan scoffs. "First, why would I need to hide

anything? Second, why do you think I would freak out *if* there were something more?"

"You lie because you don't want to have this conversation—which, too bad, it's happening. And you'd freak out because you've had a thing for Petra for the last two years. You're now married to her, and you're trying to tell me that you aren't freaking out over that? I don't buy it. Spill the dragon dung already."

It is a shame that Declan knows him so well. Though he is wrong. Lachlan is absolutely not freaking out.

Not one bit.

Okay, maybe a little bit.

"When we do see each other, we tend to watch movies or just chat about our day," Lachlan says, doubling down on his part lie.

"And…"

Lachlan coughs. "And we may have made out last night…"

"Called it!" Declan exclaims smugly.

"You called nothing."

"So, now, why are you freaking out?"

"I'm not freaking out," Lachlan lies.

Declan stares at him.

Dropping his head back onto the top of his seat, Lachlan groans, giving in. "Fine. I'm worried about us getting attached and her getting hurt. Also, it's *Petra*. I don't want to let her go now that I have her. I can't."

"There it is," Declan practically sings. "Took you long enough to admit it. How did you think this marriage thing was going to work out? There's no way you two aren't already attached. You need to discuss your feelings before you both get hurt."

"Won't that push her away, make her think I don't want something more?"

"Maybe she wants something more, too. But you'll never know where you stand or where this *thing* is going unless you talk to each other."

"I guess that makes sense. I'll talk to my wife… but only because you said I had to." Lachlan sighs like a temperamental teenager. Declan rolls his eyes at his dramatic ways. "So , tell me what's been going on with you. I'm tired of talking about me."

"I think we are going to need another beer for that. Give me a sec," Declan says, getting up to get more from the fridge.

While Declan is away, Lachlan checks his phone, feeling disappointed when he sees no messages from Petra. He slides his phone back into his pocket as Declan returns with fresh beers and a bowl of chips. He settles back into his seat and then starts telling Lachlan about what has been happening around him in the last little while, but all Lachlan can focus on is getting home to Petra.

Declan convinces Lachlan to stay for dinner, giving Lachlan the perfect opportunity to check in with Petra. He sends a message to Petra, letting her know he'll be home later—just because it's the friendly thing to do, not because it is something a husband would say to his wife when out with friends.

Lachlan does his best to avoid overanalyzing the lack of response or even just acknowledgment of his message from Petra. Yet, despite his best efforts, his brain turns to thoughts that she is avoiding him, regretting what they did the previous night. On the drive back home, the anxiousness in his body builds. Tapping his fingers on the steering wheel and bouncing his left leg, he wonders if it was a mistake.

Suppose she has decided to cut and run. Shadows start to leak out of him, creating a cloud of darkness rolling down the highway.

By the time he arrives home, his body aches to be near her, to talk about what happened; however, when he pulls up out front, all the lights are off. Entering, the house feels empty, as if its heart is missing.

As worry builds in his gut, he flicks on lights as he walks through the foyer, living room, and into the kitchen. Morris follows him from room to room, meowing, demanding attention, or most likely food. Lachlan scoops him up, scratching his chin, and carries him over to a stool to sit on.

She's okay. She's just taking some space, he tells himself, trying his best to believe it. After sitting with a glass of water on a stool next to Morris at the kitchen counter, watching the condensation roll down the glass for what feels like hours, he decides he can't stand it anymore and messages Daisy.

LACHLAN

Hey. You heard from Petra today?

Not expecting a response right away, he places his phone face down on the counter as he goes to his room and changes into his favorite gray sweatpants. He picks up a white T-shirt and brings it to the kitchen, tossing it on the stool next to him when he hears his phone vibrate. Anxiety floods his system as he reaches for it and flips it over, seeing a response from Daisy, but not one he was hoping for.

DAISY

Yeah, we went out for some cocktails this afternoon.

She left hours ago, said she was going home.

Is she not with you?

No, she's not here.

Would she have gone back to her old place?

Maybe.

Can you try calling her?

I'm not sure she wants to talk to me today, or at least she hasn't responded.

Yeah, give me a sec.

K.

Lachlan puts his phone back on the counter and puts his head in his hands, running them through his unbound hair. Why would she go back to her place? She didn't want to give it up after moving in here, but as far as he knows, she hasn't been there since they married. His phone vibrates again; it's Daisy calling him. He swipes to answer.

"Hey, Daisy," he says, trying to keep the worst-case scenario thoughts from taking over.

"Hey. She's fine. She went back to her place to grab some things and fell asleep. She said she would pack up and head back to your place. Should be there within an hour."

He lets out a sigh of relief. *She's coming home.*

"Thanks, Daisy. I appreciate it."

"No problem." He can hear the smile in her voice as she responds. "Oh, and Lach?"

"Yes?"

"She's a good one. Do what you need to keep her."

He blinks in surprise. Of all the things she could have said, he didn't expect that.

"I'm going to do my best," he tells her, hoping he exudes more confidence than he currently feels.

"I would expect no less."

"Night, Daisy. Thanks again," he replies as a sense of warmth fills him.

"Night, Lach."

He hangs up, places his phone back on the counter, takes a deep breath and lets it out, releasing the tension and dread that had accumulated within. He picks up his drink and moves into the living room, Morris following him. Knowing he won't be able to sleep until Petra is home, he turns on the TV, intending to watch something to distract himself while he waits. So he waits, aimlessly scrolling through various streaming services until finally settling on some action movie with superheroes.

A little over an hour later, he hears the door open, and Petra calls out, "Lach! I'm back."

His heart leaps in his chest. Galloping. Dancing. *She's home*, his demon sings.

"I'm in the living room!" he shouts back, trying to sound calm.

She appears in the doorway as if she were a gift from the goddesses. Even in just her sweats, sweater falling off her shoulder, her hair up in a messy bun, she's perfect. He sees her eyes flare as she finds him, stopping on his exposed chest. He may have forgotten his shirt in the kitchen. Oops.

CHAPTER TWENTY-THREE

Petra

G*oddesses' gonads!*

Petra stops at the entry to the living room, caught by surprise at the sight of Lachlan stretched out on the couch, shirtless and chiseled as if he is a statue gifted by Hecate herself. She is about to say something, but the sight of him causes her brain to short-circuit and instead leaves her mouth hanging open and maybe a bit of drool to escape.

She is silent and staring at him for what begins to feel like an awkward amount of time. Lachlan stretches one arm above his head before bending and tucking it behind the pillow underneath. A knowing smirk forms on his lips as he waits for her to regain functionality.

Her eyes roam hungrily over the corded and well-defined muscle. She doesn't count, but she's confident she sees more abs on him than should be humanly possible—which, given he's a demon, may explain some of it. His arms are god-like, and now she understands why it's felt so much like home when she has been wrapped in them, for they're nothing if not brick walls.

Finally, she realizes she's still staring, and as she shakes her head, rattling her sense of speech back into her, she catches the growing bulge in Lachlan's pants, and a little squeak escapes her lips.

"Welcome home," Lachlan says, his voice husky and wanting.

Petra clears her throat and stammers, "Huh… hi." She pulls her eyes away from Lachlan's sculpted form and focuses on a spot on the couch above his head. Even though she had his dick in her mouth a mere twenty-four hours ago, it is impolite to stare at a friend's body.

"How was your afternoon with Daisy?"

"It was good. We went out for some cocktails and had an early dinner. It was nice to be able to hang out, as we haven't had much time to do that lately," she says, keeping her eyes focused as she navigates to the chair opposite him and sits.

Lachlan laughs. "You can look at me, you know. I swear you, or I, won't spontaneously combust."

"I know I can look at you. But I'm not entirely sure it's safe to do so. Hecate may come down and smite me."

"Why would she smite you?" He flexes his chest, making his pecs dance.

Rather than answer the question and admit the many dirty thoughts floating around her brain about what she would like to do to Lachlan, Petra refocuses and broaches the conversation they need to have.

"I think, if we want…*this*"—she points between them—"and our friendship to remain intact, we need to set some boundaries."

Lachlan sits up, a mix of curiosity and disappointment on his face. "I think we crossed that line last night when I made you come with all your clothes still on."

"I know, I know. And as much as I enjoyed it, I don't think that should happen again. It was a… miscalculation of judgment."

"A miscalculation of judgment? You mean a mistake?"

"I think we both were curious, but I don't think it should have happened. It was a one-time thing to alleviate the tension between us. We need to establish some boundaries so it doesn't happen again."

Petra returns her eyes to Lachlan and notices his fists and jaw are clenched, tightening the muscles up his arms and face. This is not going how she hoped. Last night wasn't a mistake, but a long time coming, yet she can't let him know. She can't let him see how much she wants this. How right this is. Not right now. Not while everything is still on the line.

"I don't mean to upset you. I really don't. I think we have a great friendship, and I will never be able to thank you enough for marrying me. But to keep that friendship, we need to set some more ground rules," she explains.

"Ok. What do you suggest?" he asks, his voice clipped as he leans back, arms crossed over his chest.

"For one, fully clothed when in common areas."

"Don't think you can control yourself, huh?" he goads playfully.

"Could you?" she retorts.

Lachlan stares at her. Cold. Hard. Petra knows she's made her point.

"Second, no affectionate touches or glances. And third, our friendship comes first, regardless of your or my feelings. Nothing else will come in the way of that. I am merely a roommate, and our lives are to exist and continue as normal. That means you can do whatever you normally do, and so can I. Anything else you want to add?"

She has had time to think about this and can see that Lachlan may need more time to process what she has said and to decide if there is anything else he thinks they need to add.

"I can give you more time to think. I'm going to bring my stuff to my room, and we can talk again in the morning. This is for the best, Lach."

As she walks back out to the front hall where she dropped her bags, she swears she hears him mutter, "Best for who?" She's wondering the same thing. All she knows is that she can't risk losing him, and keeping him at arm's length is the only way to ensure that doesn't happen.

Petra spends the next few days living as if she were still unmarried and at her apartment. She wakes early, enjoys her morning egg sandwich on a bagel, and reads a bit of her book before getting dressed and heading to the childcare. She hasn't told anyone at work that she's now married, not exactly proud of the circumstances in which it happened, so she takes the ring off her finger, places it on her necklace, and tucks it under her shirt before stepping out the door. Thankfully, none of her eagle-eyed preschoolers have noticed the new adornment, but it will likely come at some point. How she will answer those inevitable questions, she is not sure.

Lachlan has been spending more time at the Acorn, which means they haven't had a chance to sit and talk again since the awkward conversation about boundaries a few nights ago. She doesn't want to try and have it over text, but she also knows that the opposite schedules they are on now likely aren't helping them either. Daisy, however, has not been shy about keeping Petra up to date on Lachlan's extreme moodiness and is starting to insist that Petra and Lachlan hook up already and get it out of their system. As if a single hookup would be enough to satiate what has been building.

While Petra is the one who has suggested these boundaries, she is not naive enough to believe that they will help to quell her desire. She has been so on edge since the wedding that her magic has slowly grown more and more out of whack. It now keeps misfiring, and there appears to be a developing dark pink aura around her. It was so bad at one point yesterday that when Carlos came over seeking a hug after falling and scraping his knee, he commented that it was cloudy like a frog pond around her.

When she arrives at the childcare for her shift, she is greeted by a small group of concerned caregivers, Carlos's abuela among them. This is never a good sign. She smiles kindly at them and quickens her pace as she walks by. She turns down the hall to the staff room and sees the center director and manager waiting for her.

"Good morning, ladies," she says, mustering as much brightness into her tone as possible.

"Good morning," they respond in unison. "Petra, may we have a word?" Sheila, the director, asks, though Petra knows it's not a question.

"Sure."

Sheila steps aside and motions for Petra to enter the staff room ahead of her, which she does, and they both follow closely behind.

"How can I help you? Is something wrong?"

Sheila and Rosemary, the manager, exchange a look between them. Petra swallows and places her hands behind her back, attempting to look relaxed and hide the wringing of her hands.

"We've had some concerns broached by the parents and guardians," Rosemary states.

"But nothing bad has happened," Petra interjects.

Both Sheila and Rosemary look at her; their eyes soften, and she knows they don't want to be having this conversation. They care about her, and they, along with the whole staff, have always been like family. But Petra knows this is still a job, and the goal is to properly care for the children in her classroom.

"Honey… you have a literal cloud of magic around you," Sheila says softly.

"I know. I've been under some stress."

"We understand. Unfortunately, Carlos and some other children went home and told their caregivers because they were scared. As you saw, various caregivers have come this morning concerned for their children's well-being," Rosemary says.

"I would never do anything to harm them. You know I wouldn't," Petra pleads.

"Of course you wouldn't. But we have protocols and need to consider the safety of the children. You are to be placed on a one-month leave to start. We will continue to pay you and support you. You don't have to tell us what is going on. But, take some time to sort your life out so you can come back in a better position to provide the level of care we are proud of and know you are capable of. We will reevaluate after a month, and if needed, the leave will be extended," Rosemary concludes.

Petra tries and fails to stop the tears streaming down her face. She's numb and doesn't know what to do.

"We have called Calle in to cover for you in the

meantime. So know that your children are in the best of care," Sheila adds with a note of finality.

That's it. She can't even work the day. She is to leave immediately. Sheila and Rosemary stand, waiting for Petra to follow. She has to command her legs to get herself to stand. Upon doing so, Sheila takes her hands and looks apologetically into her eyes. They walk her out, past the group of caregivers, past the yard, and to her car as if she were on a perp walk. They each hug her, wish her well, and then leave her standing next to her car, a leaking faucet about to burst open. She finds her keys in her pocket and lets herself in.

Sitting in the car, she stares over the steering wheel, watching a group of children come out with their educators. She's supposed to be in there, helping her little crew get ready. A child notices her and waves; she waves back. She hears a phone ringing through the speaker. Looking down, she sees Lachlan's name. It's only then that she realizes that upon not knowing what to do, she did the only thing she could think of: call Lachlan.

Lachlan and Daisy arrive shortly after her call for help and drive her back home. *To Lachlan's home,* she corrects herself. Though, if she's honest with herself, the last few weeks here have felt more like home than anywhere else she has ever lived. But she's choosing not to dig into that right now. Instead, she's still trying to numb herself to tell them what happened. She keeps calling on her magic to help calm her emotions, but it's clearly out of sorts and is not responding.

They check to ensure she has everything she needs before they are required at the Acorn and remind her that they're only a phone call away. In the meantime, she is encouraged to zone out with trashy reality TV and all the ice cream and junk food she wants. No judgment, they explicitly tell her. Morris joins her on the couch, curling up on her legs, shortly after they left. Within minutes, he is snoring contentedly.

Once alone, she scans through the TV options and settles on season one of *Toil & Trouble*, a reality dating competition where several single supernatural creatures date to try and find their fated mate. It's like watching a cauldron on fire, but it helps. It distracts her enough that she is no longer freaking out over being put on leave, and it helps to prevent her from catastrophizing. The last thing she needs is another shield-forming incident.

When Lachlan arrives home after his shift, she is still in the same position he left her in, with more food particles around her and half a season into *Toil & Trouble*. He changes out of his bar clothes into black basketball shorts and a dark blue T-shirt, then comes to sit next to her on the couch. He picks up her outstretched legs and slides himself underneath her feet, resting them on his lap.

"What are we watching?" He asks.

"*Toil & Trouble*."

"This season one?"

"Yeah."

"This was the best season. I totally rooted for Sylvia and Marcus from the start."

Petra's eyes snap to his. "You've actually watched this?"

"Every season," he says proudly, taking her left foot in his hands as he begins to run his thumb down her sole absentmindedly. The firm pressure releases some of the tension within and liquefies her core.

"You surprise me, Mr. Grace."

"What can I say? I don't want the drama, but seeing the shenanigans that go on, however staged it may be, on a reality TV dating show brings me joy. It's twisted, I know."

"I get that."

The silence unfolds comfortably between them as they watch couples battle it out in a sponge and bucket competition, trying to soak up as much water as they can into the sponges and squeeze it out into buckets to fill them as fast as possible so they can win a date night adventure. Lennie and Hazel win, but Marcus and Sylvia are not happy about it, claiming Lennie and Hazel cheated and that they, Marcus and Sylvia, deserve the date.

"I am pretty sure Sylvia is going to hex Lennie to prevent them from going on this date," Petra says, still enjoying the comforting and relaxing foot and now calf massage Lachlan bestows upon her.

"I thought the same thing, but apparently, the production put a 'no magic use against other contestants' clause in place to prevent potential issues."

"Smart."

"I thought so. I mean, you have a load of horny supes essentially fighting each other to find love; you need some protection plan in place, especially with how territorial we can be." He moves his hands up her calves, running his fingers and thumbs down her legs in the most remarkable ways. "So you wanna talk about what happened at work?"

"Not particularly."

Lachlan slides his hands back down her legs and resumes massaging her feet. "Valid. But I feel like you need to."

Petra releases a long breath, blowing up the hair at the side of her face. She knows he's not wrong. "I've been having some troubles with my magic, and some of the kids were worried," she says, noticing his furrowed brow as he concentrates on what she's not saying. "But anyway, they went home and told their caregivers I have been scary lately, so the parents came in and spoke to my managers. I've been put on paid leave for a month while I 'sort my life out.'"

"Damn. I know it's shitty and not what you would prefer. I know you care about those little rug rats and wouldn't do anything to hurt them," he says. "But maybe it's for the best?"

"Best for who?" Petra shoots back, repeating his words from earlier.

"For everyone. You can't care for them properly if you are a risk to their well-being. So take the time, find ways to relax…" he says, letting the word and innuendo hang in the air.

"I guess."

"I know. I'm sure it will all work out," he assures her.

"Thanks."

"Anytime."

Petra smiles at Lachlan, enjoying this moment with him. It almost seems natural, as if this is what she should be doing every night—talking to him about her day and relaxing together.

"Can I ask one other question?" Lachlan says.

"Sure."

"You mentioned you've been having some issues with your magic. What's going on there?"

A blush creeps up her neck. How can she tell him that she's been misfiring because of him? That her suggestion of boundaries between them to prevent them from making a bigger mistake and ruining their friendship when all she wants to do is climb him and ride him like a broomstick.

Her cheeks heat as Lachlan gazes at her, tilting his head curiously. The look he gives her is not helping. Instead, it fans the flames inside. She shifts uncomfortably under his gaze, causing Morris to leap off her lap and saunter out of the room. As she tries to decide what answer to give, she settles on, "It's a stress response."

"What has you so worked up?" he asks, almost knowingly, while flicking his eyes down her neck, following the heated trail left by her flushed skin.

"Um…" She pauses, answers tumbling through her misfiring brain, but none are sticking.

Lachlan runs his hand up her leg. Caressing. Tickling.

"You," she whispers.

She sees the corner of Lachlan's mouth quirk up. Pretending he didn't hear her, he says, "Sorry, what was that?"

"You," she says more firmly.

"Hmm… that's interesting. How could I be causing you stress?" he asks, his voice rougher.

"I've, um…been a bit on edge."

"On edge how?"

"You know how." She lifts her eyes to his.

"I'm not sure I do. I think you should tell me."

"Lach…"

"Tell me, Petra."

She takes hold of her sweater, sliding her hands into the opposite cuffs, running her hands up and down her forearms. Lachlan's gaze on her is heated. He's drinking her in like he'd been in the bowels of hell for weeks without liquid.

"I've been horny as fuck and hate the boundaries I put in place when all I want to do is ride that cock and come on your face," she finally says, exasperated.

"Then do it," he responds, his voice huskier, filled with wanting.

"What?"

"Did I stutter? I said do it."

"But the boundaries?"

"Fuck the boundaries," he says, lifting her legs off his lap and scooting down on the couch so he's laying with his head on the arm, "and sit on my face. Let me taste that amazing pussy of yours."

"Lach… I …"

"What did I say, Petra?"

Petra stands, disbelieving that this is happening. As she pulls down her pants and underwear, kicking them off to the side, she tells herself that this will only happen once. To take the edge off. To fill the need. She slides a hand down her stomach to her heated core, feeling her wetness. She stands before him, placing her hands on his shoulders as she raises a leg, straddling him. He leans forward, slides his tongue between her lips, and she just about buckles.

"So good."

She whimpers as he does it again.

"Put your hands on the couch arm."

She does.

He places his hands on her ass and pulls her with him as he leans back.

"Now sit."

She sits and moans as he slides his tongue inside her, lapping her up. He feasts on her as if he won't eat again for a year.

His arms wrap around the outside of her legs, with his hands landing on the inside of her thighs, holding her open and keeping her in place. His tongue is like magic. She feels her magic unwinding and relaxing as he consumes her.

"You are simply delicious," he says, taking a breath.

Petra can only manage a moan in response. She moves

her hips, grinding into him, wanting more as his tongue circles her clit. He nips her lip, and she squeaks.

He unwinds his left arm and brings his hand under her, his finger circling her slick opening. She pushes down, wanting him to fill her.

"Oh, do you want this?" he taunts.

"Yes," she whispers.

"Tell me," he says, pushing it just inside the edge and then removing it, replacing it with his tongue that he plunges inside her.

"I want you to eat my pussy while you finger-fuck me," she gasps.

"Well, since you asked," he moans, thrusting two thick fingers inside her, causing her to fold forward with pleasure as he fills her. He curls his fingers forward, pulsing them in a "come here" motion as he plants his lips around her clit and sucks, then lightly drags his teeth, making her legs twitch. He adds a third finger, stretching her in mind-bending ways, the friction as he pulses them in and out making her toes curl.

She's close.

She feels the tension building in her core as he thrusts his fingers back in and out, fast and hard. She runs one hand under her shirt, up her stomach to her chest. She palms her breast and rolls her firm nipple between her forefinger and thumb. It adds the extra bit of sensation she needs. With a final hard suck and flick of his tongue on her clit, she goes over the edge, curling forward as pleasure ripples out from her core.

"Fuck yes, Lach," she yells as she comes on his face.

"Fuck yes indeed," he says, continuing to flick her clit with his tongue as she rides out her orgasm.

The room starts to come back into focus, and she smirks

and then laughs nervously, noticing the pink sapphire sparkle around them. Too wrapped in what she was feeling, she didn't realize her magic released when she did, but she could feel it lighter inside her, rolling more smoothly, almost dancing under her skin.

"Well, then," she says, pushing against the arm and trying to move away.

"Just where do you think you are going?" He wraps his arms around the back of her legs again. "I'm not done eating yet."

Petra's eyes flare with heat.

Well, I can't let the man starve now, can I?

"As you were then," she says.

He forcefully grabs her ass and pulls her glistening pussy back into his already soaked face. Horns rise in front of her.

"You better hold on," he says.

She wraps her hands around his horns, and he groans. She begins stroking them as he feasts beneath her. Shadows rise around her, caressing her already sensitive skin. Two of them land on her breasts, floating over her peaked nipples, sending waves of magic electricity into her core.

"I hope you know what you're doing," he says, a loose threat hanging in his tone.

"I hope so too," she responds, stroking again before leaning over and licking the tip of his right horn.

CHAPTER TWENTY-FOUR

Lachlan

H*ades, help me.*

Petra tastes better than he could have ever imagined. He would spend the rest of his days here, in this moment, if he could. Already, he knows he will never get enough of her, of his face between her legs, of her taste on his tongue.

She runs her hands through his hair, grasping it and directing his head exactly where she wants it as he dips his tongue into her molten center and then licks up her folds. He flattens his tongue and pushes it against her swollen clit; she moans above him. She grinds her hot pussy into his eager face as she seeks release.

He slides three fingers into her slick entrance and feels her instantly clench around him.

"Yes," she whimpers.

He slowly slides his fingers out and then plunges them back in forcefully, hooking them slightly once fully seated to reach her pleasure center.

She sinks into his face again, placing her hands on the couch arm above his head and yells out, "Fuck me, yes!"

She comes on his fingers, clenching tightly while he enthusiastically thrusts them, sucking on her clit, and holding her in place with his free hand so she can't pull away. No, he wants her to feel every bit of this release.

He withdraws his fingers before her legs can give out, wraps both arms around the back of her legs, and swings her down onto her back while shifting himself up and out of the way.

He has never seen a more beautiful sight than her in this moment, spent, flushed, and satisfied. He leans over top of her and kisses her neck. She doesn't shy away from him, even though he is still glistening with her juices. No. She wraps her legs around him and pulls his face to hers, kissing him deeply, tasting herself on his lips.

"That… was something," she says, pulling back enough so he can look into her eyes. There's something there, but he can't place it.

She raises a hand to one of his horns and wraps it around it, stroking it slowly. Carefully.

"What does this feel like?" she asks.

Not that his horns have made many appearances in his sexual adventures, but he's never had anyone ask when they had.

"It feels amazing. Like sparks firing on every nerve," he murmurs, leaning into her touch.

"Hmm. I know that feeling," she laughs softly.

"Oh? Do tell." Lachlan resumes kissing her neck, pulling her sweater down to expose her shoulders and collarbone as he follows their path.

She places her hands on his chest and pushes him back, stopping him. Before he can ask if she is okay, she grips the bottom of her sweater in her hands, pulling it over her head, exposing her bare chest.

She's perfect.

She smirks as she looks back at him. "You're drooling, turtle dove."

He's pretty sure she's joking, but he wipes his hand along his mouth anyway, and while he wipes away wetness, he is positive there is no drool. To prove his point he licks her remnant fluids from his fingers. "I can't help it. You are stunning, wife. And might I add, delicious."

He lets his eyes wander over her, memorizing every curve, peak, and dimple.

"You are fucking gorgeous," he nearly growls as desire flares inside him again. Looking at her, he understands why men have gone to war over women, why the stars shine, and why he cannot let her go.

"Thank you." She beams, perhaps due to the two orgasms she's already had. Though if he has his wish, she will have many more before the night is over.

"But before we go any further, I want to be sure you're okay. That you want this. That you want to do this with me," he says, knowing that it always comes across as weird for a demon to seek consent from his partners.

"Lach, I've come on your face twice already tonight. I think it's pretty clear."

"I need you to say it."

She sighs in exasperation. "Yes, I want you to fuck me. Fuck me so good I forget my name."

And that was all he needed. He leans down, capturing one of her nipples in his mouth, sucking gently while he grasps her other breast in his hand, rolling that nipple between his forefinger and thumb. She arches into his touch. He releases her nipple from his mouth with a loud *pop*, garnering a single laugh from Petra. He kisses around her nipple, then nips at the tender flesh on the underside of her breast before moving toward the center of her chest. He licks between her tits and continues up, going up her neck, under her chin, and landing on her already open mouth. She gasps when he pinches her other nipple. He swallows her sounds, taking them in and matching them with his own wanting groan.

She reaches up and runs her hands down his back to grasp the bottom of his shirt and pull it over his head. He pulls away from her long enough to allow the shirt to come over his head and off his arms, then immediately claims her mouth with his. Her lips are tender and move as if they were meant for his. She wraps her legs around his hips and grinds into him. He pushes his core toward her in response, letting her feel what she does to him. She moans softly.

"Tell me what you want," he demands, his voice husky and firm.

"You," she replies breathily.

"How?" he asks, barely getting the word out as she places her hand on his still-clothed and throbbing cock and squeezes.

"For starters, naked," she replies, fumbling for the waist of his shorts and attempting to push them down. He laughs as he gently grasps her hands and pauses.

"Protection?"

"I have an IUD and got tested three months ago and haven't been with anyone since," she tells him, running her finger along the waist of his shorts.

"I tested a couple of weeks ago and also haven't been with anyone… in a while. I have condoms, but they're in my room," he says, pointing upstairs before pulling away to go and get one. She grabs his arm before he can get away.

"No condom. I want you. I want all of you. I want to

feel… all of you," she says, looking down at the sizeable tent in his shorts.

"Are you sure?"

"Yes, Lachlan. Now stop asking and take off those shorts," she demands.

Well, if she's going to be like that, he has no choice but to oblige. He reaches down and sticks his thumbs in the waist of his shorts. He smirks at her. "These shorts?"

"Yes…"

He slowly pulls them down, along with his boxers, and watches her as he frees his hard cock. Her eyes flare hungrily as it springs free. Letting his clothing drop to his feet, he palms his dick, stroking it slowly, allowing a bead of pre-cum to build on the tip. She leans forward and licks it off, then takes the tip in her warm mouth. Using her tongue to caress the sensitive space under the head, she slides her mouth to the base and hums. The vibration and sensation of being fully seated are fucking wild. He places his hand on the back of her head and waits for her to look up. She does and gives a slight nod, giving him permission.

He withdraws slowly, relishing the sucking sensation while she runs her tongue along the underside of his dick and then smiles around him. He pulls out her ponytail and wraps her hair around his hand, using it to hold her in place firmly. She looks up at him again, her mouth wrapped around the head of his cock. He grunts as he forcefully thrusts forward, using her hair to push her toward him at the same time. She takes every last inch of him, her throat opening to accept him. When he hits the back of her throat, she moans around him, which sets him off. He thrusts as hard and fast as she takes him over and over again, grinning at how wild she is driving him. As good as this feels, he knows this is not how he wants to finish, so he pulls all the way out on a withdrawal stroke, leaving her in front of him with a perplexed look.

He sits beside her and grabs her, making Petra straddle him. She doesn't hesitate. She places one hand beside his head on the back of the couch and uses the other to grasp his cock, lining it up with her soaking pussy, and slowly sinks onto it. They both groan as her heat wraps around him. *Fuck, she's tight.* It takes her a moment to fully work him in, pausing periodically to adjust to his size. Once fully seated, he tilts his head back, seeing stars. She's so fucking hot.

"That's a good girl. So fucking wet for me," Lachlan says when she's fully seated. She grinds into him in response. He places his hands on her delicious ass and pushes into her, adding more friction.

With his hands still holding her glorious behind, he pulls his hips back and draws out of her. She tries to move with him, but he holds her in place. Just as he's about entirely out, he thrusts back into her, making her take every bit of him, and he feels a shudder run through her as he does. He pulls back again, and again, and again, increasing force and speed each time. She fits him perfectly.

She leans over him, holding tightly to the couch, which gives him a perfect angle to take one of her tits in his mouth. When he plants his mouth on her peaked nipple and nips it, she whimpers and pushes her hips back into him forcefully to meet his thrust.

She pulls his hands from her ass, moves one to her other tit, laces her fingers with the other, and holds it above his head. She takes control, bouncing and grinding on his cock, taking every ounce of pleasure she deserves.

She picks up speed, bucking as she chases her release,

and he is happy to be along for the ride. Suddenly, she stops, hops off of him, turns around and lines him back up again. She sits quickly, taking him. Owning him. She brings her feet up onto his legs and leans back, grabbing his hands, placing one hand on her tit and his other on her pussy. He begins circling her clit with his middle finger and then rolls it gently between his forefinger and thumb. He shifts slightly for a better angle, and she bounces on his lap.

Bounce.

Bounce.

Bounce.

Holy Hades, she is fantastic.

He's getting close, and he can tell she is too, as her gorgeous pussy tightens around him.

With a final thrust into her, they both yell each other's names and come undone. He feels her clench hard and pulse on his cock as he shudders inside her and releases himself, firing all he has felt for her these last two years. He comes harder than he ever has in his life. She keeps going, bouncing on his cock, trying to milk every last bit from him.

When she finally stops clenching around him, she hops off him, turns around, and kneels in front of him again. She takes him back in her mouth, licking her come from his dick in the process. This sight alone could make him come again.

"Holy fucking shit, you are so hot with my dick inside you."

"It's a good thing I like your dick inside me, then," she says before continuing to suck. He's instantly hard. "Looks like you're ready to go again," she says, winking at him. She stands up and puts a hand out to him. "Let's try your bed this time."

He stands and picks her up so she has to wrap her legs

around him. He doesn't make it three steps before shoving his cock inside her, eliciting a "Fuck, yes!" from her. He carries her to his room while she starts grinding into him.

Yes, he could get used to this.

CHAPTER TWENTY-FIVE

Petra

The week goes by quickly, the days mixing with nights. Petra spends afternoons with Gammy, learning more about the council and how it functions. While she'd seen some of what Gammy does throughout her life, she'd never been privy to the council's inner workings. Having this opportunity to learn more about the role of Premier Witch from Gammy is almost as priceless as spending time with her.

Some days are more challenging for Gammy than others. She tires quickly and often needs a nap to help her get through the day. Her medications also make her feel ill and lose interest in food. Petra does her best to encourage her to eat what she can, and Lachlan makes homemade meals for her to share with Gammy. Most of it is only lightly seasoned and is meant to be gentle on the stomach, which means lots of soups and chicken with rice or mashed potatoes, as overly spiced dishes upset Gammy's stomach, both from the taste and the smell.

Lachlan has been such a doll, helping where he can, checking in, and running errands as needed. With her spending so much time at Gammy's lately, she worries that he is feeling a bit neglected, especially so soon into their new development as friends with benefits. However, when asked, he reassures her that she should be spending time with Gammy while she can.

Between naps, Gammy has also shown Petra new spells and potion mixes in her apothecary, sharing with her secret family concoctions and more of her family history. One afternoon, after sharing the family origin story with Petra and how the first Roses narrowly escaped the witch hunters before settling in and founding Leeside, Gammy pulls out an old leatherbound book. The family grimoire. The edges are dark and worn, the brown cover lined with age and wear from regular use, and the thick ivory-colored pages torn in places along the edge from years of use.

"Come, darling, sit," Gammy says, moving to a side table and chair set. "Please, bring the book with you."

Petra does as instructed, lifting the heavy tome. As she carries it to the table, she can feel the power emanating from it, stroking at her wispy magic, seeking to join it. She sits at the table, placing the priceless book between them. Gammy runs her hand along the embossed writing on the cover, her eyes taking on a far-off expression as if wading through memories.

"This grimoire has been passed down, generation to generation, upon becoming Premier Witch." Gammy stops Petra's protest before it can begin. "I know you are not the Premier Witch yet, but I am certain everything will work out, and this will become yours shortly. So I am passing it to you now."

"I... I... thank you," Petra stumbles, overwhelmed with gratitude, grief, and excitement.

The grimoire holds all of the family spells. As is

common practice across many families, young witches in the family would only have access to a select few spells in a seriously abridged version. The belief was that you had to reach a certain maturity level before being able to look through the full version, as there was concern about the misuse and malpractice of younger witches. Unfortunately for the Rose family, the sign of maturity was the passing of the Premier Witch title with the previous titleholder's death.

"You should know that upon accepting the grimoire as yours, you are bound to protect it. The responsibility should not be taken lightly. The grimoire's magic will also join with yours, adding to the power you already possess. This means you will be stronger, your magic more potent, and your abilities will have greater reach. This will happen again when you take the Premier Witch title. When your power joins with the grimoire, it may feel a bit… funny until it fully melds together," Gammy explains.

Overwhelmed with emotion, Petra finds it hard to find the words she needs. Saying thank you seems so insufficient. But its power connecting to hers now makes sense, given the tingle she felt when she carried it.

"Do you think I'm ready?" Petra asks uncertainly.

"Darling, you were born ready. We just had to wait for time to catch up." Gammy smiles, taking her hand. "I would not be doing this if I did not think it was time. You may also find some answers here to help you with the final step to seal your seat at the table."

Petra wipes an escaped tear from the corner of her eye. "I don't know what to say."

"Just repeat after me," Gammy says, sitting up straighter and placing her hands on her lap.

"Ok," Petra responds, taking a deep breath, steadying her nerves.

"I, Petra, hereby accept the Rose family grimoire as my own. I promise to protect it to the best of my ability, to keep it safe from those who wish it, or me, harm. I will keep what is written on these pages close to my heart and promise to honor it and my ancestors from this day on. May the Goddess grant me this honor."

Petra repeats after Gammy, and as she expresses each word, she feels what starts as drops of water dripping into her pool of magic evolve into a full-blown crashing wave by the time she finishes. It takes her breath away, leaving her swimming to find the surface. When she emerges on the other side, Gammy is beaming at her with pride. The world looks sharper and edgier through Petra's new, more powerful magical senses. She sends out a ripple of power, aiming to pick a single tulip from the garden, but instead picks the entire raised bed.

"Whoa…" is all she manages to say.

"Welcome to the grimoire," Gammy says, pride radiating from her. "Be careful with spells for the next couple of weeks while the joining occurs. You'll gain better control as you become more comfortable with the increased power."

"This is wild," Petra says, sensing the foreign force flowing through her like a river toward its source.

"Just you wait," Gammy tells her, beaming. "The world is about to be yours, my darling granddaughter."

CHAPTER TWENTY-SIX

Petra

P etra wakes and buries her face deeper into the pillow and draws a deep breath. Lachlan's sheets smell like honeysuckle.

She opens her eyes. She must have fallen asleep after they finally stopped fucking, spent and breathless. She feels a weight shift beside her briefly before an arm, Lachlan's arm, drapes across her midsection, curling up her body and stopping where his hand finally rests, cupping a breast. He pulls her into his hard body and curls around her backside.

"Mmm…" He groans, burying his face in her hair at the nape of her neck. "Good morning."

She sinks into him, feeling more relaxed at his touch. Running a hand along his arm wrapped around her, she pushes her ass into him, feeling his hardness against her.

"Good morning indeed, my demon-lover."

He chuckles against her.

"Demon-lover? Really? That's the best you could come up with?"

"I've been awake for all of thirty seconds here, give me a break," she says, pushing her backside against him again.

He pulls her in tighter. "Keep doin' that, and you will be sorry, witchling."

"Oh no, I'm scared," she teases, grinding her butt against him and sliding her hand between her legs to begin playing with herself.

"You are insatiable," he responds, releasing her breast, then running his hand down her side before lifting her top leg over his, lining himself up with her entrance, and shoving his cock deep inside her already dripping wet pussy. "That's my girl. Hades, you take my cock so fucking perfectly."

She moans as he slams into her from behind, stretching and filling her like he was meant for her.

They fuck hard and fast. Before long, they both are moaning together as they reach their release. Lachlan's hand is around her neck, pulling her head back to him, covering her mouth with his, swallowing the sounds of pleasure while pumping into her.

She swears she feels him getting hard again before he pulls out. It seems he's insatiable too.

Lachlan plunges his tongue into her mouth, and she meets him with equal passion. She pulls away, feeling empty as he withdraws from her core, and rolls over to face him. He softens his kiss and then kisses the tip of her nose before getting a cloth to clean her up.

As lovely as all these orgasms have been, she admits she is a bit tender when he uses the soft cloth to wipe up his deposit between her legs. He notices her slight wince as he cleans.

"Little sore?" he asks, gently kissing her between her legs.

"A bit. I can't tell you the last time I've had this much sex in a couple week period." She laughs.

"It has been a bit excessive."

"Mmm… I'm not complaining, though."

"My only complaint is that I want more," he jokes.

"I'm sure that can happen… but I may need a soak first."

I thought you said this was a one-time thing, her brain sing-songs at her.

If we never stop, then it's still one-time, she replies internally, mentally sticking out her tongue.

"To the tub!" he exclaims, pointing a finger to the ceiling like he's just come up with the best idea ever.

She puts out her hands, and he grabs them, pulling her toward him and swinging her over his shoulder in one fluid motion. She cackles as she bounces while he walks. He smacks her ass with an audible *crack.*

He sets her beside the tub while he runs it, checking the temperature and putting in some lavender bath salts. She takes a moment to pee, somehow not shy that he is standing there while she does it.

Before long, the giant tub is filled with steaming water. He puts a hand out for her to hold while she steps in. He sits and then helps to guide her to sit between his legs. They lean back and soak in the bath's heat, scent, and soothing nature.

I could get used to this, she thinks before closing her eyes, resting her head against his chest while he runs one hand between her legs and the other plays with her breast.

After deciding on sex in the shower post-soaking in the tub, they finally found themselves hungry enough to warrant food over fucking.

Sitting at the table with her plate, her phone vibrates beside her. When she turns it over, she sees a text from Daisy:

DAISY

Hey lady

How you doing?

PETRA

I'm doing okay.

Thanks so much for your help the other day. I know I was a bit shaken up and out of sorts after the work stuff.

Anytime! That's what westies are for!

Westies?? Like the dog?

No - Witch x Bestie... Westies

groan

Shut up! It's good, and you know it!

It's something....

Anyways, you wanna hang out today? Maybe do some retail therapy?

Sure. Want me to pick you up?

That would be lovely :)

Let me know when you're on your way!

Will do!

When she looks up from her phone, she catches Lachlan watching her, a small, content smile on his disgustingly handsome face and a comforting look in his eyes. She doesn't regret anything they did last night and this morning and still worries about hurting him, but she also realizes that the stupid boundaries she tried to put in place didn't help. She appreciates everything he's done for her. Her developing feelings for him will complicate things, even more so now that they've slept together. But she tells herself she can manage it. She can stay friends. Friends with benefits.

"That was Daisy. She wants to go shopping, so I'm going to head out for the afternoon," she says. She catches a look of disappointment across his features, but it quickly vanishes.

"Not a problem. Think you'll be home for dinner?"

"Not sure. I'll let you know."

"Okay," he replies, then shoos her away. "I'll finish cleaning up. You go get ready."

"You sure?"

"Absolutely."

"Thanks," she says, then leans in, placing her hand on his arm and giving him a quick peck on the cheek.

As she walks away, she turns back to see him put his hand up to where she kissed him, and smiles softly.

A few hours later, Daisy has dragged Petra into nearly every store they've passed, but despite that, they only have three bags of merchandise between them. Daisy picked up a couple of swimsuits from one store and some new jeans from another, while Petra took advantage of a sale and stocked up on chocolate bars and truffles. Petra checks her phone, sees it's approaching six o'clock, and sends a message to Lachlan, letting him know she won't be home for dinner as Daisy shows no sign of stopping.

As Daisy opens the door for the next store, letting Petra

walk in first, she asks, "So how are things at House Grace-Rose?"

"Things are good."

"That's good. How are things between you two, though? You know, since the make-out session?"

"Things are good there as well," Petra responds, turning away to try and hide her smile, but Daisy catches her.

"No, no, no. No trying to hide. What's that smirk for? Did something finally happen between you two?" she asks excitedly.

"What do you mean, *finally*?" Petra questions while flipping through the shirts hanging on a rack.

"You two have been into each other for eons."

"We have not!" Petra replies, feigning indignance.

"You have. Lachlan can't take his eyes off you whenever you are around, which, frankly, can be a pain when trying to work at the Acorn, and he's pouring booze all over the place, missing glasses and shit."

"I've literally never seen him spill a drop."

"Okay, fine, that's a bit of an exaggeration." Daisy laughs, picking a shirt off a rack and holding it against herself while looking in a mirror. She tilts her head and then puts it back. "But he completely moons over you."

"We're just friends," Petra lies, mostly to herself.

"Bullshit."

"It's true. He's helping me out, that's all."

"Uh-huh. So how was it?"

"How was what?"

"Don't play dumb. The sex. How was it? I've seen how he moves, so I'm betting it's pretty damn good."

Petra can't help but blush. It was amazing. The best she's ever had, if she's honest with herself. She thinks back to his reaction when she stroked his horns and immediately starts to feel tingly in her core. She looks back toward Daisy and finds her standing there with a large, knowing smirk on her stupid face.

"Fuck off," Petra retorts, laughter in her voice.

"I *knew* it! I want details. How many times? How long? Where? When? How big is he? He looks like he's packing some heat!" She wags her eyebrows suggestively at Petra.

"You're so… you." Embarrassed, Petra glances away, looking at a table of sweaters and picking up a pink one.

"Spill!"

"Fine. Last night, the couch, his bed, the shower. This morning, his bed, the shower. Every day for the last couple of weeks it seems. I am not complaining about his size or abilities. It has been the best sex of my life. The man loves a meal, I'll say that…" Petra winks back at Daisy.

"Yes, ma'am!" Daisy exclaims as she bounces with excitement. "Ugh, it's been too long since I've been… taken out to eat."

"What happened to the thing with Stella?" Petra asks, happy to shift the attention away from her and Lachlan's escapades.

"That fizzled out a while ago. She wanted something more exclusive than I was willing to commit to."

"Aww. I'm sorry. You should have said something," Petra says, giving her friend a one-armed side hug.

"Meh, you've had a lot going on, so I didn't want to trouble you with it," Daisy confides.

Petra turns and faces Daisy. "I'm sorry. I know it's been a lot with me lately. It feels like a giant hurricane surrounds me. But you can always come to me, regardless of what I have going on, you know that, right?"

"I do. Thanks. And sorry I didn't say anything earlier."

"It's alright. Is there anyone else on the radar for you right now?"

"There's some potential with a vamp named Vlad, but that's about it. We've just started chatting, so there isn't much to tell right now."

"Well, you let me know when that changes. I want all the details!"

"As long as you keep me updated on you and demon-boy."

Petra doesn't respond as they walk up to the cashier with arms full of clothing items. Once all is said and done, they've added another two bags each to their haul. Petra feels good about how this afternoon has gone and has barely thought about the chaos known as her life. This was precisely what she needed.

She's not naive enough to believe that retail therapy will cure all, but spending time with Daisy and feeling relatively normal again feels nice. They've finally hit the last store in the mall, and Daisy has decided she's done for the day, thank Hecate.

As they return to Petra's car, Petra spots two familiar silhouettes ahead.

"Fuck!" Petra whispers, grabbing Daisy's arm and pulling her to the side.

"What? What is going on? What are you doing?" Daisy swivels her head, trying to see what is catching Petra's attention.

Petra motions to the people walking ahead of them. "That's Sloan and Francesca. I'd rather not have a run-in with them right now."

"Got it. So what do you want to do?"

"We'll give them a minute to two to leave, and then we should be good to go."

Daisy nods in confirmation. They stay hidden among the bushes, watching Sloan and Francesca get in their car and leave. When the coast is clear, they return to Petra's car.

Petra pops the trunk, and they throw their bags in. Petra is trying to decide if they should get something to eat before dropping Daisy off at home, when Daisy calls out from the passenger side of the car. "Uh, westie?"

Petra sighs, resigning that that term is not going away. "What's up?"

"That's what's up," she says, pointing to the front tire that is very obviously flat thanks to the small dagger sticking out of it.

Petra's magic flares in anger, and a sapphire mist soon surrounds them. She knows that dagger and knows the insignia on the hilt. She bends down, yanking it out of the tire, then throws it in the trunk along with their purchases. She slams the trunk shut, and by the time she spins back around, Daisy is on the phone to Lachlan, calling in support.

"Lach will be here in twenty," Daisy informs her as she pops up to sit on the car's hood. "Looks like they noticed we were here anyway."

"It appears that way," Petra responds, seething.

"What now?" Daisy asks, waving her hand before her face to shoo away the magical mist.

"I'm not sure. But this is not okay. Sloan and her minions need to be put in their place."

"They sure do. And as the incumbent Premier Witch, you will have that ability," Daisy responds, a wicked grin forming.

They see Lachlan's familiar Jeep across the emptying parking lot a few minutes later. Lachlan hops out. "Are you okay?"

They reassure him that they're fine, and he gets started jacking the car to change the tire. As he does so, Petra fills him in, and she can see it takes everything in him not to hop back in his vehicle to let Sloan know precisely who she is fucking with. Petra manages to calm him down enough to change her tire, and when she looks at Daisy, she can see that stupid smirk again.

CHAPTER TWENTY-SEVEN

Lachlan

After putting the spare tire on Petra's car, he follows them back to Daisy's as Petra insists on dropping her off, and then he and Petra head home in their separate cars. He's still internally fuming when they return to the house, and he may have snapped at Petra in his frustration. Not his best moment, that's for sure. Now, he sits alone in the living room while she takes a bath upstairs, claiming she needs both to relax and some space from him. He could think of better ways to do that, but she, in no uncertain terms, told him not to speak to her until he stopped acting like a two-year-old.

To keep himself from thinking about her naked, soaped-up body, he tries to figure out why she was targeted. Is it related to him and the underworld? Does he need to protect her from what lies in the underworld, waiting for him?

Realizing he needs to think and knowing his fury over tonight's events would keep him up, he makes his way to the kitchen and decides to bake. Pulling out the flour, yeast, and water, he builds a bread dough, carefully weighing out the ingredients to ensure he has the right hydration. With the dough resting for the first proof, he moves to the couch.

He hears the tub drain from upstairs, and shortly after, Petra emerges wrapped in a silk bathrobe that does nothing to hide her delicious peaks but everything to excite his inner demon. He pushes down the shadows that reach out for her. Petra sits in the chair opposite him, curling her legs underneath her and leaning on one of the arms, leaving the robe gaping far enough that Lachlan can see a perfectly curved breast underneath.

"I know it's late, but I haven't eaten yet. Would you like something?" he asks, surprised there is still enough blood in his brain to form sentences.

"Are you feeling less like a troll now?" she prods.

Lachlan grunts back at her, making his best sarcastic troll impression.

"I'll take that as a yes?"

Lachlan slides his eyes toward her. He knows she is trying to ease the tension between them and lighten the mood, but he's not quite ready. He wants nothing more than to keep her safe, and while he knows he can't be around her 24/7 to ensure that happens, he feels that she should at least be able to go to the mall with a friend without being threatened. The demon within roars, pushing to rise to the surface. He fists the pillow beside him, trying to move through the tension inside him.

She leans back in the chair, crossing her arms in frustration. "Look, I get that you're concerned, but I will not have you stomping around like a troll ready to bash heads. I appreciate the concern, but I am more than capable of handling myself, and while it sucks to have to replace my tire, I'm not worried. I wasn't hurt."

"Someone stabbed your tire with a *dagger*. That's a

threat," Lachlan retorts. "What if you had been in the car when they did that?"

"But I wasn't. So they stabbed my tire? So what?"

"I just worry," he says, softening his tone and shoulders, looking down into his lap.

"I know," she says, moving off the chair to kneel before him. She takes his hand and waits for him to look at her. "I know. And I appreciate your concern. But if I'm going to be Premier Witch, I can't have you going off at the slightest bit of provocation."

Lachlan grasps her hands, kissing the back of each, before taking her face in his hands and looking deeply into her eyes. He kisses her soft lips gently and carefully.

"I'm sorry. I'll try to do better," he says, resting his forehead against hers.

"Thank you, that's all I can ask," she replies, kissing the tip of his nose. He feels the touch all the way to his toes, warming his soul and bringing him back from his edge.

Petra leans back, looking up at Lachlan. He wants to take this further but doesn't want to risk burning the place down. Instead, he slides his hands down her curves and cups a plump ass cheek in each hand, squeezing firmly with a promise.

"Fuel first," he whispers huskily into her ear.

She blushes at his hint of what's to come and then nods.

He releases his hold on her, already feeling incomplete, and then returns to the kitchen to make something to eat.

His phone vibrates in his pocket as he opens the fridge door and, without looking, he pulls it out and answers.

"Lachlan."

"Finally," the caller replies.

Fuck!

"Lachlan? Are you there?" Selene asks.

He grunts as the tension rolls through his body as his demon rises to the surface and shadows flow out around him. "Yes," he says, closing the fridge door.

"Good. We need to talk."

"No," he barks. "Get someone else to deal with it."

"Lachlan, it needs to be you. You are our leader," she pleads.

"No. Find. Someone. Else," he says before hanging up.

Guilt immediately replaces the tension in his body. He rests his forehead on the door, letting the feeling sink in. Is he being unreasonable? Perhaps. He knows he needs to spend more time in the underworld, but he can't bring himself to do so. Every time his presence is requested, he finds an excuse not to go and delegates the task to one of his staff. Thankfully he has staff who are relatively self-sufficient. Despite this, he also knows he can't keep doing this. He can't keep running from his life and responsibilities as their leader.

What kind of leader runs from his people?

A shitty one.

Maybe Selene has a point. Maybe he needs to be more present. He's spent five years avoiding everything he can that has to do with that place. Maybe it's time he try and make it back more regularly.

The bigger question that runs through his head is whether or not the beings down there would still trust him. He's spent the last five years basically telling them he wants nothing to do with them, so how would they feel now if he were to return? How can he show them that he's worthy of being their leader?

Petra

Petra picks up their dishes and returns them to the kitchen. As she bends over the dishwasher, Lachlan comes behind her and wraps his arms around her middle, folding himself over her. His hands grazed her thighs, moving slowly upward before floating over her core and continuing to land on her breasts. His hands cup them softly.

"Mmm. This robe has done nothing but tease me since you walked in," he growls, placing his head in the crook of her neck and kissing her lightly.

She pushes back into him, closing the dishwasher door. She stands upright, leaning her back into his chest, lifting an arm to place a hand on the back of his head, and opening herself up to give him better access.

"Is that so?"

"I think it's been pretty obvious," he replies wantonly, pushing his hardness into her backside. He lets go of a breast in one hand and undoes the tie on her robe.

She hears a slight intake of breath from behind. His husky, desire-filled voice says into her ear, "And here you are, wearing nothing underneath. Were you trying to entice me, love?"

Slowly moving his hand down the opening of her robe, barely grazing the flesh underneath, his other hand is busy playing with her nipple through the silky material. The sensation of the silk working over her peaked skin is scintillating. Her magic responds to the touch, sending shockwaves of electric heat to her core. She feels dampness inside her upper thigh, signaling how wet and ready she is for him.

"May—Maybe," she says, her breath hitching. "What would you do if I was?"

"Oh, I could think of a few things," he responds as his hand finds her heat. Her hands find his as he runs his middle finger down her seam, the teasing nature causing her breathing to hasten in need. "Look at you. So wet already, and I'm just getting started," he says, his voice low and gravelly as he kisses and licks along her shoulder.

She lets out a soft moan as he moves his finger in deeper, caressing the inside of her folds before landing on her nub. He circles it just the right way, with enough pressure to promise more and yet leave her craving it.

She runs her hands up his arm, firmly placing them on the back of his head, pulling him closer to her. She turns her head, planting her lips on his. He opens his mouth, his tongue meeting hers. The words unsaid between them are many, and they need to figure their shit out, but for now, this speaks volumes. He plunges two fingers inside her wet pussy as his tongue thrusts to meet hers. The mix of sensations is too much; she moans into his mouth, and he swallows every note of pleasure he is wringing from her.

Power is pulsing under her skin, aching to break free, so she lets it, which only heightens her sensations. She feels every point of contact he makes with her body, which sets her alight.

She turns, facing him. He lifts her onto the counter, and Petra's legs automatically wrap around his middle, pushing his sizeable bulge against her aching core.

He kisses her with so much care and passion. Truly consuming her, and that alone makes her toes want to curl in ecstasy. She has never been devoured like this before. There is no one else she wants to do it.

He kneels before her, placing both hands on her thighs and spreading them wider. She watches as he takes her in, looking at her like she is the goddess he worships.

He kisses the inside of her thigh, his day-old scruff a pleasing sensation as he makes his way up to his dessert. She meets his eyes as he looks up at her from between her legs. "I have been thinking about your taste on my tongue all day," he says.

He wraps his arms around the back of her legs, pulling her closer to the edge before burying his face in her pussy. She places her hand on the back of his head, pulling him towards her as he licks, sucks, and nips, devouring all of her.

She grinds her hips toward his face, feeling the pressure building at the base of her spine almost instantly. She is so close. All it takes is a hard suck on her clit from Lachlan's expert mouth, and she is over the edge, writhing into him and screaming his name. She feels his smile against her pussy as he continues to suck on her nub, causing electric shockwaves to roll through her body as sapphire tendrils dance around them.

Holy. Fucking. Hell.

"That's my wife," Lachlan says, smirking as he kisses the inside of her thighs before standing up to meet her lips.

The taste of herself on his lips is intoxicating. She tastes the sweetness of her own body and his spiciness as their tongues meet. The blend is perfect, yet never enough. She wants more. More of him. More of them. More of this.

She wraps her legs around his waist, placing her forearms on his shoulders as he leans in further, putting an arm around her back while deepening the kiss. He growls into her mouth and pushes his groin into her exposed core.

As he kisses her and palms her ass, she commands one of her tendrils back around, and it appears behind him. She uses it to loosen his pants and pull them down. He stops and cocks an eye at her as his pants hit the floor. Before he has time to respond, she has lined him up with her soaked pussy. Using her heels on his backside, she pushes his thick cock into her.

She gasps at the quick stretch. She will never get over how thick his cock is and how he feels inside her. As he withdraws, ever so slowly, the sensation has her dropping her head back. He uses the opportunity to lean down and drag his teeth on her hard nipple. She whimpers, overcome with waves of pleasure. Her electric magic dances happily under her skin, adding to the fullness of him buried deep inside her.

He grabs her around her back and thrusts hard into her, unleashing his passion into her, fucking her with everything he has. Her legs wrap tighter around him, and she writhes against him, meeting him thrust for thrust.

"Harder," she whispers, egging him on.

"Yes, wife" is his answer. He picks her up and moves her to the wall nearby, placing her back firmly against it. Her arms wrap around his neck, and he drives into her with full force, shaking the frames nearby.

His horns have magically appeared again, and she takes this opportunity to grasp them with both hands for extra leverage, eliciting a deep growl from Lachlan. She strokes them, matching his commanding thrusts.

They yell out in unison, finding their release together. Her hands clench his horns as her core does the same to his dick while he fills her pussy with his come. As the world comes back into perspective, their breathing is labored, and their bodies glisten with sweat.

Still hard inside her, she feels his deposit start to leak out of her, but she doesn't care. In fact, it's kind of hot. He moves his hips against her again, languidly sliding in and out as if they have nowhere to be. She smiles into his shoulder, breathing in the musk of sex as it mixes with his bergamot scent.

"You, sir, are insatiable."

"What can I say? You bring out the demon in me," he responds, winking at her as he forcefully enters her.

"Is that so? Well then, where would you like to fuck me next?" she asks mischievously.

He doesn't respond. Instead, he carries her over to the cleared kitchen table and withdraws himself, making her stand. She instantly feels empty and feels even more of him leaking from her.

"Bend over," he orders.

Heat fills her core again at the command. She knows it won't take long for her to come for a third time tonight. Leaning onto the table, she places her hands in front of her. She jolts in surprise when he smacks her ass. Before she can turn to look at him, he is kneeling behind her, with his hands on her cheeks, spreading them further. Then she feels his tongue as it licks her from behind.

Fuck yes!

"Please. Yes. I need you inside me."

Heated electricity shoots through her as she feels his

tongue slowly licking her as he consumes their mixed fluids. Her magic bounces under her skin, pleased but not yet satisfied. *More,* it chants. She agrees. She needs more. Always more.

He stands, running his hand up her back, gently pushing her flat onto the table. Her breasts connect with the cold tabletop, creating a scintillating juxtaposition to the heat within her. He moves her legs further apart, stepping between them. Lining his dick up with her tight entrance, he pushes gently, slowly, drawing out the sensation as he fills her again. She sees stars as the new pressure takes over, and she pushes back into him.

Her eyes nearly cross with pleasure once he is fully seated. Sparks fly from her fingers as she palms the table, wrapping her fingers around the opposite edge. The mix of cool from the table, the pressure and stretch to her slick core, and the firmness of his hands on her hips as he holds on to her are on the brink of too much. She moans lowly, breathing through the intensity.

He waits patiently inside her as she works through it. She's so tightly wrapped around him that she's sure she will break him. After what feels like an eternity, her body relaxes, and the sensations settle to a more manageable level.

"That's it, Petra. Take that dick like a good girl."

Goddess, she almost comes right then and there. Before she has a chance, he starts to rock back and forth with slow and gentle movements. His slow withdrawal and thrust forward have her gripping the table tightly and groaning beneath him.

"Hecate help me. Your dick is perfect. I love how you fill me up."

He chuckles behind her.

"Oh, I'll fill you up, alright," he says, entering her more forcefully.

When he withdraws again, she prepares, placing her palms on the table and pushing herself up. She meets his thrust forward more confidently and begins pushing back, meeting each delicious plunge with equal enthusiasm. Her body tingles and every nerve fires inside her.

Her core tightens, and she feels him tense, getting close to his release. He reaches around her legs, finds her clit with his thumb and index finger, and rolls it between them, sending fireworks throughout her body as she comes, clenching around him. He pushes inside her and releases with her.

"Oh. My. Fucking. Goddessss," she screams as she rides out her third orgasm of the night. "Yes. Lachlan. Yes."

He growls behind her as he pumps a final time, riding out the end of his release.

He leans down and kisses her back gently, caressing her.

"Are you okay?" he asks breathlessly.

"Never better." She pushes her backside back into him, enjoying the remaining moments of fullness with him still seated.

"You. Are. Amazing," he says, punctuating each word with a kiss. His hands caress down her back and squeeze her full ass before withdrawing.

Internally, she whimpers, missing how complete he makes her feel.

"Gotta say, that is by far the best dessert I've ever had," he jokes.

She stands up, stretching her arms above her head. His eyes are on her, roaming her body, and are so heated that you'd never know they hadn't just fucked twice. She looks around, trying to avoid what else his eyes are saying, and sees the mess they have left in their wake. With a flick of her wrist, the floor and counter are spotless, and the dishes are finally put into the dishwasher. As she turns to pick up her robe, which she doesn't remember taking off, he scoops her up into his arms.

"I think we are in need of a shower, witchling."

Petra can only nod in response as a wave of sleepiness overcomes her. She leans her head into his shoulder as he marches them upstairs.

Petra fell asleep immediately post-shower, still wrapped in the towel with her hair all a mess. When she wakes the next morning, she is alone. She reaches over, groggily searching for Lachlan's body, but his spot is cold, signaling he's been up for a bit.

She rolls onto her back, stretching her arms above her head and reaching toward the end of the bed with her toes. The stretch is soothing and helps to center her thoughts.

We are just fucking, she tells herself. *We are just friends who are fucking. We are just friends who got married because I needed to, and who happen to be fucking. We are just friends.*

She repeats this mantra in her head over and over until she thinks she has said it enough times to believe it. Or until she hopes she believes it.

As she is contemplating getting up, she hears the door open downstairs, followed by footsteps, making their way to the bedroom. She draws the blanket around her—she doesn't know why, it's not like he hasn't seen every inch of her already—just before Lachlan enters holding two coffees.

"Good morning, wife," he says, a bright smile spreading across his face. He is wearing gray sweatpants and a black hooded sweatshirt, and his hair is tied back in a bun. She wants to peel his clothes off and ride him right there. He is that sexy.

She clears her throat, trying to refocus. "Good morning." She smiles back.

"I went out and got us some breakfast," he says, stepping forward and holding out one of the coffee cups for her. "Vanilla latte with a caramel drizzle, lactose-free milk."

Her stomach flutters.

She sits up, reaching for the cup with one hand while still holding the duvet. "Thank you. You didn't have to do that."

"I know. I wanted to."

"Well, thank you. How did you know my order?" she asks, curious.

"Petra. We've been friends for years. I pay attention."

Friends. Friends who fuck.

"This is wonderful." She takes a drink and dances with caffeinated joy as the first sip slides down her throat.

"Why don't you get dressed, and I'll meet you downstairs? I picked up some pastries for us, too."

"Sounds great. I'll be down in a minute."

Lachlan nods and leaves the room.

Friends.

Friends.

Friends, she repeats, trying to calm the fluttery feeling in her stomach.

We are just friends. Friends with benefits.

CHAPTER TWENTY-NINE

Lachlan

Things with Petra were going well. Better than well. Obviously, the sex has been mind-blowing, and neither one of them seems to be able to get enough. He admits that demons can be known for having incredible stamina, but he's never experienced anything like he has with her. Usually, there is some kind of downtime—not long, but something—yet he is immediately ready to go again with her. Being with her is nearly enough to drive him wild. Allowing his demon to come out and play during their escapades has been freeing, and truly, it only makes him want her more. That she didn't shy away when the horns appeared says so much about who she is.

But it's not just the sex. He's drawn to her like a moth to a flame, and if he's honest with himself, he's felt that way since they first met. He did his best to stay in his friend lane, but once he offered to marry her to save her title, all bets were out the window. It was like a floodgate opened, and he couldn't stop the rush. His heart aches when he's away from her for too long. She feeds a part of him that he didn't know was starving.

He's heard people talk about what it feels like to be in love and how it can be all-consuming. How you can't stop thinking about them. How they are the first thing you think of in the morning and the last at night. How you worry about them and also want what's best. How she is the best part of his day. How she belongs in his arms. How…

Oh, fuck. I love her.

I. Love. Petra.

Heat rushes through his body as he finally, fully, and completely acknowledges how everything he has ever done for her, every interaction he has had with her, was him showing her his love.

He hears Petra making her way down the stairs. He doesn't have time to try and calm himself.

"Thanks again for the coffee," she says, entering the kitchen.

Lachlan stays with his back to her, trying to calm his body to regain composure after his revelation.

"You okay?" she asks, pausing behind him, concerned.

He clears his throat, fixing the dishtowel on the oven door and adjusting the plates on the counter. "Yes. Yes. I'm good. Breakfast?"

"Please," she says, reaching for a plate.

Finally turning to face her, he is confident she can see his thoughts written on his face. Thankfully, she doesn't say anything. Instead, she picks up a plate beside him and turns to the box of baked goodies, selecting a muffin, a mini croissant, and a Danish. She sits at the table, picking up her Danish and taking a bite. The low moan of satisfaction she lets out goes straight to his dick, making it twitch.

He loves the happy food noises she makes. He loves all the noises she makes.

"Oh my goddess, this is so good. Where did you find these?" Petra asks with a mouth full of pastry.

"At that new shop on Calvert, Krumb-Krushers," he responds, joining her at the table with a loaded plate.

"I'll have to tell Gammy about it. She will love these," she says, picking up the Danish. "You'd be surprised, but that lady loves sweets and pastries beyond anything I've ever witnessed. I remember my mom telling me once that Gammy pushed some old lady out of the way to get the last box of macarons at some high-end shop." Petra laughs, recalling the story.

She doesn't talk about her mother much. All he knows is that she died when Petra was in her early teens. He doesn't blame her for wanting to keep that part private, but he wishes she would open up more. To share some of her burdens with him. To let him carry them for her.

"So," Petra says, pulling him away from his thoughts.

"Yes?"

"You have far more experience with council than I do. Do you think Grog will ever relent?"

Lachlan leans back into his chair, crossing his arms across his chest. He tilts his head back and looks up to the ceiling, thinking through his experience as a council member.

"I would love to say I have some deep insight into the inner workings of that troll's mind, but even after all these years, I haven't been able to tap into his logistical processes. He's very tight-lipped, and I wouldn't be surprised if he has some dirt on the other council members to make them go along with whatever he wants," he muses.

"True. Maybe it's something to do with Sloan, and he's going to try and weasel her in somehow. Maybe add a secondary condition or a competition between us? Make us have a witch-off?" she suggests, semi-joking.

"A witch-off? This isn't some cheerleading movie where you have a dance battle." He laughs lightly. "I could see him changing his mind with the conditions or maybe having you and Sloan shadow each other." He sees her eyes widen at the idea of shadowing Sloan and quickly interjects, "I meant shadow as in to follow and try and find fault with each other. Not to try and take each other out."

Petra hangs her head and releases a sigh of relief. "You scared me there for a second. Thought for sure you were suggesting I kill Sloan."

"I mean, that would solve some of your problems," he jokes.

"I am *not* killing Sloan." Petra rolls her eyes at him.

Lachlan chuckles. "Fine. You don't have to kill Sloan. As for Grog, I don't think it would be beyond him to continue to push whether it's acceptable because we will both be council members. I also would not be surprised if he tried to challenge if our marriage is *real.*"

"Hmm. So what do we do to convince him we aren't just friends who got married to meet his demands?"

Just friends.

His heart aches at that phrasing. Does she genuinely believe they are still just friends after all that's happened in the last few weeks? Is he the only one who's gone deeper than that? Panic starts to rise from his stomach and burn in his chest. He has to know where she stands.

"Are we *just* friends?" he asks.

Petra's eyes go wide. "I thought that was the agreement when we entered into this. Friends first."

Okay then.

"It was, but then we started fucking, and I don't know

about you, but I've never fucked a friend the way you and I have been going at it."

Her face flushes. The rose on her cheeks reminds him of how she looks right after coming.

"Friends with benefits is a thing. We have to be friends first, Lach. I can't risk losing you. I won't be able to handle it when you inevitably leave. So, yes, we are *just* friends," she says, stressing the word so that Lachlan feels his heart break a little. Here, he thought he was in love. It turns out he is. But she sees them as *just friends*.

"Wait. Who said anything about me leaving?"

"No one did. But that's just what men do. They leave."

"Where do you get that idea from?" he asks, shocked at the level of certainty in her voice.

"Everywhere. My dad, every guy I've ever dated or cared about. They've all just left. If I let myself care about you that way, you'll do the same. And I won't be able to come back from that, so I can't be anything more than just friends with you," she responds, her eyes filling with tears.

There's that word again. *Just.* He hates that word.

The following days are cooler between them. He wants nothing more than to reach out, to shake some sense into her. Make her see what's standing right in front of her. Her past has led her to believe that she can't have anything worthwhile because it will eventually end, and, in turn, she refuses to open up to him.

His heart aches, longing to return to before he tried to define what was happening between them. He's been spending more time at the Acorn, and he's been extra surly with Daisy and the other staff, for which he's had to apologize many times.

She received another summons, why and for what neither of them knows. As the council meeting looms, he found Petra shorter with him. Her whole future rests on these meetings, and he's trying his best to be supportive. Despite how hot and heavy they had been, they'd barely watched a movie together, so sleeping together certainly wasn't happening. However, that doesn't mean he hasn't caught her lingering glances.

"You ready?" Lachlan asks, walking into the hall from his bedroom as he buttons up his shirt before tucking it into his pants.

"Just need to finish my makeup," Petra calls back.

Lachlan makes his way to her room and stops in the doorway. He rolls his sleeves up to his elbows and catches Petra watching, her eyes hungry, as he does. He smirks back at her, letting her know he sees her, but she doesn't falter under his gaze. She may say she wants to be friends, but she's not hiding the fact there's more there, even if she doesn't want to admit it. He raises his left arm and rests it above his head, leaning against the doorframe.

Petra finishes perfecting her dramatic look and approaches him, stopping when she lands under his raised arm. She leans back against the frame and looks up at him mischievously.

Oooh, she's good.

He looks down into her beautiful green eyes, raising his hand to rest gently on her face. He leans in, stopping just before meeting her lips. "You're going to knock them dead."

Is it mean to tease her? Maybe. Is he still going to do it? Absolutely.

"We should get going," he commands, adjusting his crotch as he walks away.

He hears Petra fall into step behind him. As they open the front door, the view shifts from the regular snow-covered trees along the street into the council chambers. Petra takes a deep breath beside him and entwines her fingers with his, instantly settling the bundle of nerves in his core and blooming warmth in his chest while he acknowledges her silent request for support. As they step out the door and into the council chambers, his councilor mask slips into place.

CHAPTER THIRTY

Petra

The first thing Petra notices when she emerges into the council chambers is that there is an audience this time.

"Why is there an audience?" Lachlan murmurs, more to himself than her, echoing her thoughts.

The benches in the room are filled with supernatural community members. She can see parents and caregivers from the childcare where she works. Worked? She still hasn't been back to work, and she misses it. As much as she hopes to take the Premier Witch seat, she's not sure how she'll balance her work with council duties. She spots the vampire twins who own the coffee shop down the street from her apartment, the goblins from the market, and many of her coven members.

"Welcome!" a voice booms out, calling her attention to the front of the room. "Thank you for joining us. When issues impact the community's well-being, we must have its members here."

Grog.

Grog pleasantly smiles and continues as if they have all

gathered for a family meal. It would be the most dysfunctional family in existence, thanks to Uncle Groggy, that's for damn sure. "Many of you are unaware, but Gladys Rose is fatally ill, which means we require a new Premier Witch," he says dramatically, standing to face his audience, arms outstretched to his sides, his councilor robe billowing out from some unknown wind source. His dramatics rouse a gasp from the audience. "And as part of filling that role, we have to consider those direct descendants of the current Premier Witch before looking at other candidates who have spent years demonstrating their worth."

Murmurs spread throughout the audience. As the excitement and voices rise, Grog raises a hand, silencing everyone in the room. "We, the council, met with Miss Petra Rose a few months ago and informed her of what she would need to do to prove she could take on this role. She had to show she was committed to our community, and she agreed to the terms we set for her."

Petra steps forward, eager to clarify that she was tricked, but Lachlan places a hand on her arm to stop her. A gentle warning not to do anything to feed the troll. She returns to her position, rocking back on her heels, and grumbles to herself.

"Those terms were that she needed to get married within thirty days." The audience murmurs, a mix of agreement and dissent. "Should she fail, Miss Sloan Wilks would become the new Premier Witch." At this point, all heads turn to Sloan, who stands at the back of the room surrounded by her family, all beaming as if they've won a long-fought battle. "And if she were to fail, Miss Petra Rose would also be stripped of her powers."

This final revelation in a climactic story sends the audience into an uproar. Stripping a witch's magic is only used for the most severe cases, generally where they have caused serious harm to another being—be it supernatural or human—and even then, only after a rehabilitation attempt. So, to hear it as a threat for not meeting these archaic stipulations is gravely upsetting to those in attendance. Many in the audience are now standing, even those who only a moment ago murmured their agreement at forcing her to get married, and yelling at the council, loudly voicing their concerns about that caveat.

Councilor Clellugs bangs her gavel, settling the audience. "While we appreciate your attendance this evening, you will be escorted out if you cannot contain yourself. Understood?"

"Yes, Councilor Clellugs," the audience responds, suitably admonished.

"Thank you. Councilor Grog, you may continue," they say, gesturing forward with their hand, giving him the floor.

"Now that we are all aware of the situation, we will get to why this meeting has been called."

"Yes, please do," Lachlan retorts, tension rippling through his body, his hold on Petra's hand tightening. She squeezes back in response, seeking comfort from the contact.

Grog tuts at Lachlan before continuing his presentation. "We have called this meeting because while Miss Rose met her conditions, the council has taken issue with her chosen partner. It seems that Miss Rose may not have taken the challenge put before her seriously and is attempting to spit in the face of tradition and lawful order."

"That's not true, and you know it!" Petra calls out before Lachlan can stop her. She hears him release a sigh beside her.

Grog flicks his eyes down to her, smiling, but she can see the menace in his eyes. "Now, now, Miss Rose, you will have a chance to share your side of the story shortly. Oh, I'm sorry. Should I be calling you Mrs. Grace-Rose instead?"

The gasp in the audience is palpable. *Shit.*

"Ah, yes. It appears our community members are as surprised as the rest of the council when you confirmed your marriage was to none other than a current council member, Mr. Lachlan Grace, council representative for the demon underworld." Grog steps away from his position on the council bench and walks into the middle of the room, standing between them and the other council members. "I speak on behalf of the rest of the council, though perhaps not Mr. Grace in particular since he was not part of these conversations, much like we were not part of his decision to marry you," he says, passing a dark look toward Lachlan. "You see, we find it most convenient that your new partner should be a deciding member of our council. That seems most unfair and certainly lends an air of favoritism in the decision process for Premier Witch, given, of course, that it would be your grandmother you would be replacing."

Grog pauses, letting this information sink, allowing the audience to process what this could mean and how it creates an opportunity for corruption to enter the council process. Though little do they know it's already here, alive and well.

Deciding he has waited long enough, he reaches his true reason for this session. "And so, my dear community, council members, and, of course, the Grace-Roses, we have come to a conundrum. The other council members and I find it distasteful that two council members should be married, for it opens up a whole coffin of concerns. We have to wonder how the council can remain impartial and duty-bound when two of its members are bound together by marriage. It is out of a true concern for the community that we have gathered everyone here today."

May the Goddess bless him, because holy fuck is he laying it on thick.

Petra and Lachlan turn and look at each other. Lachlan's face, where there is usually warmth and care, is nothing but coldness. His eyes are a bright gold. As her eyes wander to their clenched hands, she can see the restraint in the veins popping in his neck and clenched jaw in his effort to keep from shifting into his demon form.

"Thus, we will be opening a forum where our community members can write in or come in personally to share their opinions on the marriage of two council members. The council will take these opinions into consideration before deciding whether or not to completely accept this marriage as having met the conditions given to Petra Rose." Grog pauses for effect, eating up the audience's attention as they sit on the edge of their seats, waiting to hear the consequences. "To be clear, if the council decides to not accept the marriage, with the understanding that it poses a harm to future council proceedings, then Mrs. Grace-Rose will surrender her powers, and as an added consequence Mr. Grace-Rose shall be stripped of his title and position in the council."

Petra and Lachlan simultaneously start yelling at Grog and the council in protest. At the same time, the audience responds alongside them, some encouraging the consequences and others mystified by the extreme measures. Stripping power and position is virtually unheard of and sets a dangerous precedent.

How did he get the other council members to agree to this? Lachlan said Grog can be a pain and trolls can absolutely be manipulative tricksters. *Did Grog bribe them?*

The room refuses to settle, causing Councilor Clellugs to

end the meeting. Petra and Lachlan are forced out of the room and ported into Lachlan's living room.

Lachlan's shadows have appeared, pulling light from the room, creating a space so dark that Petra feels a cold creeping in.

"Lach! Lach! Where are you?" she yells, unable to see anything around her. She hears a shuffling nearby and jumps when a hand touches her arm.

"I'm here," he says. Though his touch is gentle, she can feel the pure rage flowing off him. Her magic responds to him, rising to the surface and sparking under his touch, protecting her. His hand vanishes as she hears him suck in a breath, presumably wincing.

"What are we going to do?" she asks softly, her voice cracking. Lachlan's shadows pull at her magic, sourcing it out, trying to leech her power. She bats a hand where she feels them connecting, but it's like batting at empty air. "Lach, the shadows. Stop them," she whispers.

The air in the room shifts as Lachlan leaves, taking the shadows with him.

The room suddenly fills with light. She's alone, with no idea where he's gone or for how long.

Petra slinks to the floor. Curling her knees to her chest, she wraps her arms around them and rests her forehead on top.

CHAPTER THIRTY-ONE

Lachlan

Lachlan sits along the bench in the council chambers, his mind repeatedly wandering to Petra, wondering what she's doing. Grog has been rambling on about one thing or another, taking periodic jabs at him for most of this weekly meeting. He's done his best to ignore it and not give him more ammo.

The meeting finally wraps, and Lachlan silently thanks the Goddess, unsure how much longer he could be in the room with Grog today. Grog is busy talking to Councilor Amare as Lachlan leaves the room. He makes it partway down the marble-lined hallway before feeling his pockets and realizing he left his phone on the desk. He turns, groaning internally, and ventures back, but as he gets closer to the open doors, he hears Grog's raised voice. Lachlan stops short before entering the room, tucking himself against the wall as he listens and calls on his shadows. Swirls of darkness surround him obscuring him from view.

"We cannot have a new Rose as the Premier Witch. She will continue to destroy everything we have worked for. Everything that *I* have been working for," Grog yells.

"Maybe it is time we support Gladys's efforts. It's time we recognize we cannot win. It has been nearly fifty years, Hegnir," Amare responds.

"You want to give up? You want to let a witch win?"

"I'm just tired. I'm tired of fighting. And my people want what Gladys has been supporting. It's time I listen to them." She sighs.

"If you abandon my efforts, you will regret it," he snarls.

Lachlan hears the shuffling of feet followed by a single set of footsteps approaching.

Did Grog just threaten Amare? Is he dumb enough to threaten a vampire queen?

"Then so be it," she says, stopping inside the door. "I look forward to destroying you."

"You'll sing a different tune when I have all the power. You'll be begging me for mercy," he growls at her.

Amare doesn't respond. Instead, she leaves the room, her shoulders heavy as she passes by Lachlan, either not noticing him or ignoring that he is there. Vampires have keen senses, so it seems unlikely that she isn't aware of him. He prefers not being noticed, though, as he's unsure how Amare would react to him eavesdropping.

He waits until he hears Grog port from the room before reentering and retrieving his phone.

Grog wants power.

Grog isn't afraid to threaten other council members to get it.

What else isn't he afraid to do?

It's been a week since that night at the council. The winds are cold, matching how he's felt since that night without

Petra. After they were launched back home that night, Lachlan could feel the rage rolling through his body, his muscles taut to the point of snapping, his mind a non-stop whirl as he tried to sort through how that all went wrong. How could Grog think what he was doing was acceptable, and why did the other council members agree? Most of all, why was he being frozen out of these proceedings?

With his thoughts clouding his judgment and his shadows frightening Petra, he felt it best to leave until he was in a better frame of mind. That is how he found himself standing outside his mother's house in Stanmore, staring at the darkened windows, wondering if he deserved to be here or if hell was where he belonged.

He hasn't heard from Petra all week, and he's been too ashamed to reach out. He knows he reacted poorly, but he needed to get out of there and clear his mind. Now, he stays because he's worried she will think less of him. She may not know it, but she has his heart in his hands and the power to crush it should she wish. How can he go back to her and risk her doing exactly that?

Sitting on the front porch, Lachlan nods along as his mother speaks. Telling tales of the old days in the underworld. How she met his father. Of him as a young demon-boy, playing pranks on other children in the neighborhood. She hasn't pushed him for information yet, giving him time to sort through his issues. She's merely happy to have him visiting.

As the daylight wanes, they venture back inside. He stands beside her and leans down, wrapping his arms around her shoulders, drawing a deep breath. *Home.* Memories from his childhood come rushing back. He pictures holding her hand as a young boy as they walked through parks, going for ice cream on hot summer days, and standing by the infernos as his dad told them stories about demons who went bad—which is an interesting thought now that he thinks about it because demons are inherently troubled so what does it take for a demon to be considered bad?

He releases her after a prolonged moment, and his mother places her hand on the middle of his back, rubbing small circles before leading him inside. He watches as she walks ahead, taking them to the kitchen and starting the kettle for some tea. She must sense he has something to say, so she's setting the stage with routine and comfort. Tea with Mom was how he and Declan worked through challenging moments when they were young.

The last few months have been beyond strange for Lachlan. Before meeting Petra, he would not have considered rushing into a marriage to help a friend. As he sits at the table trying to think about what and how he is going to share everything that has been going on with his mother, he realizes that while the suggestion to marry him was initially to help Petra earn her title, the demon in him did it to trap her and claim her. He was tired of her not seeing him, so he forced her hand.

His mother hands him a cup, steam billowing out, and sits opposite him. His hands wrap around the warm mug, and the heat flows through his fingertips and down to his toes. He sniffs deep at the familiar scent of lemon and lavender that sends him back to his childhood and unwinds the knot of tension he's been carrying around. He feels his shoulders drop away from his ears, his back relaxes, and his leg stops bouncing. He kicks off his shoes under the table and spreads his socked feet on the floor beneath him, feeling more grounded than he has in a long time.

There's just something about this home that connects

with him. Perhaps it's nostalgia or maybe the company, but whatever it is, he's grateful for it.

Finally making eye contact with his mom, he slowly breathes out, preparing for what's to come.

"You look a little rough for wear, my son. Tell me what has you tore up," his mother says softly, placing her hand on his.

"I don't even know where to start."

"The beginning is always a good place. Or the end if that is what has brought you here." She checks the clock over the stove. "We have plenty of time."

"I'm sorry for bursting in so late the other night."

"It's okay. I have plenty of time to sleep when I'm dead."

The classic joke brings a short smile to his face. "That is true. But please don't do that for a while."

"I'll do my best."

Lachlan responds with a short huff, then picks up his cup and takes a long sip. He closes his eyes and lets the flavors dance over his tongue.

"I've landed myself in a situation, and there are some serious consequences if I don't pull out ahead," he starts. "So I need to sort things out."

"You know I don't mind you being here. But what is this situation?"

"Well, you know Petra and I got married."

"Yes, I do remember being at my son's wedding," she teases.

"Yes, well, what you don't know is that it wasn't out of love," he says, watching her, gauging her reaction, but her stone face gives nothing away. " It's a whole thing, but she needed to get married to become the next Premier Witch."

"Okay. Okay. Go on."

Lachlan takes a deep breath and another sip of his tea. "As part of her conditions, she had to notify the council. Which she did. Well, now there is concern over whether our marriage is acceptable as we would both be council members. So they are starting a forum. If they find our union dishonorable, Petra will fail to take the Premier Witch title and they'll strip her of her power. What no one is saying is that all of that will also remove any status she has within the community. She'll become a pariah, and the Rose name will be forever tarnished."

His mother lets out a long whistle. "I understand now why you're here."

"Yeah." Lachlan sighs. He places his face in his hands, trying to will the complicated feelings he holds for Petra to resolve and show him how to move forward.

If they were to fail and she lost her power, he... can't even imagine. He has no words for how it would break him.

His mother leans back in her chair, looking at her fingers as she plays with the tea bag tag. "So, I guess the first place to start is figuring out where you stand with Petra right now," she says, drawing his attention back to the moment.

"According to her, we are *just* friends."

"And judging by your tone, you don't believe that." His mother raises an eyebrow. "Why?"

"I think she's lying to herself. She's holding back out of fear."

"Why?" she asks again.

He tilts his head, cocking an eyebrow at her. "Do you really want the details?"

"I'm your mother, I'm not dead. Give it to me straight."

"We've been fucking like faeries, and there is no way the sex is that good with someone you're *just* friends with. Besides, she's been through some shit, and I've been there with her every step of the way. She tries to claim we can only be friends because everyone leaves her. She's scared and won't let herself feel what's there. If she can't break through that, I don't think we can succeed."

"So, how do you plan to help her see what's there?"

"That's a good question."

"Perhaps step one should have been not leaving, especially after what sounds like a very combative council meeting."

Lachlan leans back, dropping his head onto the back of the chair, realization striking him.

"Ffffuuuucccckkkk."

Fenella's eyes find his. "Also, how does your love for her, or her love for you, impact her role as Premier Witch and the council's forum?"

"They'll claim we cannot stay on the council if we're married as we will not be able to be impartial when it comes to council decisions. Though we'd both vote for the best of the community rather than to keep each other happy."

"Can you? Or would you feel the need to side with her on every decision?"

While the question doesn't surprise him, he is taken back by the nearly visceral reaction he feels internally at the thought of not doing what is best for the community. He may love Petra with every fiber of his blackened demon soul, but he will never allow that to determine how he carries out his role and how he makes decisions for the larger community. "I can wholeheartedly say that our relationship would never be an influencing factor on me."

"Good to hear," she says, patting his shoulder as she walks by to get another cup of tea. "Now, you haven't been gone too long. Go back to her. Fix this," she says, twirling a finger in the air, symbolizing the shitstorm that is circling him, "and then get her to break down her walls. Show her how she is loved. She'll likely push against it initially but will come around."

"Thanks, Mom," he says, coming over to kiss the top of her head.

"Anytime, my son."

"Love you," he calls out behind him as he runs out of the house, into the night.

By the time he arrives home, dawn is breaking over the horizon. Lamplight is visible in the front room, but the rest of the house is in darkness. When he enters, his shadows move out, searching. They return to confirm his fears. The house is empty. Concern floods his senses. He knew that her biggest fear was losing him, that he would leave, and then he did exactly what she expected. He barely said anything to her before he left.

Dick move, Lachlan.

He enters the front room and sees a small, folded paper on the side table by the window. He opens it and reads:

Lachlan,

I will never be able to say how much I appreciate all you have done for me. I am truly honored to have been your wife, even briefly. I know someday you will make a wonderful real husband to someone, and I can't wait to see how happy you become when that happens. I said the other night that I didn't want to risk our friendship, and I think we have reached that point. I can't lose you, Lach. I will go before the council at their next open session and offer myself and my power up and inform them that I am stepping back as a candidate. I would rather go willingly and on my terms than be exposed in front of everyone.

I am genuinely sorry for all the trouble I have caused you.

With affection,
Petra

Shit. Shit. Shit.

He runs his hand down his face and growls loudly. "The next open session. Fucking Hades, that's today!"

This witch will screw everything up. Grog is too power-hungry and will never let her just sacrifice herself. It wasn't just about her not becoming the Premier Witch. No, Grog wanted to humiliate the Roses and have Petra fail publicly. Lachlan has to stop her.

He takes out his phone, pushes her name, and holds the phone to his ear.

He knows it's early and Petra is likely sleeping, but he hopes she will hear her phone vibrating and answer. He needs to talk to her. He needs to help her see the error in her plan. He just needs her.

The call rings and rings, but Petra does not answer. He tries again, but she still doesn't pick up.

He looks at the time and figures she is either at her place or Daisy's, so he doesn't have to worry about looking all over the city for her. He decides to try her place first. He runs out the door climbs into his Jeep and squeals the tires as he pulls away.

Council opens at eight a.m., and it is currently 6:45 a.m., but it takes forty-five minutes to get across town to Petra's apartment. He continues to call her on his drive over, but after the third attempt, the calls start going directly to voicemail. He leaves more than one, begging her to call him.

When he arrives at her apartment building, he checks the lot, but her car isn't there. Thankfully, Daisy doesn't live too far away. He pulls up to Daisy's house and checks the clock on his dashboard: 7:53 a.m. He launches himself out of his vehicle and dashes to her front door, where Daisy meets him, tears streaming down her face.

She nods her head, letting him know Petra's not there.

"I'm so sorry, Lach," she says through tears and potentially snot.

"Why are you sorry? You didn't do anything."

"She's not here. I tried to talk her out of it, but she…" She breaks down. The end of what she says is almost impossible to understand, but all Lachlan cares about is Petra. She can't lose her power. He can't lose her.

"How long ago did she leave?"

"About ten minutes," she snivels.

"Okay. Okay. Listen, it's not your fault. This is Grog and solely him. He has had it out for the Roses for a while. Add in the fact that he doesn't like me, and it's like a fucking holiday for him. I have to go, but know I don't blame you," he reassures her.

She gives him a slight nod before he turns around and ports out of her driveway, appearing in front of the council building, hoping he can intercept Petra.

CHAPTER THIRTY-TWO

Petra

Petra parks outside the council building. She readjusts her skirt and checks her teeth in the side mirror before mounting the steps to go inside. She places her hand on the long golden door handle and steps forward. As she lifts her foot, a familiar voice calls her name. She turns to see Lachlan running toward her.

Letting go of the door, she steps aside, allowing others to enter as she waits for him to reach her. When he does, he is breathing heavily, as if he'd just completed a marathon, and his appearance is frenzied. His hair is disheveled, unbound, and sticking in many directions. He wears sweatpants and a hoodie, his shoelaces undone.

"Lach, I said everything I needed to in the note I left," she says before he can catch his breath. "I know you are worried about any repercussions for you, but I plan to ensure that doesn't happen."

"I don't give a fuck about me, Petra," he practically bellows. "Just give me two minutes."

She reaches for the door again, saddened. She hoped she could get through this without a scene from him. It's hard enough to submit her powers in exchange for his safety. Seeing him in this state, unlike the composed man she knows, is enough to ruin her. "Lach, I have to go."

"Petra. Please," he begs. He takes hold of her hand, entwining his fingers in his. "Let's talk first, and if you still feel the same way after, I won't stop you."

A current of heat flows from the point of contact, grounding her. Calming her. She wonders how such a slight touch can have this effect. Without the touch, she would have had no problem turning her back and walking into that room. Instead, she wavers. She looks down at their hands and then up into his steely blues and nods, giving in.

He guides her to a bench just down the hall from the ornate doors leading to the council room. The hallway has emptied significantly. All that remains now are staffers and the odd community member running late, evident by the quickened clicking of footsteps on the marble floor. They sit with their bodies turned toward each other, knees touching, and their clasped hands resting between them.

She runs her free hand over his cheek, briefly cupping his face before running it back into his hair, trying to smooth it, but she only seems to make it worse. His head turns into her hand, seeking a brief embrace. A sad smile spreads across her lips. She's going to miss this, this closeness and companionship that she found with him. It was short-lived, but it felt right.

"You can't go in there and sacrifice yourself."

She huffs a breath. "Lach, I have to. There's no other way around this."

"No, you don't. Listen, Grog is power-hungry. He wants control over the council and can't do that with a Rose there. He wants to put people on the council he can control. We see that in his selection of Sloan and in the various company he keeps. We can't let him win." His voice is low and pleading.

What he says makes sense, but it would be so much easier if she just gave up her candidacy for Premier Witch. Would she be upset with the results? Absolutely. Does she know what life would look like for her, no longer a witch? Absolutely not. But for her, the risk of uncertainty is better than going through all of this to lose anyway.

"But if I sacrifice myself, everyone else wins."

Goddess, that sounded way too martyr-y.

The look in his eyes is searching, pleading for her to see he is right.

"No, they won't. Trust me. I've worked alongside Grog long enough to know that this will not be where it ends. We can find another way. We have time."

"But we don't. I don't know how long this forum will take or what they will put us through, but in the end, the result will still be the same. The council will find a way to deem our marriage unacceptable, she says, looking down at the floor rather than at him. "Besides, we don't love each other, Lach," she whispers, barely loud enough for him to hear.

He pauses for a long moment, then finally says, "Are you sure about that?"

Petra looks up at him, uncertain and tentative. "What do you mean?"

"Are you sure we don't love each other? That we aren't meant to be more than *just friends*?"

She flinches slightly, hearing the hurt in his tone. She never wanted to hurt him. She never should have slept with him. It muddied things up, and now his feelings are involved.

Petra pulls her hand from his, turning away from him.

She rests her forearms on her thighs and hangs her head, processing. Her head tells her to go into that council room and offer her power in exchange. To admit to the lie. But her heart. Oh, but her heart. Her heart is telling her to look at that man beside her. To listen to him. To give this a chance. To weather the storm.

She sighs, and perhaps, against her better judgment, she makes a decision.

She listens to her heart.

CHAPTER THIRTY-THREE

Lachlan

The nod of her acceptance is nearly imperceptible, but it's there. She's agreed to give him time.

Lachlan sweeps her into his arms, holding her tight, unsure of how many more times he can do this. Relief washes over him, grateful he convinced her to give them more time. As he releases her, they turn their heads toward the sound of heels tapping on the tiled floor, approaching them with intention.

Sloan. Her name becomes a curse in his mind.

"Stay relaxed. Don't give her any ammo," Lachlan says under his breath.

"If it isn't the happy couple."

"Good morning, Sloan," they respond in unison. "What brings you to the council building this morning?" Lachlan asks, his tone welcoming and bright as Petra takes his hand.

"Oh, you know, just trying to keep our community safe," she responds flatly, raising her hand and examining her nails.

"So you've come to step down as a candidate then. How generous," Petra says, a fake smile spreading across her lips.

Sloan's face pinches together in anger, eyes narrowing. Lachlan knows that she would be slinging curses at Petra if it were acceptable.

"How can we help you, Sloan?" Lachlan asks, his tone suggesting he is trying to keep the conversation friendly.

Sloan turns to him, rolling her eyes as she looks away from Petra. Her face softens, and an almost genuine smile replaces her angry expression.

"I'm so happy you asked, Councilor Grace. Perhaps we can find a more private location to have this conversation?" she asks.

Lachlan looks to Petra, and though he can see her hesitancy, she gives the slightest nod. Trusting him.

"Yes. That's fine," Lachlan responds before porting all of them to his office in the underworld. While this is not his favorite place, he knows there is no chance of being overheard there.

The room is a mix of black and silver, the walls covered in ornate carvings with silver accents appearing through frames and mirrors. A large dark gray sofa sits against one wall, with a small table in front. Against the other side is a large window overlooking a valley. Across from where they land are his dark-stained desk and a fireplace that sits behind it.

"As you were saying?" Lachlan prompts Sloan.

Sloan clears her throat. "See, I'm here as a concerned citizen, worried about how your…relationship," she says, waving her finger between him and Petra, "may be perceived by others in the community. It could undo much of the work done over these last few years, gaining council goodwill. To have it come out that you two orchestrated this not only so *she* could become Premier Witch but also to gain a stronger foothold in the council decisions… well, I just can't have that."

Lachlan and Petra pass a glance between them, unsure of where this is going.

"Okay… So what are you proposing?" he asks.

"Well, I am suggesting a bit of a truce. I think I can offer some assistance."

Both his and Petra's jaws hit the floor. Sloan stands across from them, waiting for them to regain composure.

"You…want to help us?" Petra asks, confused.

"Well, not so much you in particular. But we have a common foe, so I suggest a temporary alliance to help take care of the problem."

"And who is this common foe?" Lachlan probes.

"Well, Grog, of course," she says, like it's obvious.

"You want to help us take down Grog?" Petra whispers, disbelief audible.

"Yes. Look, I know you're not the brightest, but could you try to follow along?" Sloan snaps back.

"I'm sorry, this is completely unexpected." Petra shakes her head, still confused. "Why should we trust you?"

"Because I know more about his going-ons than you could ever imagine. He selected me for a reason—more my family than me—but he doesn't know that I don't want this. I've never wanted to be the Premier Witch. I know Grog's hands are dirty, and I know how to settle all this"—she waves her hand in the air—"so that you two can go about your lives again as if no one cares. Because, frankly, we don't."

Lachlan laughs humorlessly. "Give us a minute to chat, please," he says to Sloan before turning to Petra, grasping her hand, and attempting to move her away so they can talk in peace.

"No need. Here's my number." She hands them a business card with her details. "Send me a text when you decide to get your heads out of your asses. And don't worry, that card has been charmed, so no one will know we are working together." Sloan spins on her pointed red heel, attempting to walk away before remembering where she is. "Would you be so kind as to send me back?"

Lachlan smirks before snapping his fingers and sending her back into the abyss.

Petra and Lachlan remain in the center of the room for a minute as they process what happened.

"I think we need to go for drinks and figure out what we want to do," Lachlan eventually suggests.

"Lach, it's not even nine a.m.," she reminds him as frenzied laughter bubbles up from her chest. She covers her mouth in surprise.

"Right. Breakfast then?"

"Sounds lovely."

They turn and exit the room, fingers intertwined, with an almost imperceptible pep in their step and the slightest ray of hope blossoming in his chest as he leads her into his realm.

Maybe they could fix this after all.

They spend the rest of the morning at Enchanted Garden of Eve, one of Lachlan's favorite diners in the underworld. The interior appears just as one would anticipate when they hear witches run it. The tables and chairs are old, dark stained wood, with loosely draped fabric framing windows, creating a welcoming contrast of airiness to the heavy feeling of the wood furniture. Tincture bottles filled with various spices appear on floating shelves throughout the space, and hand-drawn chalkboard signs list the menu items by the cash register. But best of all, regardless of the time of day, a mystical light streams in through the front door and windows in perfect beams, highlighting the golden accents throughout so that no matter where you look, you are greeted by the "spark of life," or so the owners say.

Much to the surprise of others, the underworld isn't a place filled with only death and darkness. Life exists here, too. It can prosper here. While many inhabitants here have arrived due to punishment, a not-insignificant portion of the population chooses to live here. They select the underworld for its warmth and opportunities for growth; because so few wish to venture here, opportunities abound. The land is lush and fruitful, and it is cherished for all that it provides.

"So what do we think about Sloan?" Petra asks, poking at her salad.

"I think she can be a bit standoffish, but she's got potential."

"Ha, ha," Petra replies dryly.

Lachlan huffs a short laugh, pleased with himself, even if Petra isn't. "I think it's worth seeing what she has to say. We don't really have much else to go with right now, and she clearly wants to help—though only the Goddess knows why."

Petra hesitates. "I don't know if I trust her, but okay. We can see what she has to say. However, I am curious about what she said—that she never wanted this. Why go through all this if she didn't want to be Premier Witch?"

Lachlan nods as he leans back in his seat. "I don't know," he says. "Maybe her family was pressuring her?"

Petra picks up her napkin and starts picking it apart, her telltale sign that there's something on her mind that she's afraid to say. Rather than force her, he sits quietly, giving her time to work up to it. Knowing her as he does, and after being married and living together for a while, he knows that she will get there when she's ready. He will wait for her. For as long as she needs.

As their plates are taken away and their coffee is refilled, she finally opens up. "Can we talk about something? About us?" she asks, almost at a whisper, as if she's afraid someone will stop them.

"Absolutely. What's on your mind?"

"I want to preface this by saying I'm glad we're working together on this, but I'm struggling with what happened between us last week. The blackout shadows, the running off. The not-communicating," she says.

Lachlan lets out a long breath. "I know. I'm sorry. I let my anger get the best of me, and then I was too ashamed to come back right away."

"I know I am at fault too. Please don't think I'm blaming you. I didn't reach out to try and fix it, and instead I left you a cowardly note."

He reaches out a hand to touch hers but stops himself and instead rests it in front of himself. He wants to give her the chance to decide where they stand and how much contact she is willing to accept. "I think we both could have done better. I'm sorry I was an ass and left when you were upset, and that I scared you in the process. How about going forward we can take the moment away if needed but then we come back and talk about whatever is bugging us?"

"I think that sounds like a good plan. And no more dramatic exits? From either of us?" Her eyes find his, and he feels himself falling into them, unable to pull himself away. "What do you think? Does that sound okay?" she asks, shaking him out of his stupor.

"Yes. No more dramatic exits. We always come back to each other."

Pleased with their progress this morning, Lachlan musters up his courage and asks Petra what he's been dying to know, hoping he won't undo everything they have just worked through.

"Why are you so scared to let people get close to you?"

Petra lets loose a breath with a low whistling sound. He watches as she picks up her spoon and stirs her coffee even though there's nothing to mix in. "I don't mean to keep people at a distance," she finally says, looking down at the table, avoiding his gaze. "I've been thinking a lot about this recently, and I think it's something I do instinctively to protect myself."

"Makes sense. Probably easier to do than manifest a shield all the time," he responds, trying to keep a bit of lightness present in their conversation.

She responds with a small smile, barely lifting the corners of her mouth. "Yes."

"Why do you feel you need to protect yourself?"

She thinks for a moment before answering. "I've been hurt quite a bit in my past. From my dad abandoning me to my mother dying to bad boyfriends who have ghosted me when they felt things getting too serious. It all adds up and makes me not want to let myself go, to get too attached, because ultimately, everyone seems to leave me. Honestly, the most stable person I have had in my life has been Gammy, and don't get me wrong, I love her dearly, but at times, I feel like her taking care of me is more out of obligation than love."

Lachlan leans forward, placing his hands over hers. She lifts her eyes to meet his, and he sees the pain and discomfort in her expression. But she's letting him in, he's grateful she lets him know a piece of her. He doesn't take this glimpse into her for granted.

He doesn't want to make her retreat again, so he chooses his words carefully. "I can understand why you feel that everyone leaves. You've had a challenging past. But I have to ask, if you approach every relationship expecting people to leave, aren't you already pushing them out the door before giving them a chance?"

Petra holds his gaze and tilts her head to the side, contemplating his question. He sees the moment the realization hits.

"I hadn't thought of it that way before, that I wasn't giving people a chance. I was only setting them up to prove me right, and they did because I structured it that way. Hmm… Interesting." She removes one of her hands from under his, picks up her glass, and takes a sip. Placing it back on the table, she says, "I guess I've been my own cockblock in a way."

"That's not how I would put it, but yeah," he laughs.

Petra goes quiet, looking down at their hands. She looks back at him and says, "Okay. My turn for a question."

"Fire away."

"Why are you never in your demon form?"

"I wouldn't say *never*," he says, drawing out never into multiple syllables as he winks at her.

"Okay, yes, the horns have come out to play a couple of times." She smirks at the memory. "But the only time I've seen you even close to your full form was the night of the agreement. But you stopped yourself before you fully shifted. Why?"

"The short answer: I didn't like who I was when I was regularly in that form."

"What's the long answer?" she asks, running her thumb along the side of his hand.

Lachlan looks out the window, watching the people and cars pass by in the rain. A little boy jumps into a puddle, laughing as he splashes his parent's leg. The parent shakes their head but laughs along with him. Still looking out the window, he begins, "You know who my father was, right?" She nods her head. "Damian was a hard man. He treated most things in life like a business, and when business didn't go his way, he needed an enforcer. When I was old enough and strong enough to fight, that was me. I enforced his rule for most of my teen years and early twenties. If people didn't pay their monthly dues, they met with me, and I usually left them beaten while I walked out with a fist full of money. I was regularly praised for my size, speed, and ability to charm others. Having the power of shadows certainly helped, as they can be quite…intimidating." He pauses, taking a deep breath.

"Through this line of… work, I met Selene and Viktor, two truly heinous leaders in the underworld who were close friends of my father and ultimately ended up on his staff. I was quickly loaned out to them and sent out as an enforcer for them as well. Only they wanted more than just beatings. I refused to do anything else, though they continued to try." His voice becomes low and hard as he reaches back into his memory, unearthing the events he has worked hard to leave behind. "I don't use my demon form, and generally don't come down here now unless I have to, which is rare. It reminds me of the unhappy being I no longer wish to be."

"Wow. I'm sorry, I had no idea," Petra says, running her hand up and down his arm, trying to comfort him. She may not let people close to her, but she cares for others wholeheartedly.

"Yeah." He sighs. "I don't talk about it for obvious reasons."

"So what happened? How did you end up in Leeside?"

"I started to have a conscience." He laughs humorlessly, more to himself. "I started questioning why I was hired for these jobs and what I wanted for life. Being Damian's son meant that the world was open to me. I could do or be anything I wanted because no one in their right mind would say no to Damian." He scoffs. "I also stopped completing the jobs, allowing clients to get away or not pay. Selene and Viktor began questioning why there were so many issues. They found out I was purposefully failing. Damian defended me, but I didn't want to carry on his legacy. I wanted my own. So I left. I had visited Leeside many times as an enforcer and was always drawn to it. So I settled there and started the bar. But then Damian died. They needed a new demon council representative, and per tradition and all the bloodline shit, I was next in line. You know how it is."

He can't remember the last time he shared this side of himself. It's not a time he's proud of, and he hates to think of how others will see him when they know the whole story. But he likes to think he has changed.

"Do you think less of me now?" he asks tentatively.

Without hesitation, Petra says, "Absolutely not. Your past does not make who you are. That's what you were trying to tell me, right? So, how can I judge you?"

She sees him. Lachlan has been so afraid of letting her know this side of him. But he can't deny the warm sensation in his chest as she willingly accepts him. All of him. Without question or suggestion for alterations. He's never had that with anyone he's been with. Becoming her husband seems to have been the best decision he ever made.

After what seems like hours, the waitress finally brings

their bill, and Lachlan pays, giving Petra a look suggesting she better pull her hand back when she reaches for it. Petra turns to him as they put their coats back on and says, "So… Sloan."

"Yes, Sloan."

"We should call her," Petra says.

"We should."

"Let's make a deal with the devil and take over the world," she jests, stepping through the door he holds open.

"Thinking big, I like it. I'll make the call." He takes Sloan's card from his inside coat pocket, dials the number into his phone, and hits call. Sloan picks up on the first ring. "We're in" is all he says.

"Took you long enough. Meet me tonight. Ten p.m. at the south entrance to the Leeside Graveyard. Don't be late." Then she hangs up.

Petra looks at him, eyes wide with anticipation. "So…?"

"Looks like we have a date with the dead," he responds before taking her hand and porting them back home.

CHAPTER THIRTY-FOUR

Petra

They arrive back at Lachlan's house, landing on the front step. Petra holds on to Lachlan, taking a moment to steady herself. She hates porting. However, as she turns to look at him, she sees Daisy sitting on the front step, waiting for them. She must have been out here for a while because she is soaked from the rain. Petra, concerned, rushes toward Daisy.

"Daisy, are you okay?" She moves her hands over her, checking to see if she's hurt. "What's wrong?"

Daisy's makeup runs down her face from crying or the rain, Petra is unsure which.

"I'm okay. I'm not hurt," Daisy sniffles. "Well, not physically."

"Why are you sitting out in the rain?" Petra insists. Daisy does not cry easily, and she certainly isn't one to sit on their front step unless something is majorly wrong.

Lachlan unlocks the front door and swings it open. "Why don't we get you two inside? Daisy, you can shower to warm up, and then you two can chat."

"Yes. Yes. Let's do that. I have some clothes you can borrow while we dry yours," Petra offers.

Daisy stands slowly, nodding in agreement.

The three of them make their way indoors, with Lachlan pulling up the rear, closing the door behind them before making his way to the kitchen. Morris greets them with a howl, admonishing them for being gone for so long. Petra scoops and snuggles him as he attempts to escape while Daisy heads upstairs.

As Daisy showers and Petra changes, she can hear him banging pots and pans around in the kitchen. Soon enough, she begins to smell something delicious wafting its way upstairs. Figuring she has a few minutes before Daisy is out, she checks in with him in the kitchen, plunking Morris down in the hallway. He skitters ahead of her, and she finds him brushing against Lachlan's legs when she enters.

"What are you making?" she asks, sitting on the stool at the counter and folding her arms in front of her.

"Some chicken soup," he responds, chopping various vegetables.

"Why are you making chicken soup?"

"For Daisy. It's a comforting thing, and it seems like she needs comfort. It will also help keep her warm post-shower."

Petra holds a hand to her heart. This man. How did she ever think she could go on without him in her life? He has so much history and heartache, which could have easily shaped him into someone dark, yet he is making chicken soup for an upset friend.

How has she missed seeing this part of him?

They've been friends for what feels like forever, yet she never noticed how he moves around the people around him. How attentive he is, how he cares. Seriously, no other man she knows would do something like this for someone else. None that she can think of.

She clears her throat in an attempt to hold back tears. "Is there anything I can do to help?"

"There's some parsley and thyme in the garden box. Could you go and chop some off and bring it in?"

"Sure." She stands, coming around the counter. As she reaches for the scissors in the knife block, he reaches for another cutting board, and their fingers graze, causing a spark to shoot up her fingers. She ignores it now and goes to the back door for the herbs.

When she returns, Lachlan places a whole chicken in the pot, followed by a large quantity of water. He brings the pot to a simmer, places a lid on it, and then cleans up the mess he has made. As she watches, Petra realizes that his need for order likely stems from his need for a more comforting structure. Knowing his past now helps her see so much more of him. She feels the constant tension in her chest loosen as she realizes she wants to let him in. She wants to be accepted by him. Openly and wholly.

Warmth bubbles up inside her, her power flowing more brightly than it has in the last twenty-four hours. It pulls her toward him. As she stands there, watching him clean, it dawns on her. Her magic has been trying to tell her something all along, and she's done her best to push it down, to keep it locked away. But not anymore.

Without warning or preamble, she says, "I think I love you."

Lachlan drops his dishtowel on the floor. His mouth hangs open briefly, taking in what she just admitted before an enormous smile fills his face. He moves toward her slowly, as if she's a scared animal that will bolt at sudden movement. But she's not scared. Not anymore.

He takes the herbs from her hands, lays them on the counter, and then wraps his arms around her. "You *think* you love me?" She rests her forehead on his chest, looking down toward her feet. He lets go with one arm and places a finger under her chin, lifting it to look at him. "Please look at me when you repeat it. I need to see you when I hear those words from your lips."

"I love you," she says softly, purposefully.

"You love me," he repeats.

"Yes."

"Well, it's about damn time." He hugs her tightly, burying his face in the crook of her neck as he sucks in a deep breath, breathing her in.

"What do you mean?"

"I've loved you for two years. I never thought you would give me the time of day to be more than a friend."

She balks. "You have not loved me for two years!"

"I have loved you since you made my heart skip a beat that first day you walked in with Daisy and demanded she be hired. I may not have acknowledged it as love then, but I now realize it was."

She melts into his arms. "You love me." A statement. A confirmation. An affirmation.

"I love you," he confirms, his lips meeting hers. His lips are soft and pillowy, sending waves of fire through her body. She melts into his body, his hard planes fitting perfectly against her curves. His chest rises, pushing against her breasts as he seeks to deepen the kiss, widening his mouth and brushing his tongue against hers, tasting sweet like candy.

At that exact moment, a tear-free Daisy enters the kitchen. "Glad to see you two have come to your senses. What smells so good?"

Petra and Lachlan separate, their gazes holding a promise for later.

"Lachlan made some soup. It won't be ready for a bit yet, but in the meantime, we can chat in the living room," Petra says.

Daisy nods in response. Her shoulders fall as she turns and strides down the hall.

Before Petra can follow, Lachlan reaches out, wrapping her in his arms again, kissing her gently on the forehead. "I'm just out here if you two need me."

"Thanks," she smiles before turning away to join Daisy.

When she enters the living room, Daisy is sprawled on the oversized white couch, with a pillow over her head and a cream blanket wrapped around her like a cocoon.

"Despite your master camouflage skills, I can still see you, you know," Petra tells her, flopping onto the other end of the couch, turning sideways and stretching out her legs before her. "What's going on?"

Daisy groans. "I'm a constant fuckup," she says bluntly.

"I would disagree. I would say you are strong, courageous, and a bit of a spitfire," Petra responds. "Why don't you tell me what's wrong?"

"Do I have to?"

"Given the state we found you in like thirty minutes ago, I would say yes."

Petra picks up a pillow from the back of the couch and wraps it in her arms, resting it on her lap. Sensing that whatever Daisy is about to say will be significant; she needs something comforting to channel energy.

She watches as Daisy shifts, finding a more comfortable position. She twists and turns, flopping one way then the other, bending her legs and curving them to the side, then back out straight in front of her, arms flailing all over the place. Petra reaches out toward Daisy with her power. She whispers an incantation, sending a sense of calm over Daisy, helping her to relax. Daisy's face instantly releases the tension between her eyebrows, her jaw unclenches, and her breathing becomes more even.

"Thanks," Daisy says.

"Anytime. So tell me what's going on."

Daisy doesn't continue, allowing the silence between them to grow. Petra stays quiet, giving Daisy the space she would want when trying to find the words and courage needed to share something important. Having been friends with Daisy for as long as she had, Petra knows that sharing personal information has never come easy for her, especially after how she has been treated after her family was banished. Petra understands that desire to hold on to every piece of yourself and not to let others in. She also understands the desire not to harm those who have become close.

Lachlan comes in with trays of soup, sandwiches, and drinks. He didn't linger, considerate as always, but the look he gave Petra as he left was filled with longing.

After finishing her bowl of soup and half of her sandwich, Daisy finally feels composed enough to open up. "First of all, you better keep him. That was delicious."

Petra smiles and nods in response, not wanting to interrupt Daisy.

"Second, I'm sorry. I know this is taking a while."

"Take your time," Petra reassures her, running her finger along the seam of the pillow in her lap as she sends out her power, pulsing around the room, sensing the atmosphere, trying to gain an insight into what may be coming, but Daisy is shielding herself, not giving anything away.

Finally, Daisy blurts out, "I've been jealous of you!"

Petra is taken aback. "Jealous? Of *me*?"

"The look on your face," Daisy says with a chuckle, "says that was the last thing you expected me to say."

"It is!" Petra exclaims, playfully smacking Daisy's leg. "Why would you be jealous of me?"

"I know you see the things that have happened in your life as so much negativity, but I see you surrounded by love and compassion—and yes, some challenges too, but you have so much support that it barely fazes you. Then you're handed the Premier Witch title because of tradition. It's a lot, watching from the outside."

Petra nods. From the outside, it appears she has everything so easy. Being a Rose means she has lived a life full of privilege even if sometimes she feels the exact opposite. But she can see how it looks to Daisy.

"You have said in the past that you just want a quiet life, but I don't think that's true. I have watched you repress your magic, not really using your full power, all in the name of pushing against who you are. You are so strong and have much to offer this community, and you don't see it. Instead, you see the expectations and rebel against them. A witch with your talent and perspective needs to be making changes. We have so far to go as a community, and I say this as someone who has been on the perimeter of it for so much of their life. I see how much turmoil and dirty deeds are happening behind the scenes. No one expects the social pariah to be paying attention, but I see it all. Watching you be so flippant from the outside has been hard, and I've always felt smaller, less than, in comparison. You didn't even want to tell me about all the stuff with the council initially. Like you didn't trust me."

Daisy sits up, scrunching her legs into her chest and resting her chin on her knees. The look she gives Petra is filled with years of second-guessing her self-worth as she watches her best friend seemingly get handed everything. A burst of hurt spreads from Petra's heart to her fingertips, working out in sparkling wisps around Daisy's hand.

"I'm so sorry, Daisy. I never meant to make it seem like I didn't trust or value you. It's been a lot for me lately, and I needed to process it. I needed to think through what I was going to do. I do want to be the Premier Witch. I can see the impact I could have to help others, to help people like you, who our community has cast aside. I want a better, more accepting world for all of us. And to be honest, I think you could be a great addition as a consultant when I take on this role."

Daisy's eyes widen with surprise at that suggestion. She shifts her head lightly side-to-side and buries her face in her knees. Her shoulders rise and fall as she lets out a sob. Calling back the calming sensation, Petra places her hand on Daisy's back and rubs soothing circles. Her breathing becomes more even as her shoulders relax and the tears stop. Daisy raises her head, wiping the tears away with her shirt sleeve. When Daisy looks at her, Petra sees tentative excitement grow, sparking something new within her.

"I assume you would like that?" Petra asks, a gentle laugh floating out of her.

Daisy nods quickly while a smile forms on her lips. "Does that mean you will fight to take Premier Witch?"

"Well, I wouldn't say I'm fighting for it. I mean, I hope there's no bloodshed," Petra replies, grimacing, "but you're right, I need to accept my role and acknowledge the privilege and power I have. I plan to take what is rightfully mine, regardless of what these old farts want to throw my way to prevent that from happening."

CHAPTER THIRTY-FIVE

Lachlan

Petra and Daisy have been in the living room most of the afternoon. After Lachlan brings them lunch, he isn't sure what to do with himself because, well, the only thing he wants to do is filthy things with Petra. Of course, he couldn't do that with Daisy in the house. Thus, he resigns himself to cleaning, and eventually, when that is all done, he opts for a workout, hoping it will take some of the edge off. As he lifts heavy weights and runs on the treadmill, he keeps coming back to the meeting they are to have with Sloan this evening.

They agree to meet with her, yes, but the logical side of his brain is saying they need to approach it carefully. She said she wants to help them, but she has proven to be anything but trustworthy in the past—so why the change of heart now, he wonders? What are her motivations? What does she get out of boosting Petra to Premier Witch?

As these thoughts swirl around his mind, he realizes they should chat with Gladys. She's been left out of many of these details, and she almost certainly has connections that can help them uproot the current council of cowards.

He finishes his workout, sweat running freely down his chest, making him glisten like a vampire in the sun. He picks up a towel and dries his face, making his way to the living room to check in on Petra and Daisy and to suggest she reach out to her Gammy.

When he walks into the room, the chatter stops abruptly. Daisy covers her eyes and yells out, "Oh goddess, put a shirt on!" before making retching sounds. Petra, however, licks her lips slowly, her eyes flaring with heat. While he came here with different intentions, he's not unwilling to let her ogle him, even with her friend pretending to barf next to her. As she continues to stare, her cheeks turning a gorgeous flush from what he can only assume are the filthy thoughts running through her mind, his dick twitches and begins to stiffen.

Not the time! he tells himself, moving his towel down to hide the growing bulge in his shorts. Petra notices his intentional movement and smirks at him. *That little witch.* He returns the look, hoping it sends the message that she's gonna be in trouble for that later.

"If you guys are done eye-fucking each other…" Daisy interjects, breaking their stare down.

Lachlan clears his throat. "Sorry," he says sheepishly. "We should probably get ready to go."

Petra nods and turns to Daisy, "Are we okay?" She asks.

"Absolutely," Daisy responds.

They hug briefly before Petra stands up and walks toward where Lachlan is standing by the entryway. She doesn't look at him as she passes, though he sees a small tick up in her lips as she strides past. He reaches out and grazes her bottom, sending sparks of heat up his arm and straight to his dick.

Mine! his inner demon demands.

They pull up to the cemetery gates a few minutes early. The full moon shining through the spotty clouds creates moving shadows as the light shifts over the headstones and monuments. They step out of the Jeep onto a gravel path, crunching underfoot as they make their way to the closed entrance.

"It doesn't look like Sloan is here yet," Petra says, a shiver running down her spine.

"She'll be here," Lachlan states, more certain than he feels. A twinge in the back of his mind wonders if this is some kind of setup. As he reconsiders if they should have trusted Sloan so freely when history has shown that they should do the opposite, he hears footsteps approaching on their right.

Emerging from the darkness, moving between headstones, is Sloan. Dressed in all black, she appears as if born of the shadows. With the presence she commands, even among the dead, he considers that she would have been a great addition to the underworld. Her stride is confident and nearly silent. She would be an absolutely terrifying hunter.

Sloan reaches forward, twisting her hand in the air, unlocking the gate. As it swings open with a loud whine, Lachlan looks behind them as they enter, hoping the sound doesn't alert anyone nearby. They enter the cemetery proper, with the gate whining and clanging shut behind them.

"I could have done that," Petra says under her breath as they approach Sloan.

Although Petra can't see it in the darkness, Lachlan

smirks, amused at her petulance. He senses a protective shield slide over them. Calling on his shadows he sends a smoky tendril to push against the invisible barrier that moves with them. Solid.

She whispers, "just in case. And you can thank the new grimoire strength later."

He snorts. *This should be fun.*

Sloan leads them deeper into the cemetery, passing by headstones of various ages. Some are so covered in centuries-old grime that the names of the dead are no longer legible, while other, newer ones gleam in the moonlight, the granite and marble sparkling like witch lights as they pass by. Lachlan follows behind Petra, careful not to step on any of the graves so they do not upset the tenants. With everything going on, the last thing they need is a haunting because of a misplaced foot.

When Sloan stops, it is in front of a large stone mausoleum with a heavy-looking door set back between two Corinthian columns. Carvings and sculptures of various gods and goddesses adorn the archway overtop. Barely visible above the door, carved into the stone, are the words *Nomen Defendit Nos. Name Protects Us.* Sloan approaches the doorway and whispers the protective phrase; the door unlocks and slowly swings open.

Petra looks to Lachlan questioningly, "Think she's brought us here to bury us with her family?"

Lachlan stifles a snort. "I mean, it's not a bad plan. The last place anyone would think to look for us is in their crypt."

Petra and Lachlan pass a glance between them, only mildly confident that they aren't about to step toward their doom in a creepy mausoleum that belongs to the family vying for Petra's rightful title. Black wings emerge from

Lachlan's shoulder blades, a precautionary measure of protection his demon pushes out. Sloan follows closely behind, and as she steps over the threshold, the door shuts behind her. Witch lights ignite around the room, casting a flickering golden glow and dancing shadows on the walls. Petra shivers, rubbing her arms with her hands.

"You alright?" Lachlan asks.

"Yeah, just the whole being entombed with a chamber of dead people and my nemesis is setting my nerves on end."

Lachlan places a comforting hand on her back, gently rubbing it up and down her spine, and feels her relax into his touch. She looks up at him and smiles, and his heart clenches.

Sloan clears her throat, drawing their attention.

"So it is real," she says.

"What is?" Lachlan asks.

"You two," she responds, pointing a finger between Petra and him. "Grog will look like a fool when he sees he's caused all this fuss for nothing. It will be glorious."

Petra looks confused. "What do you mean?"

"I mean, you two are clearly in love. Aside from how you keep looking at each other, I can literally feel it emanating from you both. The mix of light and shadow is ridiculous, and for Grog to have ever doubted this, thinking he could use it to replace the Rose Premier Witch, is beyond me."

Petra's hand reaches for Lachlan's. He interlocks his fingers with hers and squeezes her hand gently three times.

I. Love. You.

"Your family hasn't exactly been innocent in all of this. Pushing for you to take Premier Witch, threatening me and my family, and so on," Petra says.

"I know, I know. That's part of why I'm here. Honestly, I

don't want to deal with all the bullshit you have to do as a council member, and I don't want the responsibility of Premier Witch. My parents have pushed for this because they want the prestige, and they think this is the only way to get it, to garner the power that comes with it. But I'm done playing their games."

This is not what they anticipated from Sloan. Petra stands in disbelief, chewing on her bottom lip.

"Yeah." Sloan laughs. Maybe he's had Sloan wrong all these years. "Anyway, my family has been working with Grog, trying to replace the Roses as Premier Witch for years. They've done whatever they can to create animosity between our families and to feed stories throughout the community, creating mistrust in yours. I don't want to be a part of that anymore. I've hated you most of my life, and I really don't know why. So I'm here with some information and to help you claim your rightful title."

Petra steps forward, cautiously reaching out to Sloan. She gently grasps Sloan's hand, and he notices Sloan flinches slightly under her touch. "Thank you," Petra says, "truly. I appreciate this more than you'll ever know."

Sloan genuinely smiles at Petra, making her appear kinder and less harsh around the edges. It may just be the witch lights, but Lachlan swears she sees Sloan glow just a little before the smile is quickly extinguished.

"So. Obviously, Grog has given you an ultimatum. But the bigger concern here is the whole community forum questioning your marriage now, and some other things have been happening, right?"

"Yes," Petra responds, more enthusiastic than she thought she would be. "Francesca tried to bribe Lachlan, my tire was slashed, and the general animosity from Grog and his minions as he tries to undermine me every chance he can."

"Yes. Grog is behind it all. From what I have overheard in my family's conversations, he plans to overrule any positive response from the community. The forum is all a farce. He will use his power on council to negate any positive outcome."

"Do you know why?" Lachlan asks.

"I know he has a history with your grandmother," Sloan answers, nodding to Petra. "I don't have many details on him since he's pretty slick, and while my family has been involved, I'm often left out or given bare-bones details so that I can't be implicated. All of that to say, that's why no one has been able to connect it all to Grog. You may do well to talk with your grandmother and see what she can tell you for any next steps. And she'll know proper protocols to follow."

Lachlan tries to think through the various policies and protocols that he agreed to follow when he became a council member, but he draws a blank. He can't think of a single policy they would be able to use against Grog.

"Okay. Okay," Petra says, touching her chin with her index finger. He sees her mind at work as she closes her eyes, processing the information and trying to piece it all together to make sense of it. The crinkle of skin between her eyebrows means something isn't quite right. She puts her hands down by her sides, opens her eyes and looks back at Sloan, breathing deeply.

"And you, master of shadows," Sloan says, turning to face Lachlan.

"Yes?" He bristles as shadows appear to swirl at their feet.

"You may do well to use those connections of yours to see how Grog is connected to your world."

"What do you mean?"

"His hands are dirty, and I know he's somehow connected in the underworld and using that to his advantage in council proceedings. I'm sure it won't take you long to figure out what he's up to," she explains.

"Noted."

He knows she's being vague on the details for a reason, leaving it up to them to do what they will with the crumbs she's providing. But he would be lying if he said he didn't think there was truth to what she was saying. He's heard rumblings over the years but never looked into it. Maybe he should have.

"Anyway," Petra says, her posture relaxing, "thank you. This is helpful. I need to call Gammy tomorrow. Is there anything else?"

"Keep it quiet. If Grog gets word that you are looking into him, who knows how dangerous he could get."

Petra and Lachlan both nod. "I think it's time we go," Petra says to him.

He nods in agreement and then faces Sloan, trying to determine who she really is. She's shown herself to be open and honest here tonight, but can they trust that this meeting won't come back to bite them in the ass? Only time will tell, unfortunately.

"Thank you. If you need anything, you know how to reach me," Lachlan offers. "I owe you one now."

"Noted," Sloan replies. The witch lights extinguish, and the door opens before them.

As they walk out, Petra whispers to Sloan, "Also, thank you for not killing us and leaving our bodies with your dead relatives."

"It was a possibility, but I didn't want to deal with the punishment that would come from that sort of embarrassment," Sloan deadpans, turning on her heel and walking the opposite way from where Petra and Lachlan came in.

Lachlan laughs deeply. The sound billowing out of him in raucous waves. Tears are building at the corner of his eyes, which he wipes away with the side of his index finger.

Petra glares at him, not finding this as funny as he did. "Are you about done?" she asks, annoyance fully evident in her tense expression.

"I think I like her," he says, still laughing as they walk back to the car.

Petra reaches out and pushes him toward the graves as they walk down the path, narrowly missing stepping on one.

CHAPTER THIRTY-SIX

Petra

Petra wakes with the not-so-light pounce of Morris on her stomach as he launches himself from her nightstand onto the bed. She folds in half, letting out an "oof" as he carries on about his business, walking down her duvet-covered legs to curl up at her feet.

"You are a menace, you know that?" She grumbles, rolling over to look at the clock on her nightstand. It reads 6:32 a.m., which is about two minutes past when he demands to be fed.

"That's no way to talk to your loving husband," Lachlan mumbles, his face buried in the pillow beside her. He reaches forward, wrapping an arm around her, pulling her into his chest. Scents of honeysuckle fill her nose as she kisses the tip of his nose.

"I need to go feed the cat before he tries to eat us," she says.

"Waiting five more minutes won't kill him."

"No, but he may kill us," she responds as Morris lets out a loud squawk in protest. "See, he's already demanding your head. I will remember you fondly, my love," she jests, kissing his forehead before slipping out of his arms and out of bed. Morris leaps off the bed with a loud thump when he lands, then scampers ahead of Petra. He winds between her legs as she reaches into the cupboard for his food and meows loudly in anticipation. Petra scoops his food, and he bumps his head on her leg in excitement and then gives it a lick. She brings his dish to his feeding spot, and he howls at her in thanks as she places it on the floor. She runs her hand along his back as he digs in.

"I love you too, buddy," she says.

Petra picks up the coffee carafe and starts making coffee. As she moves around the main floor, opening windows to let the fresh crisp winter air in, she feels warm arms wrap around her stomach. A familiar scent of bergamot envelops her as Lachlan's face nuzzles into the crook of her neck, causing goosebumps to travel down her body.

"Mmm. Good morning, wife," he says, pulling her hair aside to kiss her neck. "How are you doing?"

"I'm so happy Morris decided to let you live. I would have missed you terribly," she responds, placing a hand on his head and leaning her head to the side, giving him better access. "I'm surprised you're up so early."

"I wasn't going to get back to sleep with you out of bed. Though I do have an idea of something else we could do with this extra time together."

"Oh, really?" Her breath hitches as his hands slide down the front of her stomach, grazing the sensitive, exposed flesh between her shorts and the bottom of her tank top. Maybe the distraction is exactly what she needs.

He pulls her into him, allowing her to feel exactly what he has in mind. She puts her hands behind her, feeling down his torso to his legs. "You aren't wearing any clothes, Mr. Grace," she says, grinning.

"True," he responds, sliding his hand underneath the front of her shorts and slipping a finger between her already wet lips. "And you appear to be wearing too many."

"Is that so?"

"It is," he says as she arches into him and feels his firm cock pressing into her lower back.

"Well, then. How do you suppose we fix that problem?" She moans as he slips a finger inside her heated core.

Rather than answer, he withdraws his finger from her wetness, slides his thumbs into the hem of her shorts, and pulls them down. She leans over, placing her hands on the window as he grabs her hips and pulls her back. He kicks her feet apart before kneeling and putting his face between her legs and licking her wet pussy to her tight hole. She pushes back into him, asking for more.

"Greedy one this morning, huh?" he teases.

All she can manage is a gasp as he thrusts two fingers into her slick center as he continues to lick her wet heat. She leans over further, the sensations running wild within her, begging and pleading to be filled with him. Her toes tingle as he curls his fingers inside her, hitting just the right spot.

"Please," she begs.

"Please, what?"

"I need more. I need you."

He withdraws his fingers, leaving her feeling empty and incomplete. He grabs her hips as he stands behind her. She places her hands lower on the window, providing better balance as he bends her over. She feels him line up with her entrance and moans as he roughly thrusts into her, entering her fully. He's so thick and hard that she feels every ridge of his cock, filling her in a way she never knew was possible. She doesn't think she will ever get used to this. How he moves inside her, gliding and thrusting, giving her exactly what she wants. What she needs.

"Play with yourself," he orders.

She moves one hand in front of her to be more central, keeping her balance as he slows his movements, drawing out the sensation while he withdraws and then quickly fills her again. She takes her other hand and places it on her soaking pussy. She uses her index and middle finger to slide down her core, feeling the sides of him as he moves in and out. He groans behind her, enjoying the extra touch.

"I said, play with yourself."

She moves her hand up and begins circling her clit with her middle finger. Sparks build in her toes, shooting up her legs and spine. The additional pressure and sensation rapidly bring her closer to the edge.

"That's my girl."

Her head hangs down, chasing the release while he bucks into her, firmly holding onto her hips, punishingly stretching her with every thrust. She picks up the speed and rubs her clit, pushing more firmly.

"I'm so close. Fuck me harder."

"As you wish, wife," he says. He spreads his legs, giving himself more purchase for each thrust. Placing a hand on her breast he rolls her nipple between his fingers. The pinching adds a new dimension to everything she's already feeling, and she arches into him, always wanting more. Using his other hand, he holds on to her hips hard enough that she knows she will have bruises later on as he fucks her with every last bit of energy he has. "Make sure the neighbors know who is making you come, love," he says slamming into her.

She flicks her clit in time with his rapid thrusts and goes over the edge, sparks of ecstasy shooting throughout her body as she screams. "Lachlan!" Her mind spins with euphoria, unsure which way is up or down as she rides out the pulsing waves of electric heat working through her. He continues thrusting, chasing his release and grunts her name in response when he finds it. She will never get over the sound of her name on his lips as he comes undone. Her name on his lips sounds like a promise. That he belongs to her and will remain hers until the end.

"Fuck, I love how you feel wrapped around my dick," he pants, leaning over, lazily sliding in and out of her.

She responds by clenching around him, eliciting a deep-throated groan.

He withdraws from her, his deposit seeping out of her. Rather than clean her up as usual by conjuring a cloth from somewhere, he slides his fingers inside her, pushing it back in. That is the first time he has done that, and it is so unbelievably hot that she comes again with just the simple touch. Her toes curl as she whispers his name, riding his fingers and chasing the sparks that flow through her body as she releases. She turns and faces him, taking the hand he was using to stuff himself back in, and licks his fingers, tasting their mixed fluids. She moans around his fingers, her eyes rolling back as she clenches again and again with the second orgasm.

Taking it as an invitation, he removes his hand from her mouth and picks her up, wrapping her legs around his waist. He lines up with her core again, slides her down his still-hardened length, and presses her back against the window. They groan in unison as he fills her, her wet pussy clenching around him, claiming him as hers.

"Hades, you are perfect," he grunts, punctuating each word with a thrust.

She moans in response, grinding into him as he holds

her under her ass and thrusts deeply. It isn't long before she is screaming his name again, louder this time, letting everyone know who is the source of all her pleasure, as she comes on his dick for the second time this morning. He is breathless, sweaty, and grinning when he follows with his release.

"What are you grinning so madly about?" she demands as he withdraws, setting her on her feet.

"Just thinking of the show the neighbors got so early in the morning."

"We really should put up some glamours so they can't see in. Especially if you plan to regularly fuck me senseless in visible places."

"What's the fun in that?" he teases.

She shakes her head at him. "I should probably shower and clean up before meeting with Gammy for breakfast."

"I can help with that," he says, raising a mischievous eyebrow and taking her hand, leading her toward the stairs.

"I bet you can." She raises her hand to flick her wrist and clean up their mess on the window and floor, but he grasps her hand, stopping her. "Leave the window prints," he says, his voice heated. She smirks at him, knowing he likes it as a little reminder. She does as he suggests, then follows him upstairs, where they fuck again in the shower, bringing her morning orgasm count to four. He tries to get her to five, but she is running late and promises him another round later.

After getting dressed in dark jeans and a cream sweater, she puts her hair into a messy bun and kisses him goodbye, yelling "Love you" behind her as she runs out the door to meet Gammy to talk about a troll.

Gammy has been busy with medical appointments, and as much as Petra has tried to come and see her the past few days, Gammy has done her best to keep Petra away, not wanting to be seen in the rougher days after her treatments. She says it usually takes a few days to start feeling close to normal again, so she suggested waiting to meet until she was feeling up to it.

Petra shudders in the winter morning cold. As she approaches the door, she remembers where she is and that this is likely Gammy's last winter. The last time she will feel the changing crisp winds. This realization stops Petra's hand as she reaches for the door handle, ready to push down the latch and step into a home she has known since she was a teen. She shakes off the incoming feelings of loss and grief, reminding herself that Gammy isn't gone yet. Not sure what to expect of Gammy when she walks through the door, Petra plasters a fake smile on her face and prepares herself for the worst.

She finds Gammy basking in golden rays in the sunroom at a small bistro set with a teapot and two teacups. When Gammy hears Petra approaching, she turns her head and smiles lovingly. Petra smiles back and hugs Gammy gently, though she notices that Gammy's eyes seem slightly sunken, her hair not quite as shiny, and her posture not quite pristine. A soft gray blanket adorns Gammy's shoulders, which Petra assumes is to keep her warm in the cooler space. In the middle of the summer, this room is almost a sauna, which is great for the flowers and herbs she keeps in here as part of her apothecary.

"Sit, my darling," Gammy says, gesturing to the chair across from her.

Petra gladly obliges, angling her body to the side and crossing her legs under the table. "Would you like me to pour us some tea?"

"Please," Gammy responds.

Petra picks up the teapot, placing her other hand underneath to help it remain steady as she pours. She moves one teacup before Gammy and picks up the other for herself. She adds a small dollop of honey to her cup.

"Thank you," Gammy says softly, sliding her index finger through the handle and lifting it to her mouth to take a sip. "To what do I owe this pleasure?"

Petra sips at her tea, enjoying the floral notes mixed with the added honey. She notices Gammy's breathing is particularly labored this afternoon. "Gammy, how are you doing?" she asks, her body flooding with concern. It's only been a few months since Gammy first told Petra of her illness. It seems like so long ago, and yet, as if no time has passed, making her decline seem all the more sudden.

"I'm okay, love, just tired. It's been a long day."

Petra doesn't fully believe Gammy, but she accepts the lie anyway. "I'm not sure how much you know about everything that has happened with me in the last week or so. It's okay if you don't. I have been a shitty granddaughter by not visiting often enough." She raises her hands, stopping Gammy's protest. "No, I have. I have been wrapped up in my own things, and I'm scared. Scared of watching you fade away. I'm not ready to lose you, so I've been keeping some level of distance, telling myself that you needed the rest and had help and I would only be getting in the way. For that, I want to apologize. I love you and love everything you have done for me. Taking me in when you didn't need to, helping me to develop into the witch I am today. I will never have the right words to capture how much you mean to me."

Petra picks up the napkin on the table, unfolding and wrapping a corner around her index finger, using it to dab away the tears that have surfaced. Admitting her negligence as a granddaughter is hard. Acknowledging that she is losing Gammy is harder. She's not gone yet, but the crack in her chest is already opening, creating space for the inevitable earthquake of grief that will shatter her world and hollow her out.

"My darling granddaughter, I know this," she says, motioning to herself, "is not easy for you. But know, I do not hold any harsh feelings toward you. I knew you would come when you were ready. Remember, I have also done what I can to try and keep you at a distance, so you are not the only one to blame. I can only hope that you will not have ill feelings toward me for doing so."

"I could never," Petra sniffles.

The two clasp hands over the center of the table, the teapot warm beside them. Not knowing how much longer she will be able to do this, Petra holds on as long as she can, wishing things were different and that she could change the course of destiny. Sometimes, the Fates are cruel, but she knows they have chosen to take Gammy away for a reason, whatever that may be.

Gammy uses her free hand to lift her cup and take another sip, her eyes closing briefly as she savors the moment. "Since I am behind on events, why don't you fill me in? What has been happening with you, darling?"

Petra takes another sip and launches into everything that Gammy was unaware of, including the threats and that she has fallen in love with Lachlan. Gammy smiles at the admission. "I'm not surprised at all. There was always a spark between the two of you, and I wondered if there was more on his side when he offered to marry you."

"It's been wonderful getting to know him this way. The move from friends to something more was scary, but I realized I couldn't keep him as just a friend anymore. I was continually drawn to him, my magic pulling me that way, knowing he was the one long before I did. Or at least, long before I would listen," she laughs, embarrassed at her reluctance.

Petra explains why, aside from seeing Gammy, she wanted to meet today. "We— that is, Lachlan and I—had an interesting meeting with Sloan Wilks yesterday."

"Really? How did that go?" Gammy responds, her eyes widening with curiosity.

"That's the thing. It was… good. She offered to help me and Lachlan, and surprisingly, she followed through. That's kind of what I wanted to talk to you about today. She informed me that the person behind everything is Grog."

Gammy sucks in a breath.

"Gammy?" Petra asks, panic rising. "Do you need something?"

Gammy exhales, trying to steady herself. She shakes her head. "No, no. I'm fine," she says, waving Petra off. "Yes, Grog and I have been on the council together for quite some time and have history that I have shared with you before. I was hoping this wasn't him." She twirls the ring on her middle finger, looking down at the table.

"Do you think there is any way to take him down?"

"I'm not sure. It is hard to be removed as a council member. These are typically lifelong appointments. If you could collect enough evidence of his wrongdoings, you may have a better chance of defeating him if you could orchestrate it so it is an ambush. Less chance of him running."

Petra nods, making a mental note of this information, planning to talk to Lachlan later.

"When is your next council check-in?" Gammy asks.

"I am not sure. There should be a summons soon for a final decision about whether our marriage is allowed to stand and if we will be able to remain council members."

"Okay. Let me know when you are summoned."

As they sit in quiet for a moment, Petra's brain fires with an idea. "Oh, and Gammy?"

"Yes, darling?"

"You said that council positions are lifelong. I know they are appointed based on bloodlines."

"Yes?" Gammy responds, sleep threatening to taking over her voice.

"Is it possible to change that practice? Could we change the way that council members are chosen and create a more democratic and inclusive practice?" Petra asks as inspiration takes over her. Pink sparks at her fingertips, eager to create change. To prevent others from being subjected to this life like she has. Not that she regrets it now, but it still would have been nice to have had a choice.

Gammy is silent for a long time. So long that Petra is sure Gammy has fallen asleep. "That is an interesting proposition. I suppose it could be done. You would need to do some serious campaigning and sway the council to your side. But yes, I think it could be done," Gammy responds, a proud smile blooming on her delicate features. "And I think it would be good for the community."

Petra tucks that nugget of information into the back of her mind, into a place where it can continue to grow and take shape before she decides to move forward with it.

The noon sun has warmed the sunroom considerably since she first arrived. She notices a small bead of sweat at the corner of Gammy's brow, and her eyes appear heavy. While Petra doesn't know exactly what the treatment looks like that Gammy is going through, she imagines it takes a toll on her.

"Gammy, would you like to go rest?"

"Yes, please. I think a little lie-down would do me well."

Petra moves to her side and puts out her arm for Gammy to hold on to as she stands. Helping her inside, Gammy instructs her to take her to the plush sofa in the living room.

As Gammy settles on the couch, Petra lays a light blanket over her. Gammy's eyes start to close, her breathing slowing. Petra picks up a mystery novel from the side table and sits in the matching chair, curling her legs underneath her. Opening the book, she begins to read, listening to Gammy softly snore.

CHAPTER THIRTY-SEVEN

Petra

Petra leaves Gammy's a little earlier than usual on one afternoon. She's slowly been adjusting to the new powers from the grimoire, and Gammy is extremely helpful as she navigates her new abilities. It turns out that the grimoire didn't just strengthen her power but also gave her new skills. She has developed a new affinity for elemental manipulation along with the calming magic she already possesses. She can now do things like control fire and heat. Using these new skills, she's even been able to turn water into ice by manipulating heat levels within the water. Gammy says should Petra continue to develop this new skill, she may even able to control things like the weather.

She arrives at her work for a follow-up meeting with Sheila and Rosemary. As she walks from the parking lot to the front door, she passes by the play yard full of children. Many of them, including those from her preschool group, charge up to the fence, excited to see her.

"Miss Petra! Miss Petra!" they call out.

"Hi, friends! I've missed you all so much," she says, stopping and squatting down to talk to them.

"Miss Petra, where have you been?" Max asks.

"I had to take some time off. I wasn't feeling well."

"Are you feeling better?" Seraphina queries.

"Much better, thank you for asking. I have to go talk to Miss Sheila and Miss Rosemary, but I am so happy to see you."

"Bye, Miss Petra!" they yell as they run back to play.

Her heart smiles as she watches them leave. She didn't realize how much she missed them all. How much she missed being here and watching them grow.

Upon entering the facility, she is greeted by Sheila, who pulls her into a warm hug. Sheila releases her and holds Petra out at arm's length, her hands on Petra's shoulders.

"I am so happy to see you, dear. You look well."

"I am well, and it's good to see you too. I didn't realize how much I missed being here. It's been good to be away, but I'm ready to return."

"Come, come. Rosemary is in the office. We can talk there," Sheila says, walking ahead of Petra into the office. Petra follows and is greeted with another hug from Rosemary when she enters.

They settle in the chairs in the corner of the room. A brief, awkward silence fills the room as they wait for the other to start. Rosemary eventually takes the lead.

"As we've said, we are so happy to see you. You truly do look well," Rosemary says.

"Thank you."

"How are things going with you? Has the time off been beneficial?" Sheila asks, clearly seeking whether Petra is fit to return.

"It has. I cannot thank you enough for recognizing what I needed and forcing me to accept it. I didn't think I was that bad. I tried to keep my chaotic life from trickling into my work, but we know that is virtually impossible," Petra shares. "The time off allowed me to focus on what I needed to work on, and in doing so, I found more of myself and believe I have grown into a better person and will be a better educator."

"That's wonderful, dear. We are so happy to hear it," Sheila says.

"I would love to come back if you'll have me."

"We would love to have you return. Your children have missed you, and we are certain they will be happy to have their Miss Petra back!" Rosemary tells her.

"Does next week work for you?" Sheila asks.

"It's perfect."

"Wonderful. We will let Calle know that she will be moving over to toddlers. Maya is about to go on maternity leave, which is perfect timing."

Petra stands, her heart feeling full. "I can't wait. Again, thank you. I will never be able to express how much this means to me. I'll see you next week."

"We're just happy to see you more yourself," Rosemary says as they walk together to the door. "We have missed you."

Petra smiles and nods, turning to the door and leaving. The children wave at her as she walks back to her car. She can't wait to be back with them.

"Lach!" Petra calls out.

No response.

"Lachlan!" she calls again. As she checks the living room, she finally hears him call back from the gym's direction, and she heads in that direction. "There you are," she says, leaning against the door of the gym.

"What's up, witchling?"

"I've been summoned. A week tomorrow, we get the final vote on our marriage."

He drops the weights in his hands and comes to her. She hands him the paper so he can read it himself.

"Okay, we'll at least have some time to gather everything that we need."

"That was my thought. I would not have put it past them to yank us there whenever they felt like it."

"No kidding. Have you told Gladys yet?"

"No, I just saw it. I'm going to head over and check in on her. She wasn't doing well the last time I was there. I think the end is closing in," she says, her eyes glistening.

"Do you want me to come with you?" he asks, the warmth in his tone a sense of comfort in the impending doom.

"You wouldn't mind?"

"Absolutely not. Let me go rinse off and change. Leave in like ten?"

"Sounds good," she responds, wiping away an escaped tear. He kisses her quickly and tells her he loves her before dashing out of the room. She follows slowly behind, finding Morris asleep, sprawled out in a sunbeam on the floor in the library. She sits beside him, petting his soft belly while she waits.

She can't put her finger on it, but something doesn't feel right. When they arrive at Gammy's home, the sense of wrongness intensifies. The air feels heavy, like an extra weight has been added to the world. She looks to Lachlan and notices the tension in him, his shoulders and arm tight, his jaw set.

"You feel it too?" she asks, dread creeping up her spine.

"Do you want me to go in first?"

Swallowing her fear, she shakes her head no. "I should be the one to go first." He nods his acceptance, though she can tell by how the side of his mouth quirks down that he disagrees.

She takes a deep breath and steps toward the door, holding his hand as he won't let her go. Silently, she thanks him. She opens the door, and her suspicions of the sense of wrongness are confirmed. She doesn't need to see Gammy to know she is no longer in this world.

They walk through the house, hand in hand, quietly, slowly, trying to stave off the inevitable. Petra follows the faint, lingering trail of magic to Gammy's bedroom door. She looks to Lachlan, her pillar of strength. With a final steadying breath, she places her hand on the doorknob and turns it, opening the door and stepping into the room.

Inside, Gammy lies peacefully on her side on top of the blankets, legs slightly bent and a hand tucked under her pillow on the bed.

Her essence is gone.

Petra clasps her hand to her mouth, a loud sob escaping. Lachlan turns her into his chest, holding her tight as her heart breaks, a large hole taking shape where Gammy once occupied.

"She's gone," she wails, clenching Lachlan's shirt in her fist. He doesn't respond. Instead, he remains stoic, holding and running his hand along her back.

"Do you want to say goodbye?"

Petra nods into his chest.

Sniffling, she turns away from him, running a sleeve over her face to wipe the tears away. Silently, she moves to the side of the bed, Gammy facing her. Petra slides in beside her, curling her body to face her. Tucking a hand under her face, she reaches out with the other, taking hold of Gammy's free hand.

Cold. She's so cold.

"I'm sorry, Gammy," she squeaks, tears spilling onto the pillow. Clearing her throat, she continues, her voice breaking, "I love you. I'm sorry I was such a shithead sometimes as a teen. I will do my best to approach the rest of my life with the tenacity and compassion you taught me. I hope I'll make you proud."

He's been quiet, but Petra knows Lachlan has stayed with her, leaning on the doorframe so as not to intrude. She hears a slight sniffle behind her.

Petra stays on the bed, holding Gammy's cold hand for a while longer. How long, she isn't sure. Eventually, Lachlan comes to her, placing a loving hand on her hip and crouches down behind her. "We should call someone," he says.

"I know."

"Do you want me to call?"

"Please. I want to stay with her a little longer," she tells him, her voice thick with emotion.

"Ok. I'll call and be right back." He leans over as he stands, kissing the side of her head. "I love you," he says before turning and leaving the room. She hears him make a call; the rumble in his voice carries, though the words are indistinguishable. He returns shortly, letting her know they are on their way.

Petra stays holding Gammy's hand until the coroner arrives. As reality sets in that she will need to let go, the world around her becomes muffled. She hears them talk to Lachlan, likely asking him to move her, worried that she will hinder their ability to take Gammy away. Before he can come over, she whispers, "I love you. Goodbye, Gammy."

She releases Gammy's hand, pushes herself up and slides off the bed. Lachlan is at her instantly, catching her as she falls to the floor. One arm on her back, he sweeps the other under her legs. Curling into his chest, he carries her out of the room. They settle in the sitting room on the main floor, Petra still wrapped in his arms, tears flowing freely from her eyes onto his shirt.

It takes about an hour for the coroner to remove Gammy's body. They quickly check for any signs of unnatural passing, then wrap her and place her in the body bag. Petra, fingers laced with Lachlan's, follows them out and watches as Gammy is loaded into the van.

"We are sorry for your loss. Do you have a preferred funeral home to which you would like her brought?"

Petra looks to Lachlan. She hadn't thought of where Gammy would be going.

"Take her to Last Walk Funerals. Tell them to call Lachlan Grace for details."

"Got it," the coroner responds, writing down the information on his clipboard. "Again, I'm sorry for your loss."

"Thank you," Petra responds, her voice tired.

The coroner opens the driver's door, hops in, and leaves, taking her Gammy with him.

Petra spends the next few days in a haze of grief. Thankfully, Gammy had planned ahead, and many arrangements for her service and aftercare are already set. The casket, music, flowers, service location, and who would be doing the service were already chosen by Gammy, which Petra was thankful for. She's not sure she would have been able to make such delicate decisions on her own.

Lachlan has been a loving source of strength during these few days, providing a shoulder to cry on or making decisions when she couldn't. He took control of sending out notices to important people and writing the obituary for the local paper. She would not have made it through these days without him.

On the day of the funeral, Petra dresses in a soft blue flowing dress with a flower crown made of conjured wildflowers. While funerals are generally a sad affair, Gammy requested no black. She wanted to be celebrated for who she was rather than mourned for no longer being here. The celebration of her life was to take place at sunset in the Leeside forest, a place where she felt most connected to the earth and her power.

When they arrive at the location of Gammy's celebration, Daisy meets Petra and Lachlan at the entrance to the forest. Petra hugs Daisy, and then Daisy moves to stand on her other side. The three of them forming their own family, bound together by circumstance, trauma, and love.

Petra stops, speechless, as she looks over the large crowd gathered in the trees. Trolls, shifters, vampires, and many more supernatural creatures stand shoulder-to-shoulder with humans. Gammy has touched everyone here in some way during their life. Petra's eyes well up, but they are happy tears for the first time in days. Knowing how much of an impact Gammy had on everyone here fills her with hope. She can only hope she can maintain this legacy as she steps forward in her own life.

After the celebration, many beings come to Petra, sharing their condolences and stories of how they knew her grandmother. She hears stories of how Gammy saved their lives, helped them in time of need, and lent a compassionate ear when needed. She feels the hole in her chest fill little by little with each story. Gammy may be gone, but she will live on in all of these beings. She learns so much more about her grandmother, understanding her in ways she never did before. She was a truly remarkable woman.

After everyone is gone, Petra walks to the now-closed casket with Lachlan and Daisy, her misfit family, at her side. She places her hand atop the coffin and recites a parting spell to help carry Gammy on in peace. As she draws power from the earth below, swirls of sapphire pink magic work their way around the casket, sealing it, before it takes Gammy's body into the afterworld.

CHAPTER THIRTY-EIGHT

Lachlan

Daisy has been spending the past couple of days at their place, keeping close to Petra. She's managed to get Petra to agree to go out for the afternoon. Lachlan would give anything to be able to help make it all better, but he knows all he can do is be there for her. So he is. Every minute he can be.

Without Petra home for the day, he takes the time to review some council business he has been avoiding. He spends the afternoon working his way through various requests ranging from the need for accessible entry ramps to funding new businesses from community members. Some of them, like the ramps, are a no-brainer and are immediately accepted; others, like building permits and business funding, are put in the "need review" pile, and then others, asking for the right to refuse service to people they don't like are outright denied. Closing his eyes, he leans his head back on the top of his chair, pinching his nose in frustration. The gall of some of these people openly asking for permission from the council to discriminate against others.

The jockeying for position at the top of the supernatural

being tower is wild to Lachlan. Maybe it's because of his experience in the underworld and knowing that every being ends up there that helps him to see that the disdain for others is pointless. If his dark life in the underworld has taught him anything, everyone deserves a chance. A chance to be loved, valued, and seen as living beings, regardless of any abilities. Even the worst of the worst are loved by someone. He's also aware that the most heinous beings deserve to suffer the proper consequences of their actions. But no, he will not sanction hatred.

He'll have to bring this up at a council meeting. The thought alone causes his head to pulse with the beginnings of a headache. The council used to be something worthy and important in the community. But with all of this chaos from Grog, it's becoming a farce. They need to find a way to get rid of him. He's ruining what the council is meant to stand for and instead is turning it into the Grog show, which would never get greenlit for public viewing.

He grumbles under his breath as he looks at another request from a community member. This one is from the Goblin Market owners asking to extend their space. Unlike many others, they have included a complete development plan, how the new area will be used, and a tentative timeline for construction and cost. They are requesting some added funding from the council, claiming that the community would greatly benefit from the new space, given how frequently it is used. While he knows he should put this in the review pile, he is pleased with the effort and planning the owners have gone and forcefully stamps **APPROVED** on the front. If Grog can create chaos, he can use his power to do good within the community.

"Fuck you, Grog," he says, tossing the file on the approved pile.

He's made good headway on the paperwork, but a daunting stack remains. As he pulls yet another bare-bones request from the pile, his phone vibrates beside him. Declan.

DECLAN

Answer your door.

LACHLAN

Sounds sus.

Ha. Ha.

Let me in.

You could be a murderer. Posing as my little brother.

Yes, because a murderer would text first.

All a part of the plan to trick me into letting them in.

Just let me in, asshole.

Lachlan chuckles as he opens the door to Declan's less-than-amused expression.

"Seriously. Such a dick," Declan grumbles, stepping through the entryway.

A deep laugh breaks from Lachlan's chest. "Had to be sure you weren't here to kill me, that's all."

Declan rolls his eyes at Lachlan and walks further into the house, leading them to the kitchen, where he opens the fridge and helps himself to a drink.

"Welcome. Would you like something to drink?" Lachlan asks sarcastically, taking a seat at the counter.

"Don't mind if I do," Declan responds, sticking his tongue out.

"Nice to see you too. What's prompted this unscheduled visit?"

"Can't I just want to see my brother?"

"Other people could, but not you." Lachlan ducks the roll of paper towel flying toward his head. "Hey!"

Declan comes around the corner of the counter, pushing Lachlan off his stool, and continues into the living room, sitting in an overstuffed chair.

"You should clean your windows, man."

Lachlan sputters his drink. "I'll get right on that," he says, smirking, joining Declan in the living room.

"So, how are things with the wife?" Declan asks, leaning back and placing his free hand on the arm of the chair.

The smirk changes to a genuine smile at the mention of Petra. "The past couple of days since Gladys's passing aside, honestly, it's better than I imagined. We've come a long way in a short time, and I am enjoying getting to know this new side of her."

"What do you mean?"

"Well, obviously, we had been friends for a while before all of this marriage stuff. We had some challenges at the start and had to talk about our communication, especially after realizing we had feelings for each other that went beyond friendship. We needed to figure out what our relationship looked like and what we wanted from each other. Moving past that friendship barrier to something more was hard for her. She's been hurt a lot in the past by people she's cared about. But setting those expectations of communication has helped wonders. No secrets, no suddenly leaving when we are upset. It's something else," Lachlan explains.

"I'm happy to hear that."

"Thanks. Don't misunderstand me: do I wish things may

have come together differently? Absolutely. Marrying a woman out of obligation was never my goal or plan. But I'm happy with where we are, a couple of months in."

"You mean you didn't have it planned out to offer yourself to a random woman who was being forced to get married so she could claim top witch status? How strange."

Lachlan laughs heartily. His brother jokes, but the smile on his face is unbreakable. Petra brings a light to his life he never thought possible. She is sunlight casting his shadows aside.

"How about you? How are things? What brought you out here?" Lachlan rambles off.

"I'm doing okay. I've signed up for a 10K race next weekend. You should come and watch," Declan says.

"Doc says that's okay? You're all healed, and what not post-surgery and physio?"

"Yep. Doc and therapist signed off about a month ago. The therapist was helping me get back into running shape. We worked on it through physio and built the training I'd need into the plan."

"That's awesome! I'll be there," Lachlan says enthusiastically.

"Also…"

Here it is.

"As you know, I've been specifically asked to weigh in on the community forum," Declan says.

"Yes…"

"Well, I'm just a little worried that I'll say something to fuck it all up. I'm not good with these council things like you are." Lachlan scoffs. "And I don't want to say something dumb that will ruin everything you two have been working for."

"Be honest. They aren't looking to trap you. They want

a general community opinion on whether or not Petra and I would be able to remain impartial when on the council together. You know us both. Share what you know."

"They won't try and shut my shop down or retaliate in some way if I side with you two?"

"Not at all. I understand your concern—both for yourself and for us—but none of this will fall back on you, I promise," Lachlan says, hoping he is being reassuring.

"Okay," Declan responds, still sounding unsure, but he doesn't continue, so Lachlan lets the topic fall away.

A loud howl from the hallway announces Morris's presence before he enters the room. Morris strolls over to Declan and jumps onto his lap without ceremony. Morris lays down, curling his paws underneath himself, turning into a loaf and drifting off to sleep as he purrs softly.

"I hope you didn't have any other afternoon plans," Lachlan says. "He's not pleasant when he's woken up. Or when he's hungry. Or most other times."

"I guess I'm stuck here then?"

"Yep. I'll get you another drink, and then we can put a movie on. Get comfy," he laughs, shaking his head as he leaves the room.

CHAPTER THIRTY-NINE

Petra

"Welcome, Mrs. Grace-Rose. You understand why you have been summoned here this evening?" Councilor Clellugs asks.

"Yes," Petra responds. She sits on a witness stand in the chambers, wearing a reserved light-gray knee-length pencil skirt, cream blouse, and black heels. Her hair is pulled back into a tight bun adding to the refined look she was going for. She hopes she appears poised and collected, yet her insides twist, sending shivers up her spine.

"Good. Shall we begin?" the councilor asks, looking down the line of members. They all nod in response. "Good. Good. For the record, Mrs. Grace-Rose, as you know, you have been summoned to this forum because you were provided with an ultimatum back in the fall wherein you were required to marry as a means of fulfilling tradition and demonstrating your commitment to the council and larger community. Upon doing so, you would be deemed a worthy candidate and promoted to Premier Witch, giving you a seat on this council, replacing your grandmother upon her passing, and allotting you the power and responsibility with the mentioned title. We, the council, are concerned that your marriage may not be what it seems, and the legitimacy of your marriage is now in question. The forum into whether your marriage is acceptable has been ongoing, with various family and community members being questioned about the perception and possible ramifications of your relationship. It is now your turn to be questioned, which is why you have been summoned today. I want to be clear: should your marriage be deemed unacceptable at the end of this forum, you will no longer be a viable candidate for Premier Witch, and your powers will be stripped. Do you understand?"

Petra swallows. "Yes."

"Are you ready to proceed?"

"Yes."

"Ok. We each have questions and will work through them as we go. This should take about an hour."

"I understand."

"Good. Councilor Amare will begin," they say.

"Thank you, Councilor Clellugs," Amare starts. "Mrs. Grace-Rose, can you start by telling us how you met Lachlan Grace?"

"I first met Lachlan about two and a half years ago. I was with my friend, Daisy Hale, and she was looking for a new place of employment. We entered the Bittersweet Acorn together, where she was putting in an application. As you know, Mr. Grace owns that establishment and was there that day, setting up. Walking in Bittersweet Acorn that day was the first time we met."

"Thank you," Councilor Amare states, finishing writing her notes before continuing. "Next, please tell us about your relationship with Mr. Grace. How did your relationship start, and when did it become more romantic?"

Petra picks up the water pitcher on the desk before her, pouring herself a glass and takes a long sip. The action allows her to collect her thoughts and prepare to say something that won't harm her.

"As I mentioned, we met at the Bittersweet Acorn, and after Miss Hale was hired that day, we began to see more of each other as I would attend the establishment a few evenings a week to attend events and be able to see my friend. As I frequented his business more often, we began to converse and ultimately became good friends. We would spend time together outside of the Bittersweet Acorn, going for coffee or visiting farmer's markets regularly as friends tend to do. I began to develop feelings for him about a year ago but didn't think the feelings would be reciprocated. I have since learned that he had been interested in me for some time. I would say we moved from friendship to a romantic relationship a few months ago when all of the Premier Witch conditions started," she answers. Most of what she has said is true; the timelines may be slightly smudged, but they don't need to know that. If she were completely honest with herself, she would say she's been linked to him from the moment they met, she just didn't realize it.

Councilor Amare nods as all the council members quickly jot down their notes. The shifter representative, Councilor Knight, speaks next, followed by the faerie, werewolf, and goblin representatives. Because Lachlan is not present due to his involvement and the Premier Witch seat is empty due to the loss of her Gammy, that leaves the final round of questions coming from the troll representative, which means Councilor Grog has the last stab at her.

She looks him squarely in the eye, doing her best not to show any fear or discomfort of facing him despite all that he has been doing and organizing against her. He smirks at her, looking like he thinks he has her trapped.

"Hello, Mrs. Grace-Rose. Thank you so much for joining us today," he says, a sneer evident on his stupid lumpy face. "I only have one question for you."

She perks up a bit, feeling a sense of relief wash over her. She's almost done; she can get through this.

"Please tell the council why you and Mr. Grace decided to get married. I want to remind you that you are here because the ramifications of this marriage are being called into question, so lying would not be prudent."

Petra releases a slow, calming breath. She could lie and say it was love, even if it was unknown. But she decides to go with the truth, hoping that it will bring the council members to her side, helping them to see the position she was put in and that it was the only way she could see to respond to an impossible challenge. She feels her newfound power well up inside her, giving her the confidence to say what she needs, knowing it is right.

"Thank you for the reminder, Councilor Grog," she says, looking him in the eye, showing no fear. "I would like to remind the council that Councilor Grog set this challenge to marry, and refused to let me hear the full set of terms before I accepted. As you know, I had thirty days to find a spouse. As discussed in this meeting, I was already in a relationship with Mr. Grace, albeit a *friend*ship, and now I was faced with this impossible task. I was not instructed that I had to find love, but that I had to get married. The fact that the acceptability of this marriage is being questioned is frankly absurd, as that was never part of the conditions. I had a dear friend offer to help me. After some personal struggles and wavering on this offer, I finally accepted, knowing it was the right choice so I could be the next

Premier Witch. If you were in my position, I would be interested to see how you would have responded to this ridiculous stipulation. I may not have married for love initially, but I have found it. My relationship with Mr. Grace has only grown since we married. I adore going to bed next to him every night and can't wait to wake up and share the new day with him. We complement each other. He provides strength for me, and I soften his edges. And as council members, we would continue to provide balance in a position that often requires us to choose sides. We would make our individual choices based on what our community is telling us and what we each believe would benefit the community. We do not agree on everything, and I can assure you that would continue as council members. Whether you accept this marriage or not, my world has changed forever by having Lachlan Grace in it. Thank you."

The sneer on Grog's face vanishes, and if they could, Petra is sure there would be steam billowing out from his ears.

"Thank you, Mrs. Grace-Rose. That is all. Again, thank you for coming in. We still have a few more interviews to go, but we should have a decision for you in a few weeks. You are free to go," Councilor Clellugs says.

Petra stands, wiping her hands down her thighs. She makes to step down from her stand and instead is pushed through a portal, ending up on Lachlan's—no, their—front step.

Home.

CHAPTER FORTY

Lachlan

A breeze flows through the trees, rustling branches. These quiet mornings spent with his coffee, book, and Morris have become some of Lachlan's favorite moments. He's learned to cherish tranquility and peace after years of chaos in the underworld. He sips at his coffee, turning the page of his book, content in the home and the life he and Petra have created here.

Petra joins him a little later, having fallen back asleep after Lachlan rose to meet Morris's demands for food. She opens the sliding door, garnering his attention, and while she's only in shorts and a sweatshirt, her hair in a messy bun on top of her head, she is the picture of beauty. She tiptoes to his seat as he opens his arms, welcoming her. She slides onto his lap, wrapping an arm over his shoulders, leaning in and delightedly kissing him good morning before turning and stealing a sip of his coffee.

"Good morning, love."

"Good morning, peach pit." She smiles, happiness radiating from her like the morning sun. He dramatically rolls his eyes at her new attempt for a nickname.

"What has you so happy this morning? It can't be me because I have yet to have my dick inside you," he says, his cock twitching beneath her, earning him a giggle.

"I'm just happy to see you, sugar plum. As good as your dick is, not everything revolves around it, you know," she responds sarcastically.

"But I love it when *you* are wrapped around it."

She rolls her eyes at him and makes to leave, but he wraps an arm around her, keeping her in place, letting her feel what she does to him. She squirms in his lap, laughing brightly, the sound filling his soul in a way he never expected to experience. He laughs along with her, unable to keep the unbridled joy inside. It bubbles up from his core, escaping in fits and starts as he wraps his arms more firmly around her center, nuzzling into the crook of her neck.

She finally relents, gasping for air as she feigns disappointment, pouting that plump bottom lip out. He places his hands on either side of her face and nips that perfect lip with his teeth. She moans, leaning into him, meeting his mouth with hers. She opens her mouth, brushing his tongue with hers, deepening the kiss. She pushes her ass into his crotch, and he growls hungrily. As he gets worked up, his dick at full attention, hoping to slide into her soft heat, she breaks the kiss, leaping off his lap and heading inside.

It takes a moment for his kiss-fogged brain to catch up, but he is up on his feet, following her into the house. "Where do you think you're going?" he growls.

"Me? Oh, I have to get ready to meet Daisy," she says over her shoulder before running upstairs, leaving him hard and wanting.

"You're in so much trouble, witchling," he yells after her.

All he hears back is a cackle as she starts the shower.

Breathing heavily, sweaty, with his muscles like liquid, he pauses his run and stands on the shores of the lake. It's been a while since he has run this route, usually avoiding the lake because of how busy it can be, but it's oddly quiet this late morning. As his breathing slows, the steady waves ground him.

"Lachlan? Lachlan Grace?" he hears someone call out behind him. His back stiffens, recognizing the voice. This can't be good. He hopes they will think they have the wrong person if he doesn't respond. Only they call his name again, markedly closer. *Shit.*

He turns to see Selene striding toward him.

Fuck me.

"It is you! How lovely to see you, old friend," she says, stopping before him, her voice like a snake winding through his chest, squeezing out every last bit of growth he's made over these past few years. "Don't be like that," she says, noticing his tense stance, locked jaw, and the growl rumbling in his chest.

"Is that what we are?"

"You always were such a joker."

"I didn't realize what I did for you and Viktor was a joke," he says through clenched teeth, barely keeping his shadows at bay.

"Come now. I hear you have made a nice little life for yourself here. You own a bar, have friends, and even found yourself a pretty little witch for a wife."

"You leave her out of this," he barks, letting go of his hold, shadows emerging from the ground, winding toward her.

"Oh, put those wispy things away. I came here as a peace offering."

He draws the shadows back, allowing them to shift and flow around his feet. A warning that he's ready should she try anything funny.

"How so? As far as I remember, you know nothing of peace."

"Things change." She examines her nails. "I hear you are looking for information about a certain troll."

He folds his arms across his bare chest. "What of it?"

"I happen to know something about what he has been involved in in our world. How he's been using the underworld to do his bidding, including harming other council members."

"At what cost? And what do you mean harming council members?"

"No cost. As I said, a peace offering," she says, her tone softening, almost apologetic. "To protect my sources, all I can say is there is a reason Gladys was unable to be healed. If you agree, I will tell you everything I know and help you in any way that I can."

"Why?"

"Well…it's not the same without your regular presence in the underworld. Not because you were great at what you did, but because people trusted you. It's gone to shit, and we need you back."

"Why would I return when you and Viktor did everything possible to turn me into a monster like you?" he asks, years of buried pain rising to the surface.

"It's not the place you remember. The community needs to see that there are alternatives to what we did. What we no longer do. That's why I've been trying to reach you these last few months. I have done what I can to keep things going in your absence, but I can't do it alone anymore. The people need you."

He admits that supporting the people of the underworld would be a wonderful way to contribute to their community. As the council representative, it has always been an odd feeling to be connected to that world but still an outsider in many ways. This could be a way for him to pull it all together. To help demons like him find their way.

"Does Viktor know you're here?" He asks.

She hesitates a moment. "He died. Last year."

Her answer is like a wound starting to heal. He's never wished for anyone to die, but hearing that that monster is no longer terrorizing the underworld eases a small part of him. "I'm sorry you've lost someone you cared about," he says diplomatically.

"Thank you. Anyway, I won't keep you, but let me know when and where you need me, and I will follow through on my offer. You know how to reach me," she responds, turning and disappearing before he can thank her.

He pulls out his phone and sends a text to his love.

LACHLAN

We have Grog.

Sliding his phone back into his armband, he takes one last look at the lake before running home.

CHAPTER FORTY-ONE

Petra

Petra stares, gobsmacked, at her phone. The message from Lachlan only sparks questions and curiosity. How? What does he mean?

"Earth to Petra," Daisy calls, waving her hand in front of Petra's motionless face. She snaps her fingers next to Petra's ears, finally breaking her out of her thoughts.

"Sorry, sorry. I'm here."

"Questionable. What was all that about?"

"Lachlan found a way to out Grog. Somehow. Somewhere. I'm not sure. All he said was this," she says, showing Daisy the message he sent.

"That's huge!"

Surprise floods through her, sending shockwaves of excitement from her head to her toes. This is real. They can put an end to Grog's terror. The realization makes her giddy, restless tension filling her body.

"I feel like I need to celebrate, but I'm not sure what exactly to celebrate or how," Petra laughs.

"Do we need a reason? Let's celebrate you!" Daisy responds, leaping up from the floor to make drinks. She returns a moment later with two mixed drinks. Petra doesn't bother to ask what's in them, trusting Daisy's expertise. "To you!"

"To me!" Petra responds before taking a sip and coughing. "Smooth," she rasps.

"Sorry. May have been a bit too excited and made it a heavy pour."

Clearing her throat, Petra smiles. "S'all good." She takes another sip, this one more tentative, letting the mixture of whiskey and bitters linger on her tongue before swallowing. "Delicious."

"So what's the plan?"

"I'm not decided on all the minute details, but I think the plan is to out Grog at a council meeting. We hope to present our information to the council and push for an emergency vote on his position."

"Do you think it will work?"

Petra shrugs, taking another sip, the burn of the alcohol more welcome now that she knows what to expect. They continue to discuss what becoming Premier Witch means, what she hopes to accomplish in the role, and what changes she would like to implement in the council.

As they continue talking, a slow realization dawns on Petra. Wanting these changes and thinking about all the things she can do with the position of Premier Witch is wonderful. However, she recognizes she will have to do it all without Gammy guiding her. She won't be here to see what she can do, how she can improve their world, or how she will continue to grow into her powers and abilities. A wave of grief takes over her, tears forcing their way through her shell.

"Wait. What's happening? What's wrong?" Daisy asks, noticing the change in Petra's demeanor.

Sniffling, angrily brushing away the escaped tears, she slumps forward, her face in her hands. "Gammy."

"Oh."

"Gammy isn't here," she says.

The loss of the family matriarch and the person who has cared for, shaped, and loved her isn't easy. In moments like these, the reality of a future without Gammy hits her and leaves her wondering if she's ready. Wondering if Gammy will be proud of her.

CHAPTER FORTY-TWO

Lachlan

Lachlan arrives home from his run, power flooding his veins. Pulling a towel from the closet, he wipes the sweat from his face and chest. As usual, with Petra out, the house feels empty, like it's missing its heartbeat.

Victor is dead. The news from Selene is surprising. A part of him wonders how it happened. Who gets to claim the victory of finally ridding the world of him? At least, Lachlan assumes someone else did it and that it wasn't natural causes. That monster had so many enemies. Living the way he did, it was bound to happen that his name came up on someone else's list. It's a testament to Viktor and his reach that it didn't happen earlier.

Morris struts around the corner, brushing against Lachlan's leg. He looks up at him with a look that says, "You'll do." Lachlan reaches down, scratching behind his ears the way he likes. When he stops, Morris looks disappointed, like he isn't ready for this petting session to be over.

"Come on, little man. I'll get you some treats."

Morris takes off, bounding for the kitchen, his little paws

sounding like a herd of hippos charging through the house. While he's never had a cat before, Lachlan is under the impression that they are supposed to be light on their feet. With the way Morris moves about the world, he would not make a good hunter, that's for sure.

Morris howls for Lachlan to hurry up. Rather than risk his life, he does as requested. Reaching the kitchen in record time and depositing a satisfactory number of treats on the floor for his majesty.

Leaving Morris to his snack, Lachlan showers and dresses in gray sweatpants and a white T-shirt. He makes a turkey sandwich on a bun with pesto and sliced tomato and brings it to the patio in the backyard. As he eats his lunch, he rolls through everything that has been weighing on him. He thinks about Petra and the upcoming decision, Selene and her offer, and that little nugget Selene planted that is quickly growing in his brain.

The idea of going back to the underworld being a guide for other members is not something he ever thought about doing. But Selene is right; he has managed to turn his life around. Darkness and danger no longer lurk at every corner. He no longer worries about tomorrow being his last day. He can finally say that he is fully happy. And helping to adjust to the underworld and supporting those who seek change sounds exactly like what he is meant to do.

He spends the rest of the afternoon going through more paperwork from the council and the bar, approving some requests, declining many more, and filling out order forms. As the afternoon light turns into the oranges and pinks of sunset, he hears the front door open. "Lucy, I'm home!"

Meeting her in the hallway, he says, "Lucy? Please, if anyone is Lucy, it's you," He kisses her gently. "I've missed you."

"I missed you too," she responds, smiling against his lips. She curls her arms under his and up his back, leaning into him as he wraps his arms around her. They stand, embracing, breathing each other in. The scent of cherry and vanilla fills his nose.

My heart.

When they finally release each other, Morris is heard bounding down the hall, coming to greet his preferred human. She leans over, scooping him up and nuzzling her face into his soft fur.

"Hello, my little man. Were you good for Daddy today?"

"Daddy, huh?" Lachlan says, smirking as he leans against the wall, arms crossed, watching their interaction.

"You effectively adopted him when you agreed to marry me. Thus, Daddy."

"I like it when you call me Daddy," he says.

She rolls her eyes at him, as usual. "I can call you some other things if you'd like," she says, winking at him before going to the living room and flopping on the sofa with Morris in her arms. He wriggles free from her arms and curls up in her lap, content and demonstrating it is possible for him not to be an asshole.

Lachlan sits at her feet, lifting them to rest on his lap, his hands finding them as he massages her soles. "How was your day with Daisy?" he asks, running his thumb along her arch.

"Good. We gossiped, had a breakdown, figured out how to solve world hunger, you know, the usual."

"What caused the breakdown?"

"We were celebrating 'me' after you sent the text about Grog, and I realized Gammy isn't here to see me become Premier Witch," she says, picking at the non-existent fluff on her shirt.

"Ah. That tracks."

"Yeah."

He tugs on her big toe to get her to look at him. He can see the watery layer begging to break free when she meets his eyes. She's stronger than she gives herself credit for. "You know she is going to be so proud of you. She may not be here to see it in person, but she'll be with you every step of the way, cheering you on and telling you when you've done something stupid. She already knew you were capable and was so proud of you. You should have seen how she talked about you when you were not around. She beamed as if you were the sun that keeps the world alight and she made sure everyone knew it."

A sad smile forms on her face, the glisten in her eyes lessening. "Thanks for that. I know she's proud of me, she told me all the time. The reality of her being gone hit hard today as I realized she won't be here to see everything I plan to do."

"I know. It's hard to accept, especially when she's been a big part of your life. But that woman," he says, whistling, "she was tough. I would not be surprised if she refuses to leave completely and instead haunts us all."

Petra laughs, the sound pleasant and amused. "That's true. She would totally haunt us."

"One hundred percent," he says, leaning over to kiss her cheek. As he leans back, he senses another notch in his life sliding into place. This life with Petra, this moment here, being here to support her, to be by her side, regardless of what she may be facing, is where he is supposed to be. This is what he has been waiting for. No, longing for. He'll never understand how he lived, let alone survived, without his heart with him.

"So. Tell me more about Grog. How? What do you have on him?"

"Oh, this is good," he responds. He goes into the story from this morning, Selene tracking him down and her offer. But one thing Selene says still sits uneasy in his mind. "She also said that there was a reason Gladys couldn't be healed."

"But how did she know?"

"I didn't ask. Honestly, I don't even want to know," he says, churning this over in his mind.

"Do you think Grog is somehow behind Gammy's illness?"

It's as if a fire ignites inside him. His demon pushes to the surface ready to fight. That has to be what Selene meant. Grog orchestrated all of this. "I think that's exactly what happened," he nearly growls, fighting against the raging tide inside him.

Surprisingly Petra is calm. He catches a flare of anger flash across her face, but that is it. "Why are you not angry?"

"Getting angry doesn't help me against Grog. If it is true, it is absolutely devastating to know he hated her, and by extension me, so much so that he would willingly cause her not only harm, but death. But the anger right now serves no purpose. I need to remain levelheaded until we get through this. Now, do you think we can trust her?" Petra asks, doubt floating through the air with her words.

"She seems genuine. Like she wants to help. I think she's feeling lost without Viktor and maybe seeing she has more enemies than she likes. By reaching out to me and offering support, she may be hoping for some protection as she tries to change."

"Will you protect her? After all that she put you through?"

"I don't know. I've moved past the blind hate for them—

well, for her now—but I don't think I would offer support that way. She also said she wanted me to come back to the underworld. To have a more consistent presence there again and help people change their lives like I did."

"I mean, you've talked about creating positive change. That would be a great way to accomplish that. I'd also like to see more of where you came from," she says. He can see her mind at work, rolling the idea around, watching as it takes shape. "Maybe as a council, we could create an incentive or program to help community members facing life challenges?"

"That's a great idea. We need you to be Premier Witch first," he says, his chest glowing with pride for this woman he is lucky enough to call his wife, "but I think that would be a wonderful step forward."

"All right. So what do we do now?"

"I'll reach out to Selene tomorrow. She'll have mechanisms in place to do what needs to be done when the time comes, but at least she'll know it may be a quick turnaround as the council doesn't like to give us lots of warning."

"Great. Dinner thoughts?"

"Mmm. I do have one," he says, picking Morris off Petra's lap and placing him on the floor.

Her eyes flare with heat. "Oh. And what would that be?" she asks, placing her hand on his head and running her fingers through his hair.

"You," he responds, hooking his fingers atop her pants and pulling them down.

Over the next few days and multiple conversations, Selene confirms her information and promises that when the time comes, a quick text to her will deliver her sources. Lachlan hasn't asked how she found these sources, but he knows Selene well enough not to question whether she will follow through.

He may not have enjoyed or felt good about what he did when he worked for Selene and Viktor, but he can't deny they brought a sense of family in a time of turmoil. An odd sort of bonding occurs within criminal organizations like theirs that, even years later, and upon threats of death, a sense of loyalty remains. Lachlan reasons loyalty is part of what brought her back to him, hoping he will respond and help her. He hopes that all she wants is for him to help support others trying to better themselves. Regretfully, he doubts he will ever be that simple. It may not happen soon, but eventually, she will come back asking for a favor.

"Are we all set?" Petra asks, coming to join him in the library.

"Yeah. Selene said to text her when we need her to deliver. Now we need the summons from the council."

"Have they not mentioned the decision when you've been at the standard meetings?" Petra questions over her shoulder while perusing the shelves.

He leans back, clasping his hands behind his head and putting his feet on the desk. "No. They've been surprisingly tight-lipped about it, but I can sense discomfort among the other members. I think Grog bit off more than he can chew and may have alienated his allies. I wonder if it will be easier to rid him from the council than anticipated, especially if there is already so much tension and if he's been threatening them all like I heard him do to Amare."

"Wait? What do you mean he threatened Amare?" Petra asks.

He had forgotten to tell her about that. He fills her in on what he heard all those weeks ago between Grog and Amare. Her eyes are wide by the end.

"That fucking scum."

"Yeah, no kidding. I knew he was dirty but didn't think he was dumb enough to threaten the other council members. If they see him brought to a vote, it could easily go our way."

"That would certainly make things easier. Any idea who they may choose to replace him as the troll rep?" Petra asks.

"There's no clear bloodline successor, but I've heard some rumblings about a few candidates. Why? Worried they'll be just as bad?"

"A little," she confesses, pulling a book from the shelf and reading the synopsis on the back. "It's more than I'm not sure how we can guarantee that any new rep won't turn out like Grog, filled with hate and making it his new life mission to cause harm."

Moving over and wrapping his arms around her from behind, he rests his head on her shoulder. "We can't be sure," he says gently, "but we may be able to put protections in place, spells, to prevent him from causing damage."

"You mean like bind him? Can trolls be bound?"

"I have no idea, but maybe your grimoire can tell you something about it."

"Hmm. I'll have a look. Just in case."

CHAPTER FORTY-THREE

Petra

"Remember, no matter what they say in there, I love you and I'm very glad to be married to you," Lachlan says, brushing her cheek with his thumb.

"I love you too, snickerdoodle."

He smiles and rolls his eyes at her ridiculous nickname. "I will also snuff them all out if I need to." A low growl rumbles under her hand resting on his chest.

"Let's try to avoid that part if we can," she says. While Gammy has been gone for a little while now, entering these chambers and knowing she isn't there causes a wave of grief to wash over Petra, heaviness settling on her shoulders. She knew she would have big shoes to fill when she took over for Gammy, but on days like today, she still feels the need to call for Gammy like a sick child calls for their mommy.

The doors to the council chambers open, beckoning them in. She pushes thoughts of Gammy aside, hoping that what she is about to do will make her proud. So with a final look, Petra and Lachlan nod at each other, clasp hands, and walk in united as a family.

"Welcome, Mr. and Mrs. Grace-Rose," Councilor Clellugs greets them. "Please, have a seat," they say, pointing to the table and chairs to their left. Petra and Lachlan take a seat, their faces devoid of emotion. Petra spares a glance at Grog, who sits in his elevated seat, looking down at them smugly.

"Thank you for coming in today and for your patience as we worked through this community forum," Councilor Clellugs says.

The acknowledgement is kind and appreciated, Petra glances at Grog, who rolls his eyes. Refusing to let him get to her, she smiles and thanks the councilor.

"Are you ready to proceed?" they ask.

Lachlan squeezes her hand reassuringly. "Yes," they answer in unison.

Councilor Clellugs begins reading points from what Petra assumes is a summary of their final report. "As you know, we have interviewed many people you know, including your family members, close friends, and yourselves. We have also interviewed other community members who knew you separately and together from establishments you frequent or your workplaces. Through all this, we have developed a picture of you both, individually and as a couple. We have come to find that this relationship may be new, but many interviewees reported knowing you two were bound to get together. A years-long friendship existed, but it always had an underlying attraction. Close friends, family, and community members reported you were drawn to each other early on and would spend time together regularly."

Petra and Lachlan glance at each other, and he runs his thumb along hers, silently saying *I'm yours.*

The councilor continues, "Mrs. Grace-Rose, you admitted in your interview that the marriage to Mr. Grace-Rose was initially for convenience, and we appreciate your honesty. You also shared that while it started that way, your real feelings soon emerged, and your love for him helped you see not only the man in front of you but also your self-worth."

Petra sucks in a breath, knowing a decision is about to be awarded. Fearing this will have all been for naught, she looks away from the council bench, down at her hand clasped with Lachlan's.

"After much deliberation and admittedly great tension between council members, we have come to a decision."

Lachlan squeezes her hand three times. *I. Love. You.*

"We, the supernatural council, vote, in a 3-2 decision, in favor of your marriage fulfilling the conditions of your challenge, and Petra Grace-Rose, you shall officially be granted a seat on the council as the witch representative. You will occupy the seat left empty by the passing of Gladys Rose and will be granted the title of Premier Witch, gaining the power and responsibility allotted as such."

Petra weeps, happy tears for the second time since Gammy's passing. Lachlan grabs her face, kissing her excitedly. "You are the next Premier Witch," he says against her mouth.

The celebration is short-lived, however, as it is harshly interrupted by a collection of supernatural beings deposited into the center of the council room. Dazed and disoriented, the newly introduced group bounce off each other, trying to find a way out, but they are held in place by a cage charm.

Without thinking, Petra tosses a shield around her and Lachlan. She knows this was orchestrated by them, but the timing from Selene could have been worked out a little better.

"What is this?" Councilor Amare shouts over the confused voices.

Petra looks to Grog, who is doing his level best to avoid making eye contact with her or any of the strangers in her protective dome. He shifts uncomfortably in his seat. Before Grog can speak, trying to play off his guilt as confusion, Lachlan stands. "Sorry for the interruption, but we needed to bring along a little surprise. The beings in front of you are, shall we say, close personal friends of Councilor Grog and have been working for him for many years. Most recently, some of them have been employed to intimidate and threaten harm upon Mrs. Grace-Rose while making it appear that it was Sloan Wilks's work. Grog has been using these beings to strike fear and uncertainty in Mrs. Grace-Rose, hoping she would relinquish her right to the Premier Witch title so that he could put someone in place that he could control."

"That's preposterous!" Grog shouts. "They are clearly trying to undermine all of the work I have done over the years, and want to use their new combined power to sway council decisions!" He comes out from behind his seat and into the main space in the room. "I knew allowing your marriage to continue would be trouble. I warned you all. But you wouldn't listen. Now they are coming after me."

He's scared, Petra realizes. He didn't anticipate them exposing him. Now he's trying to turn it around on them.

Lachlan ignores the scene Grog is creating, and looks along the bench, pausing at each council member, before continuing, "Additionally, he has illegal ties to some of the others here and has been in business with them collecting and selling illegal wares, and has used them to gain information to bribe various council members to sway votes." As he says this, various council members look down, attempting to avoid being noticed. "And finally, he is the one responsible for the incurable illness and ultimate death of Gladys Rose. We have evidence and accounts from those in his employ of the mixtures used to weaken Gladys over time, leading to her unfortunate passing." The room erupts into chaos. Council members yell at each other regarding the allegations and their potential involvement; Grog threatens the deposited guests, and the guests scream back at him.

"As a council member, I motion for an immediate vote to remove Councilor Grog as a member and to move forward with banishment to prevent harm against other community members. All in favor of the said motion, say 'Aye,'" Lachlan orders.

"Again, these are all lies," Grog proclaims.

"The troll doth protest too much, I think," Petra calmly counters, letting an amused smile emerge while she stares directly into his cold eyes. The mention of her beloved Gammy sparks a pain in her chest, but seeing Grog finally have his comeuppance and get what he deserves is satisfying.

Spit flies from his mouth as he points at her, spitting out, "You! You are behind this. Getting Premier Witch from your bitch of a grandmother wasn't enough, huh?" An audible intake of breath is heard around the room as those present get to see the true side of Grog.

"I think you are confused. My grandmother, may the goddess care for her departed soul, was a witch. W-I-T-C-H."

Lachlan moves to step between them as Grog closes what little distance exists between him and Petra. She makes eye contact with him and shakes her head slightly, telling him not to intervene.

"Oh, ho, ho. You think you're funny, huh? Think you managed to pull one over on the big bad troll? You have nothing. No one here will speak against me. They know better," he says. Petra's eyes widen at that little bit he let slip, but she doesn't say anything. No. She will let him bury himself. "You have no proof of these allegations. I am the smartest troll in existence. I would never leave any kind of trail to be discovered," he declares. "You know, your grandmother tried to shut me up when she was new to the council. And then she continued to try and prevent me from doing what needed to be done throughout her tenure. But guess what? It didn't work out so well for her now, did it? What makes you think you could do what she couldn't?"

Petra doesn't respond. Instead, she looks around the room at the other council members. They are all staring at him, mouths slightly agape, with looks of shock that could be etched of stone. The creatures deposited by Selene have moved to the room's edges, trying to keep their distance from the wild troll with sweat on his brow who is now pacing back and forth.

Grog continues as if he needs to fill the silence or risk the room turning on him. "Despite being able to fulfill the conditions to be Premier Witch, you will never be worthy. You've never cared about the supernatural community, and you will never amount to anything."

Petra's power surges, seeking an outlet. Her skin tingles as Lachlan steps in behind her and places his hand on her back in an attempt to ground her, clearly sensing the electric current she barely holds on to.

Grog turns to the other council members, saying, "I request that we remove both Petra and Lachlan Grace-Rose from the chambers, and effective immediately they are to be banned from the council." He sounds so sure of himself that it would be laughable if it weren't so pathetic. "They have falsely accused an upstanding member of council with heinous claims, only demonstrating their inability to be effective council members. All in favor, say 'aye'" He turns briefly glancing at Petra, a cocky smirk plastered on his disgusting face. Only when he turns back to face the council does he realize no one has said a word in support of him. He steps toward Petra, poking her shoulder as he punctuates each word. "You should have been taken out with your grandmother."

Lachlan steps forward, shadows flooding the room. Petra splays a hand at her side, placing a barrier between Lachlan and Grog. Her other hand twists as her hand extends out before her. Dark pink tendrils of magic, surging with her anger, burst forth and wrap around Grog, pulling him away from her. They bind his legs and tie his slimy arms behind his back before suspending him six feet in the air. She closes her fist, tightening her hold as he squirms in her binds. In doing so, she also draws out his magic into her own, weakening him.

"What! What's going on? Put me down!" he barks. Realization dawns on his face as Petra leeches his power from him and he is unable to fight back.

Her voice comes out low as she says, "You have been warned not to touch me without my consent. While I could let my husband handle you, I want you to be sure that you know who you have pissed off. I am no wallflower. I am Gladys Rose's granddaughter, and if she taught me anything, it was not to let anyone make me feel anything less than a Rose." Grog spins in the air as she speaks. If it's possible, his face looks greener than normal. She hopes he doesn't puke. Bringing him back down, she releases her hold on him just before he touches the ground, causing him to thump like a wet cloth on to the floor.

A handful of the beings Selene rounded up step forward, and one of them, a goblin, says, "I know we don't have a vote, but we would like to side with the Grace-Roses. We have spent years under the toe of Councilor Grog and are prepared to share all details related to his misdeeds, regardless of any consequences we may face."

"Ha, see!" Grog says, standing up and clearly having misunderstood. The room is silent, waiting for him to realize what just occurred. It takes him a few seconds before he understands that the goblin was speaking against him, not for him. "Wait! I misunderstood!"

"Clearly," Councilor Amare responds dryly.

Panic crosses Grog's face, and he charges for the door. In his attempt to make it to the council chamber doors, he is abruptly stopped when a thick pink tendril wraps around his feet keeping him in place. The vine-like structure winds up his body, wrapping around him like the snake he is. He twists and turns, struggling against the hold she has on him. Tilting her head, she narrows her eyes as she watches him attempt to fight against her magic. It's no use, really. Even with what magic he possesses, it will always be a lesser power to what she can control.

"Hegnir," Petra says softly. Saying his name causes him to stop. His eyes snap to hers, full of surprise and something that resembles…sadness? She wonders when he last heard his name in a more friendly way. Stepping toward him, leaving him bound just in case, Petra says, "Hegnir, from what I know from my Gammy—may the goddess bless her soul—you have spent years trying to undermine the council and have worked hard trying to pit community members against each other. She spent years trying to help you build a stronger community, and you returned the favor by slowly poisoning her with troll magic, making her unable to be healed. You turned against one of your own. And for what?" She wipes a stray tear as it starts to roll down her cheek. "You even tried to trap me in a situation with ridiculous conditions with the hope that I would never be able to meet them. And despite all this effort, you've never been successful. Don't you think it's time to give it up? You are clearly intelligent; no one denies that. But I have to wonder if those abilities could be better used. Don't you want to support our community, to help it grow and prosper?"

His features shift from something resembling understanding into pure malice. His nostrils flare wide with each heavy breath he takes while his eyes narrow and his chest puffs out, pushing against the bind Petra maintains around him. "Everything I have ever done has been to protect our community," he bellows. "Your bitch of a grandmother did everything she could to stop me, so I did what I could to stop her from passing down the power. Only I didn't count on you, the weak, avoidant witch that you are, to actually rise to the challenge. My mistake. But I won't make that misstep again. No. The Wilkses have your number and will continue to do my work," he sneers. "They were always the better family."

Petra, tired of his tirade, opens a portal behind him. "If you continue to speak ill of the Rose family, I will banish you myself." Tendrils of magic fill the room, pulsing in response to her anger.

Grog's face drops. Apparently, he is still underestimating her.

"Alright, enough. You have both said your piece, and

frankly, Grog, you are not helping yourself in the slightest. Aside from what I know from our interactions, the fact that you are trying to run proves your guilt to me. These reported actions are disreputable, and you disgrace this council. In response to Councilor Grace's request, I say aye," Councilor Amare says.

Four more votes of agreement follow her response. Petra's magic calls her to action as she takes hold of him, placing him inside a shielded dome.

"I do not wish to add any additional charges. I leave it to the council to decide the terms of his punishment, setting the conditions he must meet and consequences should he fail," Petra finishes, stepping back to stand with Lachlan, interlacing her fingers with his. Lachlan snaps his fingers, and folders of evidence of Grog's business deals, threats, and bribery material land before each council member.

He looks to Petra, raises a hand to her face, and kisses her, "My wife," he whispers. Turning back to face Grog, he tells him, "You may have orchestrated this whole ordeal that led to Petra and me marrying, but rather than get angry, I wish to thank you. See, I found my partner. And while you were too busy with your head up your ass trying to tear the council apart, I found strength. I am going to spend the rest of my life with this witch. And for the rest of our lives, we will remember how some little troll tried to ruin us, but the only thing he ruined was himself."

Petra beams at him. Does she need him to defend her? No. But it sure feels nice that he does so willingly and publicly.

Councilor Clellugs calls the room to order and nods to Lachlan and Petra, silently thanking them and wishing them well. Once again, Lachlan is to be excluded from this decision, as he is involved in bringing it forward. How they plan to handle the proceedings, given Grog has threatened and bribed at least a few of the council members, Petra doesn't know. She is simply grateful that he is finally going to get what he deserves.

"Let's go home, turtle dove," she says.

He takes her hand in his, kisses her forehead, and ports them home.

Epilogue: 10 Months Later

After everything with Grog went down, the council decided that he was to return to his homeland, Gerulleon, with restrictions on his interactions within the larger supernatural community. His powers were also stripped. He was ordered to partake in training and education to hopefully broaden his perspective and help manage his anger. While Petra doubts that education will truly help him, she hopes that some time away from the community at large will give him time to reflect and grow. His involvement in Gammy's passing did not go unnoticed. While others advocated for harsher punishment, Petra chose grace. Punishing him further would not bring Gammy back. Instead, she chose to focus on how she could continue Gammy's legacy through her own work, and in doing so, she would continue to prove Grog wrong.

A few days after they received the decision and Grog's sentence was handed down, Petra was officially sworn in as Premier Witch. In doing so, her power grew exponentially, the depths of which she is still figuring out. The council apologized to her for everything they let Grog put her through, and while the apology didn't fix it, she appreciated it nonetheless. It opened up a great discussion about the practices of the council, how they choose members, and whose voices are important.

While adjusting to being Premier Witch has taken some time, Petra jumped in with both feet just like Gammy taught her, immediately advocating for changes to the practice of council. It has taken some time to convince the few members who were closer to Grog, but Petra feels she is finally in a good place to put forth her first major motion. Or the first two major motions, today.

"Happy anniversary, my lovely wife."

"Happy anniversary, my banana cream pie," she says, wrapping her arms around his neck before kissing him softly.

"Are you ready for your first big day as Premier Witch?"

Premier Witch. While she's been in the role for close to ten months, it still feels odd to hear herself referred to in that way. But at the same time, it feels right, like a properly fitted dress that hugs her in all the right places. Or a warm hug from Lachlan, easing her worries. Or sharing a loving cup of tea with Gammy in her sunroom.

While Gammy has been gone for these ten months, the hole she occupied in Petra's heart still exists, and Petra is certain it will always exist, changing and evolving as she does. Some days she is perfectly fine, and others she may have moments—even the whole day—where she is deep in the waters of grief. Wishing Gammy was here to guide her through this new phase. Petra lost her mom when she was young, and that grief still remains, but the loss of Gammy has hit differently. It's shaped differently. As much as there is pain, she recognizes the beauty in the grief as well, that it is love that remains unexpressed.

Petra steps up onto the council member bench and takes her seat. As she sits, a gust of wind pushes her hair from her face, the scent of lavender washing over her. Though she can't see her, she knows that it is Gammy wishing her well.

"Welcome, council members. Today we are discussing a motion being put forth in collaboration from our newest council members, Mrs. Petra Grace-Rose, Premier Witch, and Miss Ecia Damari, troll representative," Councilor Clellugs shares. "The floor is yours, Councilors."

"Thank you," Petra and Ecia respond. Petra stands to make her first motion.

Lachlan's gaze provides added strength as she steadies herself, calming the nerves and power bubbling inside. "As my—no, our," she corrects herself, looking to Ecia and smiling, "first official motion, we propose a new bylaw. As you are well aware, I did not choose to become Premier Witch. While I accept my role and will do my best to be the best Premier Witch I can be, if given the choice, I would have wished to have more time before assuming the role. Ecia has shared the same sentiments, and so together we have created a new practice that we are calling to a vote to have it become supernatural law. This law would change the practice of council positions being attached to power and bloodlines, and would instead move for a more democratic practice. Willing candidates could apply for an open position, which would be determined by an election, voted by both the council and community members. Ecia and I feel it is important that council members desire to be here and that the community has a say in who will represent them. As an addition to this, we are also requesting that the human community also have a representative on council as it is important for them to have a voice in a space where decisions are constantly made that impact them." She hears some of the council members shift in their seats uncomfortably, but she presses on.

"As our second motion, we would like to bring Daisy Hale in as a consultant for a new program to help outcast community members. We believe we have been doing a disservice to our community, and that many members have been shunned for one reason or another, creating unnecessary hardship where we have the resources and ample ability to provide support. I have a program plan here, and if you could open your packages"—she snaps her fingers, making documents appear in front of each member —"and turn to page one, we can review the program summary together."

After returning to work at the childcare, Petra realized that she truly loved interacting with the various families and providing support for them as they and their children grew and evolved. The more she sat with it, the more she wanted to find ways to extend these opportunities to the community. The plan she is suggesting to the council will be the first step, of hopefully many, wherein the community members, both human and supernatural, feel cared for. She hopes this plan will prevent others from experiencing what Daisy has and will be the steppingstone needed to help Lachlan with his endeavors to support underworld members in turning their lives around.

As she resumes her seat, Lachlan beams at her from the opposite side of the bench. Getting here felt like a long road, but she would not want to be anywhere else. Finding the balance between her work at the childcare and her council duties will take some time, but she knows now, with her whole being, that this is exactly where she is supposed to be. And that she is meant to have Lachlan at her side.

She looks across the bench at Lachlan and takes a deep

breath, settling in as she begins reviewing the plan's summary. He winks and taps three times on the desk.

I. Love. You.

She taps four times in response.

I. Love. You. Too.

Acknowledgments

First and foremost, I wish to thank my loving husband. Sean, you have been a light in my life, and I am absolutely sure I would not be where I am today without your consistent and unconditional love, support, and cheerleading. Thank you for continuing to show me what love looks like. I love you, my honey bunches of oats.

Second, I wish to thank my amazing editor, Sarah Pesce of @loptandcropt editing. This story would be nowhere without you.

Third, I wish to thank some friends who helped along the way. To Amanda A., Megan McSpadden, Tam M., and Karla H.—you have been so supportive and listened to me vent, share my concerns, and have just been wonderful friends as I've embarked on this new journey. I kept this adventure fairly close to the chest, and I'm so thankful you were there and helped me keep going. The enthusiasm, encouragement, general excitement—I couldn't have done this without all of it. So thank you. I appreciate your support far more than words can describe.

Finally, I want to thank you, reader, for giving this story a chance. I can only hope that you grew to love Petra, Lachlan, and the larger Leeside community (minus Grog, of course!) as much as I have. I couldn't do this without you, so thank you from the bottom of my heart.

About the Author

Isla is an enigma—even to herself—and is figuring all this life stuff out as she goes. She enjoys spending time with her husband and furry family of two cats and two dogs. When she's not reading or writing, she's likely playing Mario Kart or Stardew Valley.

If you enjoyed With This Witch, please be sure to leave a review on Goodreads and/or Amazon!

Want to receive updates on upcoming projects? Sign up for Isla Winter's Newsletter

You can also follow Isla on the following social media platforms (she is most active on Instagram):

instagram.com/islawinterwrites

tiktok.com/@islawinterwrites

facebook.com/author.isla.winter

www.ingramcontent.com/pod-product-compliance
Lightning Source LLC
Chambersburg PA
CBHW061629190726

48289CB00006B/1541